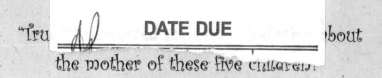
"Tru⟶ ⟶bout the mother of these five children."

"Well, she'll be home with them." He started backpedaling almost before he finished the sentence. "It's not a political thing, barefoot and pregnant and forced to bake pies. I just think that if you're going to have children, you might as well raise them yourself. My mom was a single parent, and it was not a good scene. It's nice for kids to have someone at home."

"Sure, it's nice for the *kids*. But what happens when happily ever after breaks down and Mom is stranded in the middle of nowhere with no job and no income while Dad takes off with some popcorn-obsessed chippy?"

He waited patiently for me to settle down. "No *Waltons* for you?"

"Can I get a 'hell no'?"

We studied each other across the table.

"Hmm," he said.

"Hmm," I said.

Exes and Ohs **is also available as an eBook**

Also by Beth Kendrick

My Favorite Mistake

Exes

~ and ~

Ohs

Beth Kendrick

doWn tOwn press

New York   London   Toronto   Sydney

An *Original* Publication of POCKET BOOKS

 DOWNTOWN PRESS, published by Pocket Books
1230 Avenue of the Americas
New York, NY 10020

ISBN: 0-7434-7035-4

First Downtown Press trade paperback edition March 2005

10 9 8 7 6 5 4 3 2 1

DOWNTOWN PRESS and colophon
are trademarks of Simon & Schuster, Inc.

Manufactured in the United States of America

Designed by Jaime Putorti

For information regarding special discounts for bulk purchases,
please contact Simon & Schuster Special Sales at 1-800-456-6798
or business@simonandschuster.com

For Larry,
my true love and fellow lollygagger

Acknowledgments

My undying thanks to:

Dr. Terry Wilson and Dr. Kenneth Schneider, who patiently answered my questions about cognitive behavioral therapy.

Kresley Cole, my primal scream buddy.

Amy Pierpont, my fabulous editor and comrade in bad-air-travel karma.

The girls from "the lab that's too loud": Sara, Alyssa, Osnat, and Kim, who can turn five solid hours of statistical analysis into a party.

Murphy and Roxie, world's sassiest dogs.

And the usual suspects: Irene Goodman, Susan Mallery, Barbara Ankrum, Megan McKeever, Paolo Pepe and the brilliant team at the Pocket art department, and of course, the Chicago Cubs.

1

The first time I ran into Dennis after the infamous nonwedding, I was wearing a coffee-stained tank top, no makeup, and baggy red track pants that made my ass look as big as Montana. I ordered a double espresso, collected my change, turned around to grab a napkin, and lo and behold, there was the man who'd "needed to talk" after our rehearsal dinner six months before.

I should have known this day was coming. UCLA is a big campus, but the medical plaza is a small world.

It was not good. We gaped at each other, both of us mute and rooted to the sun-bleached concrete. His gaze slid away from mine, so I focused on the small blue name tag pinned to his white coat: DR. D. SCHELL. We were standing, fittingly, in The Bomb Shelter, which is the café adjacent to the med school.

The silence between us stretched into eons. Stars flared up and extinguished in the heavens. Species evolved and died out. It became tragically apparent that the Big One was not going to hit right now, swallow me up into the San Andreas Fault, and save me from the raw humiliation of this moment. I had to say something. Anything.

"How's Lisa?" Those are the words that actually came out of my mouth.

He startled when I said her name. "She's good. She's . . . you know."

I nodded at his left hand, which, although tan and sprinkled with thin dark hair, remained ringless. "Still not married?"

"No." He scuffed at the ground.

"Good to know. And actually, as long as we're on the subject, I still have a few bills I could use some help with. As you know." I smiled at him, sweetly. The expression on his face suggested that I had sprouted pointy, glistening fangs. "The photographer, mostly. The engagement ring paid for the jazz band and the catering, and I sold the bridesmaids' gowns on eBay, but I took a loss, so . . ."

He flinched. Couldn't bear to think of my platinum-set Tiffany diamond ring sparkling away in some second-rate North Hollywood jewelry shop. Poor baby.

He cleared his throat, pulled his Palm Pilot out of his pocket, and commenced poking at it with the plastic stylus. One of his nervous little tics. That and pulling on his earlobe. "I want to help out with that stuff. I kept meaning to call you, but . . ."

"Lisa." I nodded briskly. "I know."

"Listen." He finally raised his gaze, up to about my chin, as he gestured to the café counter. "Can I buy you something?"

"Like what?" I planted my hands on my drawstring pant waist. "Chai? Latte? No thanks. You've done enough. Just pony up ten thousand bucks, and we'll call it even."

His big brown eyes were those of a puppy cowering in the face of a rolled-up newspaper. "I deserve that. I know. Listen, Gwen, I never meant to—"

But I was already walking away. Strutting my stuff in red track pants and a messy ponytail, trying to make an imperious Miss Thang exit before I burst into tears. Which I did, approximately four minutes later, when I reached the campus botanical gardens and caught sight of the quaint little mission-style chapel across the street. A bride and groom were posing for photographs on the church lawn.

Late Friday afternoon was an odd time for a wedding, but sometimes the church and reception site are cheaper if you're willing to book a Sunday or a Friday. Just another fun fact I'd amassed on my long, meandering, and ultimately aborted trip down the aisle.

The bride was tiny, disappearing in swaths of white lace that I recognized from the *Modern Bride* special issue on Vera Wang. The groom was tall, lanky, a little goofy. Both of them looked stunned in the afternoon sunlight filtering through green leaves. Shocked by the final fruition of all those months of strategizing and bickering over centerpiece ideas. They were married, for better or for worse. Off with the wedding gown and on with the rest of their lives.

I sat down right there on the sidewalk and rummaged through my bag until I unearthed my cell phone, then speed dialed my roommate (and would-be maid of honor) Cesca. At times like this, a girl needed to hear someone say things like "When he asked about the ring, what you *should* have said was, 'Pawned it. Went to Hawaii and slept with a cabana boy.'"

What a girl did *not* need was to discover that she had forgotten to recharge her cell phone last night, and consequently had no battery power left.

Where was the justice? I was already pinballing around rock bottom. Literally kicked to the curb with no dignity and no Kleenex. Were a few ions of Nokia lithium really too much to ask?

I swiped at my eyes with the back of my arm and checked my watch. I had fifteen minutes until my meeting with my research adviser, who, much like a pit bull, would lunge for my jugular at the first sign of fear or weakness. I needed to talk to Cesca. Now.

"Come on." I punched the phone's power button one more time.

The phone beeped angrily and gave me the technological equivalent of the finger—the "please charge battery" message. Then the illuminated screen went blank.

"Come *on!*" I pressed the power button again. Nothing.

A sleek black limo pulled up across the street. The Vera Wang brigade piled in amid a flurry of tulle. Guests streamed toward the parking lot, no doubt headed to a gala reception with champagne fountains and ice sculptures, where the groom would manfully blink back tears while toasting his new wife.

I couldn't even get thirty seconds from Verizon.

So I did the only thing left to do. I hurled my cell phone into the middle of Le Conte Avenue, where it was promptly run over by a forest green Saab. The driver, a blond beach bunny with dark sunglasses, honked her horn and flung her cigarette butt at me as she vroomed away.

"Okay." The time had come to take a minute and ask myself, What had I become?

Since the night of my (unnecessary, as it turned out) rehearsal dinner, I had turned into the kind of woman who commits phonicide and willfully creates road hazards just because she sees a glowing, happy couple who apparently registered at Good Karma, Inc.

And the truly horrible part was, I missed him. He had lied to me, cheated on me, and humiliated me in front of a rented reception hall's worth of friends and family, but I missed him anyway, and I could never admit it to another living soul.

"Swear to God, Gwen, if a guy ever did that to me I would cut off his penis. And then FedEx it to his new girlfriend." That's what Cesca had said, and she had a point. Part of me knew that he didn't even deserve my chilly courtesy—that what he in fact *deserved* was to have his nether regions severed, sealed, and delivered—but another part of me was still holding on to what we'd had: the sunny Sunday mornings brunching at Gladstone's while watching the tide roll in. The postsex, late-evening showers we took together, dueting "Summer Lovin'" at the top of our lungs. The safe, even spaces between his breaths when he slept.

We had been in love, you see.

Or, at least, I had.

But now "we" had been reduced to me, the dead cell phone, and the limo tracks of another couple's dream wedding.

I heard footsteps on the pavement behind me as a long, dark shadow engulfed my little patch of sidewalk. I craned my neck around to see who had witnessed my curbside meltdown. Praying—to God, Buddah, Gaia, anyone who might listen—that Dennis hadn't followed me out here.

Wincing, I forced myself to look up. My eyes skimmed over khaki pants, a blue button-down shirt, and the face of a man I'd never seen before. Midthirties, with dark hair and dark eyes. He seemed concerned.

"You look like you need to borrow a cell phone." His voice sounded all deep and East Coast. The kind of guy who'd been on the crew team at prep school.

I blinked up at him, hoping we could both ignore the fact that my eyes were red and puffy. "What?"

"Do you need to make a call?" He offered up a silver Motorola with one hand, but his eyes never left my face.

"Oh. Not really." I started tucking strands of hair behind my ears. "There's no emergency. I just wanted to call my roommate. To . . . tell her something."

Ooh, pithy. Why wasn't anyone chiseling this down in stone?

"What's the problem?" He reached out to help me to my feet. His grip felt warm and steady, but not too tight. Obviously, he was practiced at making people feel comfortable and secure. I wondered if he was a doctor, like Dennis.

"It's kind of a long story." I hitched up my track pants and pasted on a smile.

He continued to stare, and I was feeling less comfortable and secure by the second. Finally, he nodded and said, "You're Gwen, right? Gwen Taylor?"

I took two giant steps back and shaded my eyes with my hand. No matter how I squinted, this guy's face did not ring any bells. "Gwen *Traynor* . . . why?"

Already my eyes were darting around, trying to find the best escape route. Had I been dumped by my physician fiancé only to be slain by a stalker from Banana Republic?

He laughed at my expression. "Don't worry. We haven't met, but I recognize you. I saw you in your office when I visited the mental health clinic."

This did not go a long way toward calming me down.

He laughed again, the corners of his eyes crinkling up. His skin looked tan and a bit weathered. Probably from all that yachting down at the asylum.

"I'm Alex Coughlin." He offered his hand. "I'm the new trustee on the children's clinic board. Dr. Cortez showed me around the new building this morning, and he took me by your office. We just peeked in, but I remember you. Dr. Cortez said you were one of his best new therapy interns."

Oh.

"Well, I try. When I'm not having meltdowns in front of the new trustees." I sighed. "Listen—"

He smiled. "Don't worry about it. I know how much pressure graduate school can be."

"Oh yeah? What fancy degrees do you have slapped up on your wall?" I sized him up and took a guess. "M.B.A.?"

He blinked. "Maybe."

"Definitely."

"How do you know I'm not some nice anthropologist who just happened to wander into the medical plaza?"

I nodded at his wrist. "Anthropologists don't wear Patek Philippe watches. And all that brushed twill—it's a dead give-away."

"Damn. You psychologists have quite the eye for detail. All right, I admit it—I'm a preppy M.B.A. who wears an ostentatious watch." He turned both palms outward. "What can I say? It was a gift from my mother, and it does keep good time."

I willed my puffy eyes to deflate. I hadn't worked up the nerve to flirt with anyone in the six months since Dennis had dumped me. But maybe it was time to dive back in the dating pool. Maybe all was not lost. Maybe, just maybe, I wouldn't have to grow old alone in Los Angeles just because I was an academic with a head for useless facts instead of a serene *Modern Bride* or a Britney Spears backup dancer.

I smiled back at him, feeling attractive for the first time in weeks.

Then I glanced at the ostentatious watch. "Oh my God. Is it really five o'clock? I'm late for a meeting with Dr. Cortez."

He paused for a second. "I just came from a meeting with him myself, so if you'd like, I could call and tell him you're showing me around the campus. We could go grab a cup of coffee."

My eyebrows shot up. "Are you asking me for a date?"

"Yeah, I guess I am."

I looked at him, and then I looked at the chapel and the cell phone laying disembowled on the pavement, and shrugged. "Fair enough. Let's go?"

"Such enthusiasm." He followed my gaze to the Great Nokia Massacre of 2005. "You want to tell me why that cell phone had to die so young?"

"I might as well. You should know what you're getting into." I lowered my voice to a whisper. "*That*—I'm sorry, what was your name again?"

"Alex."

"*That*, Alex, is what eight months of wedding planning leads to."

He looked confused. "But you're not married?"

"Nope. I was all wedding, no marriage. I learned my lesson."

"Got it." He nodded. "Well, I don't know about weddings, but I always thought it'd be nice to settle down, move out to a ranch in Colorado, have a bunch of kids, and live happily ever after."

"Really. Well . . . that sounds great too," I assured him. But inside, I was like, *Good luck with those catering bills, suckah.*

Yes, right from the beginning, the big red flags were there.

As we strolled two blocks over to Café Chou on Wilshire Boulevard, Alex called my adviser and told Dr. Cortez I was graciously providing a "walking tour of the campus facilities." Shiny, late-model Boxsters and BMWs whizzed by on their way to Bel Air and Beverly Hills. I examined the fractured pieces of plastic and metal that had once been my cell phone and wished, not for the first time, that I could add a little impulse control to my life.

"Done." He snapped his own phone shut and grinned at me. "He bought it. We are officially playing hooky."

I closed my eyes and turned my face up to the golden sun. "How can something so wrong feel so right?"

"So you're that kind of girl." He opened the glass door to the coffee shop and ushered me into frigid, mocha-scented air-conditioning. "Fiesty."

"That's one word for it."

He ordered a large coffee, black. I opted for herbal tea, as my system clearly did not need any more stimulants of any kind. We waited through a long, awkward pause at the counter while the server prepared our drinks, then found our way to a table by the café's front window, where he shook his head at my phone and tossed it into the trash bin.

"Hey! I need that!" I protested. "I mean, I know I should have thought of that before I chucked it in the street, but I could still fix it . . . maybe." The truth of the matter was that I couldn't *afford* a new phone, but he didn't need to know that I lived off a meager fellowship and a lot of boxes of orange macaroni and cheese.

He raised one eyebrow. "God himself couldn't fix that thing. So who *is* this guy who drove you to such senseless violence?"

"Oh, let's not go down that road." I tried to avoid broaching this subject with strangers, as I tended to go off on long, frothy-mouthed, spirally eyed rants.

"We're going down that road. Drink your tea and start talking."

I flushed. "Let's just say that he was *not* worthy of the many hysterical breakdowns I had over whether the wedding invitations should be white or ecru."

"Really?" He shook his head, his eyes bright and intense. "How can planning a wedding be that bad? What's to do? Call a few churches, buy a few cases of booze, end of story."

"Ha." I sipped my tea. "The bride needs a few cases of booze before she even gets to the bachelorette party. You have no idea. Guest lists, church decorations—"

"Come on. Church decorations? Buy a few rolls of crepe paper, some duct tape, problem solved." His smile was so disarming that I forgot I was bitter for a second and smiled back. "I don't see the need for hard liquor yet."

"And then there's the dress." I covered my eyes and shuddered. "First fitting, second fitting, final fitting . . ."

"Fittings?"

"Yeah. You know, so the bodice stays on and the hem is short enough that you don't trip."

"Well, just buy some extra duct tape and you're good to go."

I rolled my eyes. "Of course. I can't believe seamstresses all over America are letting their most precious resource go to waste on plumbing facilities."

"I'm serious." He feigned great earnestness and masculine consternation.

"Duct tape. Honestly. What would Emily Post say?"

"She's dead. She doesn't get a say."

"Listen, I've seen the dark side of 'I do,' and it is 'I don't.'

Uttered the night before the ceremony, when the erstwhile groom decides that his true destiny lies with his ex-girlfriend, a massage therapist who makes popcorn mosaics on the side." I waved my spoon for emphasis.

He looked skeptical. "Popcorn mosaics?"

"With shellac and spray paint and stuff. Apparently, it's her true calling."

"What's her medium? Pop Secret? Redenbacher? Does she have a corporate sponsor?" His laughter was contagious.

"You know, I don't believe that 'true art' and 'corporate sponsorship' mix."

"I guess you're right." He rubbed the emerging stubble on his chin. "To keep it real, she'd have to get a grant."

"A few well-placed patrons and she might be able to move on to her pasta period and take the L.A. art world by storm."

"Yeah. And then on to rice, legumes—who knows what poignant sorrows lie within the humble lima bean?"

"You wanna hear my sad little story, or not?"

He pretended to debate this for a minute. "I'll hear the sad little story."

"Very gracious of you. *Anyway,* long story short, my ex couldn't resist the siren call of *his* ex, and by the time the dust settled—"

"Don't you mean 'the kernels settled'?"

"—the only thing I needed duct tape for was to box the gifts back up and return to sender."

He saluted me with his coffee cup. "And you still have your sense of humor."

We lost eye contact.

"I'm over it," I agreed.

"You're better off without him."

"Totally." I stared down at the gold-speckled Formica table-top, my thoughts turning inexorably to the wedding dress still moldering away in my closet. The bridal salon wouldn't take it back. Apparently, all Amsale gowns were final sale, even if Dennis wasn't.

Morning after morning, as I selected the day's ensemble, I was greeted by the ivory silk reminder of my failure and disgrace.

Dennis had found bliss with a "less complicated" woman, some other euphoric bride-to-be would soon be flashing my pawned ring, and still I hung on to the hand-beaded fabric that tied me to the life I'd almost had. The life I'd wanted so badly that I'd been blind in my faith and careless with my heart. The life I'd wanted so badly that I'd—oh, God, the shame—literally *begged* Dennis not to leave when he said he was meant to be with Lisa.

On the sidewalk in front of the rehearsal dinner restaurant, I'd sobbed that my life could never be the same without him. And he had cleared his throat and said, "I love you, Gwen, but I *need* Lisa."

Well, I'd been right about one thing. My life had never been the same since that night.

I yanked myself back to the date in progress and Café Chou and smiled at Alex in what I hoped was a winsome manner. "Let's talk about something else. Like you, for instance. Let's talk about you."

He leaned back in his chair. "All right. What do you want to know?"

"Well . . . what do you do with your time when you're not playing hooky on Friday afternoons or stewarding the clinic?"

He groaned. "*Stewarding* the clinic?"

"Isn't that what you do?"

"Technically, yes, but *stewarding* . . . it makes me sound like I smoke a pipe and wear an ascot and I've got one foot in the grave. I'm only thirty-five."

I laughed. "Okay, then, what do you do when you're not, ahem, *charitably donating* your time to the psychological improvement of young minds?"

"I'm a financial analyst and consultant."

"Oh." Pause. "That sounds really . . . um . . ."

"Boring?" He laughed. "It's not as dry as it sounds. I love the challenge of turning around companies on the brink of disaster. Kind of like bailing out the *Titanic* with a hand bucket."

"But how on earth did you end up working with the clinic?"

"I was tricked. One of my friends roped me into helping out on the board of a children's charity, and somehow I just got sucked in deeper and deeper. And now I enjoy it."

"Wow. That's really generous."

He shrugged. "Not really. It's kind of a personal thing for me."

Ah. I could see where this was going. "You have children?"

This question surprised him. "No. I've never even been married."

"Obviously not, if duct tape is your idea of a pew decoration."

"I almost got engaged once." He seemed suddenly mesmerized by the bottom of his coffee cup.

I pounced. "*Almost?* What happened?"

He tapped his fingers on the table. "We went our separate ways before I actually bought the ring."

"No way are you getting off that easy after I spilled my guts all over this table. What happened?"

"Oh, you know how it is with L.A. dating. She was beautiful, I was a sucker for a pretty face, neither of us had any common sense. One thing led to another and . . . we're much better off without each other. The end."

"Alex." I tossed a sugar packet at him. "Come *on*. I got dumped for a box of Jiffy Pop. You gotta give me something here."

"I'm not discussing this," he said, hanging his head sheepishly.

I gave him a look.

He lowered his voice. He looked to the left. He looked to the right. "The woman I was dating—Harmony—"

"Harmony?"

"Like I said. L.A. dating. She's a soap opera actress, if that tells you anything. I met her at a black-tie dinner for one of the companies I worked with." He leaned in closer. "We were just different personalities."

I nodded. "Which is the polite way of saying she was stark raving mad."

He shrugged. "She was a force of nature. A gorgeous, charismatic—and okay, crazy—force of nature. I made the classic male mistake."

"Not reading the instruction manual?"

"Letting good looks get in the way of good judgment. I kept telling myself that a woman that beautiful had to have some redeeming qualities." He was still communing with his coffee mug. "I saw what I wanted to see, instead of who she really was."

Hmm. He sounded quite reasonable and insightful. (For a man.) I couldn't decide if this meant he had unlimited romantic potential or if, given that he had once dated a woman so good-looking that people were willing to overlook her full-blown psychosis, he was wholly out of my league and I should just give up now.

Further investigation was warranted.

The two of us huddled together. The passersby on the other side of the plate glass must have thought we were planning a heist.

"And? What happened?" I prompted.

He straightened up in his seat. "I shouldn't say any more than I already have. It was a long time ago, and it's not worth remembering."

I nodded knowingly. "Bad breakup?"

"Only if you consider finding another man's sopping-wet boxers in your bathtub 'bad.' But on the bright side, I stopped being such an idiot about dating." He placed his mug back into the saucer with a definitive, end-of-story clink. "So the short answer to your question is, no, I've never been married and therefore have no children."

"But, you know, some people don't get married before they

have kids," I pointed out. "Look at Calista Flockhart. Heidi Klum. Look at *everyone*."

The J. Crew smile blinked on again. "We shouldn't even get into this. I don't want to scare you more than I already have."

I made a big production out of bracing myself against the table with both hands. "No, no—bring it on. I can take it."

"Just remember, you asked for it." He met my eyes. "I'm old-fashioned. I've always wanted to find the right woman and get married. Big believer in two parents, family dinners, the whole *Waltons* scenario."

"Yeah, yeah, yeah. Ranch in Colorado and all."

"Exactly." And he got that look on his face that guys get after they watch too many McDonald's commercials featuring precocious blond moppets playing catch with their dads. "All that fresh air and room to run around. What a great place to raise a family."

I signaled the guy at the counter for another tea. "Why Colorado? Did you grow up there?"

"Nope. Born and bred in SoCal."

"So why . . . ?"

He shrugged. "I don't know. It just sounds nice—all the trees, the slower pace . . ."

"You've heard, of course, about the Colorado winters."

"Sure! I'll teach the kids to ski, take them tobogganing."

"How many kids?"

"Oh, five or so."

"Five! That ranch house is going to need a lot of square footage."

17

He shrugged. "Real estate's cheap, compared to Los Angeles."

"True." I narrowed my eyes. "And what about the mother of these five children?"

"Well, she'll be home with them." He started backpedaling almost before he finished the sentence. "It's not a political thing, barefoot and pregnant and forced to bake pies. I just think that if you're going to have children, you might as well raise them yourself. My mom was a single parent, and it was not a good scene. It's nice for kids to have someone at home."

"Sure, it's nice for the *kids*. But what happens when happily ever after breaks down and Mom is stranded in the middle of nowhere with no job and no income while Dad takes off with some popcorn-obsessed chippy?"

He waited patiently for me to settle down. "No *Waltons* for you?"

"Can I get a 'hell no'?"

We studied each other across the table.

"Hmm," he said.

"Hmm," I said.

He pushed back his shirt cuff and consulted the controversial Patek Philippe watch. "Listen. I've got to get back to the office, but I'd love to finish this discussion later. How about next Friday night? I have Lakers tickets."

I must have looked hesitant, because he added, "I solemnly swear not to chain you to the stove in the ranch house. Until the third date."

I laughed. "All right, I'll go. But I ain't bringing no pie."

We shook on it.

*   *   *

Later that evening, while I was finishing up some final case notes and preparing to go home for the night, a courier showed up at my office door with a small package and a release form to sign. When I unwrapped the box, I found myself staring at a brand-new, top-of-the-line cell phone. The thing weighed like two milligrams. The message included read:

> *Thought you could use the latest model—*
> *it's shock absorbent.*
> *See you Friday.*

He had attached the note with duct tape.

I sank down in my chair. My heart was doing a little flutter kick that I hadn't felt in so long, I wasn't sure if it was infatuation or the early symptoms of cardiac arrest.

I had survived the breakup with Dennis along with all the accompanying humiliation, despondency, and self-doubt. And now I was getting all melty and blushy over a cup of tea and a glorified walkie-talkie. It would appear I was ready for another spin of the roulette wheel of love.

The human heart is either really resilient or incredibly masochistic.

2

"R-E-B-O-U-N-D, find out what it means to me!" Cesca did her best Aretha impression and followed it up with a heaping spoonful of Cheerios. It was the Monday morning after I met Alex, and my roommate felt it was her right—nay, her duty—to interrogate me about the new prospect. And to editorialize.

For the last four years, Francesca DiSanto and I had shared this squalid shoe box of a two-bedroom apartment in Westwood. True, it was on the ground floor of a building overrun by rowdy undergrads and it occasionally smelled like mold, but it was in a safe neighborhood, we could walk to campus, and we could (sort of) afford the rent. Due to space constraints and the fact that neither one of us had ever gotten around to buying a kitchen table, we had fallen into the habit of eating breakfast standing up and leaning against the counter.

"I'm not rebounding," I protested. "I'm done with Dennis. It's been six months. That whole debacle is dead, buried, and decayed."

"Ha. No one can pile on the denial like a psychologist." She jabbed her index finger at me. "How many times do I have to tell you? If you have man problems, the answer is never another man. You have to stop this vine swinging."

"I'm not vine swinging," I huffed. "How dare you?"

"You've gone from boyfriend to boyfriend to boyfriend from the day I met you." She paused for another bite of cereal. "And that was a very long time ago."

We had been thrown together during our freshman year of college, both of us rolling our eyes in the back row of the Psych 101 class we had been forced to take to fulfill our social science requirement. Nine years later, we were both working on our doctorates in clinical psychology. But our attitudes had not improved.

"Woman. You've been single for like, eight months, grand total, since you hit puberty."

"Hey! I am *not* one of those annoying girls who always has to have a boyfriend!"

"Well . . . you're not annoying, anyway."

I gasped in outrage.

She tilted her head. "What's so scary about being single?"

I busied myself with rinsing off the dishes in the sink. "You didn't meet Alex. He seems really nice. He's smart and well mannered, and—"

"*Re-bound,*" she intoned like a foghorn.

I played my trump card. "He has season tickets to the Lakers."

Her eyes lit up. "Are you serious?"

"Would I tease you about the Lakers? Do I look suicidal?"

"All the more reason you should steer clear of him. And give his number to me."

As the lone girl in a family with four brothers, Cesca tended to be loud and obsessed with sports. Despite her dainty appearance (think Audrey Hepburn with an olive complexion and a cute pixie haircut), she was the only female I had ever known who looked forward to Thanksgiving and New Year's Day "because I am ready for some football, baby." And for a chick currently wearing an extra-large Lakers T-shirt as pajamas and ankle socks with lavender pom-poms on the backs, she was awfully judgmental.

"So let me get this straight." She pushed a clump of dark brown hair out of her face. "This guy sees you going postal in the middle of Le Conte Avenue—"

"On the *sidewalk,*" I corrected.

"—having a hissy fit and wearing those hideous red track pants—"

"They're comfortable. I had a chapter due to Cortez."

"And he asks you out for coffee? And calls Cortez to get you out of your meeting?"

I nodded. "Yes, your honor, that is correct."

She planted her hands on her hips. "Well, what's his story? Does he just cruise the campus looking for damsels in distress?"

"No. He's a new trustee for the clinic."

"Just what you need—a romance with a guy who's all buddy-buddy with the adviser from hell. Do yourself a favor and give yourself some more grieving time."

I tried to play defense. "Listen, missy, don't you have a qualifying exam to study for or something?"

"Don't remind me." She grimaced. "I have three more days to come up with some endless paper on the efficacy of cognitive behavioral therapy versus antidepressants."

"Well, it sounds like you better get your ass to the library." I stuck my head into the fridge and started scavenging for something to pack for lunch. I snatched up a can of Diet Coke—actually, better make that two cans, okay, four—a peach and a container of yogurt. These would go nicely with a Kit Kat from the clinic's vending machine.

A Cheerio came sailing over the refrigerator door. "Don't try to change the subject. What are you going to do about this?"

"I'm going to go to the Lakers game with him. I like him and I'm giving him a chance." I cleared my throat. "Despite his reactionary worldview."

"Reactionary . . ." She tossed her bowl into the sink. Milk sloshed up onto the counter. "What the hell does that mean?"

"Well. He clearly watched too much Nick at Nite as a child and now envisions marriage and family life as some black-and-white, Eisenhower-era wet dream."

"Ward Cleaver meets Carrie Bradshaw. Yeah, this'll solve all your problems."

I shoved the yogurt and a spoon into my black tote bag.

"Sarcasm is very unbecoming this early in the morning."

"Mark my words: this is only going to lead to trouble." She tugged at her T-shirt. "Tell you what—get out while you can, and *I'll* go to the game."

"Your advice is neither solicited nor appreciated," I said primly.

"But it *is* right on the money."

I scowled at her.

"I'm just saying, this guy seems too good to be true. And when they seem too good to be true, they usually are."

I headed for the door. "Did you get that directly out of Ben Franklin's autobiography?" I sighed and turned around, one hand on the doorknob. "Listen, Ces, I appreciate what you're trying to do here. But I don't think you understand what I'm dealing with. I mean, when you broke up with Mike—"

"Do not speak that man's name in this house," she warned. "He's dead to me! Him and his stupid eight-track collection."

"Well, if you think you were upset about breaking up with him when you did, imagine how much worse you would've felt if you had planned to *marry* him."

She crossed her arms. "I have to go to the library."

I crossed *my* arms. "And I to the clinic."

And with that, the Dysfunctional Future Therapists of America meeting huffily adjourned.

"Gwen?" Julie, the clinic receptionist, stuck her chignoned head into my office. "Your ten o'clock's here."

"Oh. Okay." I finished my first Diet Coke of the day, shuffled through the papers in my bag, and tried to focus on the task. Which was salvaging troubled young psyches. Not to be confused with obsessing over the petty nuances of my own love life. "I'll be right out. Give me one second."

I scanned the information sheet the clinic director had left for me and tried to get into Work Mode.

My newest patient was a four-year-old boy, L. St. James, who'd been referred by his preschool teacher. He was described as displaying irritability, negativism, and "attention problems." Could be depression, which, in young children, often manifests as pouting, defiance, or chronic crankiness.

Well, I'd have to see. I wouldn't be meeting L. St. James himself for another week or so—today, I had asked to meet only with L.'s "primary caregiver," who was listed only as "H." St. James (nice record-keeping system we had going here), so that I could ask her about recent changes in her son's behavior and get an idea of their home environment.

Most moms of depressed kids are exhausted and absolutely at the end of their rope from trying to deal with their unruly children. So when I stepped into the toy-strewn waiting room, I was expecting to find a woman who looked like she'd been pulling her hair out between shots of bourbon. But I saw no one fitting that description. Only a little boy in a baseball cap and a young lady, barely out of adolescence, with a sandy-colored French braid and a placid, milkmaid face.

The girl looked up at me expectantly. She looked far too young to have a four-year-old, but hey, this was life in the big city, right? The child didn't look up from the toy truck he had overturned on the blue carpet. He turned the wheels round and round with the palm of his hand.

"Ms. St. James?" I ventured.

"Oh, no. I am not Ms. St. James." The girl smiled. She had a lilting European accent I couldn't quite place. Swiss? "I am her au pair. My name is Nell. This is Leo. Leo, say hello."

The little boy looked up at me. His face was nearly hidden by the brim of his red and blue cap, but his brown eyes were huge and serious. "Hello."

"Well, uh . . ." I stared at the information sheet in my hand, hoping for instructions on how to handle last-minute au pair insurgencies. "Where's his mother? I'm supposed to be meeting with her today."

Nell turned her palms up helplessly. "She is at work. She asked me to come with Leo here, so I do."

I gave her my very best fair-but-firm smile. "Well, I appreciate your time and effort, but I really can't start with Leo until I've had a chance to meet privately with his mother. It's very important. So I'm afraid you'll have to take him home now, and I'll call Ms. St. James to set up a new appointment."

Nell looked worried. "But I don't have a car. Ms. St. James dropped us off. She will pick us up in another hour."

I sighed. "I thought you said she was working."

"She has a break before lunch." The au pair started to shred a stray magazine subscription card. Thin strips of paper fluttered to the floor. "Should we just stay here until she comes?"

Grrr. Of all the days for my supervisor to be on vacation.

I took a deep breath. "All right. Let's start over." I turned to the kid on the carpet. I couldn't do any clinical work with him yet, but we might as well have a breezy little meet-and-greet. "Leo, how about you come with me? I've got some really fun toys in here."

"Okay." He abandoned the truck and followed me without a backward glance at Nell.

As we headed toward my office, I peered down at the head obscured by the red and blue baseball cap. Fringes of downy blond hair curled out over his T-shirt collar.

"I like your hat, Leo. What's that on the front?"

"Fider-Man." He pointed at the masked web slinger embroidered over the bill. "Everybody loves Fider-Man."

"What's not to love?" I opened the door to my office. "So Leo, my name is Gwen and I'm—"

"I know." He nodded solemnly. "You're a side-kick."

I blinked. "I'm sorry. What?"

"A side-kick," he repeated. "Like on TV. The lady that talks to kitties."

"Oh! You mean the pet psychic?"

"Yeah. On TV."

"No, I'm a psychologist. Not a psychic." I ushered him into the room. "Psychics are people who can see the future and guess what other people are thinking. I can't do that."

"Are you sure?"

"Very sure." Just ask Dr. Dennis Schell. "So this is where we're going to play today."

He scrunched up his mouth as he surveyed the piles of paper on the windowsill, the children's drawings on the wall, the big corduroy cushions piled in the corner. "It's kind of messy."

"Yeah, I guess it is, but since we're going to be playing, it doesn't have to be totally neat. You can help me straighten up when we're done, if you want. When your mom comes to pick you up."

He looked up at me with a glimmer of anxiety. "How long 'til she gets here?"

"Don't worry, she'll be here soon. Now, what do you want to do first? We could color, or play with Legos . . . I have some dolls and stuffed animals, too."

He mulled this over for a minute. "Color."

"Okay." I broke out the paper and a plastic bin full of crayons. We settled down on the floor with our supplies and waited for inspiration to strike.

His big brown eyes were shaded by his hat, but I could see that there was a lot going on in there. He was obviously an intense and watchful kid. Cute too. He had round, peachy cheeks and the kind of eyelashes that maiden aunts everywhere would describe as "wasted on a boy." But the Precious Moments exterior didn't fool me—I'd met a lot of preschoolers in my day, and this kid was macho and fearless as only a four-year-old male can be.

He silently selected a red Crayola and drew a long, thin, continuous spiral on his white piece of paper.

"Wow." I nodded at his design. "That's pretty cool."

He didn't look up. "Mm-hmm."

"Want to talk about what you're making?"

Apparently, he didn't. Still no eye contact. Another loop added to the coilings of red crayon.

I tried again. Sometimes directives were a better way to go with young kids. "Tell me about what you're drawing."

He sighed deeply, as if I had just interrupted progress on the Sistine Chapel. Shooting me a look of great condescension, he explained slowly, "It's a snake."

Duh. "Oh. That's a very long snake."

"Yes." He seemed pleased. "The longest snake in the world. Thirty-two feet."

Because I was not a Freudian, I let this comment slide. But he was on a roll.

"Snakes," he announced, raising his index finger like a pint-size Confucius, "are very dangerous. Not all of them. Just some of them."

"That's true," I agreed.

"That's why I'm never going to the desert. Or the jungle. Or the woods. Or the ocean."

I raised my eyebrows. "The ocean?"

"That's where the sea snakes live."

"You certainly know a lot about snakes."

"Yes." He paused to pick at a Band-Aid on his elbow. "I'm very smart."

Well, at least we knew he wasn't suffering from low self-esteem. I hid my smile and started doodling with a gray crayon on a spare sheet of paper.

Leo stopped progress on his serpentine scribbling and stared at my sketch. "Miss Gwen?"

"Yes?"

"What're you drawing?"

Busted. I felt a warm blush creep into my face as I stared down at my Crayola creation. "It's, uh, it's a cell phone."

He wrinkled up his face. "A cell phone?"

"Yeah. Because I got a new phone on Friday, so it's on my mind." I dug the item in question out of my bag and showed it to him. "See? Here it is."

"Oh." He walked across the floor on his knees and hunched over the phone until his face was mere inches from the antenna. "Can I call my mom?"

Uh-oh. "No, Leo, I'm sorry. But she's going to be here soon." I hoped. "Don't worry."

"*When* is she going to be here?" he persisted.

I consulted the wall clock. "In about half an hour."

"Okay." And after a final look of longing at the cell phone, he resumed coloring. "I'm going to draw a picture of my dog. His name's Jellybean. He died."

My ears pricked up. "I bet you felt pretty sad."

"Yeah."

I tried to continue the conversation, but the life and times of Jellybean were apparently not up for further discussion. For the next thirty minutes he acted quiet and placid, not the sort of demeanor you'd expect from a kid who'd been referred for treatment by his preschool.

At 10:05, Julie rapped on my door and ushered in Leo's mother, who was, hands down, the most beautiful woman I had ever seen outside the pages of *Vogue*.

I noticed the contrasts first. The waist-length black hair streaked with gold in the front. The simple sleeveless white dress accented with a black leather belt and strappy high heels. Her diminutive stature and the way her ripe, almost cartoonish curves managed to fit into some ridiculous, nonexistent clothing size like zero. Scratch that. This chick could wear a negative two.

The tawny tones of her cheeks and forehead set off startling, ice blue eyes. And yeah, she was wearing too much makeup, but so what? This was the kind of woman who had a heavy metal ballad written for her. The kind of woman a man might leave his fiancée for. She looked, I realized with a flash of raw red déjà vu, the way I'd always been afraid Lisa looked.

Thus, I wanted to hate her on sight. But I couldn't. She just seemed so delicate and, well . . . vulnerable. Charisma oozed from her every perfect pore.

"Mama!" Leo looked relieved to see her but did not, I noted, run over to her.

"Hi, pookie." She tilted her head and smiled down at him. Her teeth were perfect, dazzlingly white and evenly spaced. "Were you good for Dr. Traynor?"

His eyes widened for a second. Since I had introduced myself only as Gwen, he had no idea who this Dr. Traynor character was. But he decided to hedge his bets. "Yes."

She turned to me. "I am so, so sorry I'm late. The receptionist already yelled at me."

"Well, no one should *yell* at you. It's just that, for an initial interview, I really need—"

"To talk to me, I know, I know." She ducked her head with a naughty-kitten grin. "But I was running late this morning, because I couldn't find anything black or white to wear, and my spiritual adviser says I should only wear black and white for the next lunar phase."

I tried to remain poker-faced.

She ran her hands through her artfully tousled tresses. "And then I just couldn't get the director to rearrange my shooting schedule this morning, but I thought I'd at least send Nell and Leo."

Oh, Lord. "Your shooting schedule?"

"Yeah." She stopped and shook her head. "Oh, of course, I'm sorry! I work in television. That's why I'm wearing way too much makeup way too early in the morning." She laughed. "You probably haven't seen my show—you don't exactly look like the type to watch daytime dramas."

Had I just been complimented or insulted?

"I work on *Twilight's Tempest.*" She struck a pose and offered up a dainty, French-manicured hand. "Harmony St. James."

"Okay, okay, there's no need to shriek." Cesca switched on her turn signal and ruthlessly cut off the minivan behind us.

"No need to shriek?" I shrieked. "Did you hear what I just said? Her name is Harmony St. James and she looks like a digitally enhanced Carmen Electra."

"I hear you loud and clear." She flinched and stomped on the brake as traffic slowed to a crawl. She yanked open the Civic's glove compartment and threw a roll of Sweetarts my way. "Have some candy. Good God, woman."

I popped a Sweetart in my mouth, washed it down with my

customary late-afternoon can of Diet Coke, and grimaced as the sugary tang seeped into my mouth. The 405 Freeway was rapidly turning into a parking lot, as it did every day at the stroke of five o'clock. Much like Cinderella with the pumpkin, except with insane auto insurance rates and horrible gas mileage.

I blinked at the sunlight glinting off the bumper of the Volvo in front of us and tried not to hyperventilate. "I don't think you comprehend the gravity of this situation. You did not see this woman, so you could not possibly understand, but she could have her own swimsuit calendar. She probably *does* have her own swimsuit calendar."

"Don't you think you're losing perspective a little here?" Cesca patted my arm. "You have no idea if this is the same woman Alex was talking about—"

"How many soap opera actresses named Harmony do you think there are out there?" I demanded.

"I don't know! Maybe in soap opera world, 'Harmony' is the equivalent of 'Sarah' or 'Jennifer.'"

"That is such bull—"

She put a hand up. "All I'm saying is, we don't know. So until we do, stop screaming the house down."

"How the hell am I supposed to compete with Carmen Electra?"

"You can't." She shrugged. "You don't. Alex doesn't want her, he wants you."

I tipped my head back and let loose with the bitterest laugh in the world. "Where have I heard that before? Oh yeah. My *ex*-fiancé."

"You have some real trust issues, you know that?" Keeping one eye on the road, she dug a Tootsie Pop out of her purse and unwrapped it.

"You and your damn candy," I muttered.

She batted her eyelashes at the BMW convertible next to us until the gray-suited yuppie in the driver's seat let us pull in front of him. Then she readjusted the lavender Lycra sports bra she'd donned for the gym. "If I didn't eat candy, I wouldn't need to go work out, and then I wouldn't get to feast my eyes on Polo, the Pilates instructor."

I banged the back of my head against the seat. "Oh my God. You dragged my ass out into five o'clock freeway traffic to go mack on some guy named *Polo?* What the hell kind of name is Polo?"

"I think he's Brazilian or something." She grinned. "Besides, if anyone ever needed to work off some stress, it's you. You'll thank me for this later."

"This isn't even our regular gym," I pointed out. We could have walked to the UCLA fitness center, our usual routine, but this week she'd suddenly gotten a bee in her bonnet about wanting to try a Pilates class in Marina Del Rey. Now the truth was out. "Polo. Unbelievable. Polo and Harmony. They should hook up. Hippie children, unite."

"If you can't say something nice . . ."

"Bite me." I slouched into my seat and cranked up the air conditioner.

Cesca turned on the radio. The upbeat female announcer informed us that there was "a bit of a delay" on the 405 southbound. I glanced at the car's speedometer. Sure enough, we were still going 0 mph.

"So? Have you heard from your main rebound man today?" she asked.

"Who? Alex? President of the *Twilight's Tempest* fan club? No, I have not. And I probably never will, since apparently he only dates pneumatic bimbos who look like they've starred in movies called *Vixen Sorority Girls Unchained*."

She pulled down her sunglasses and gave me a look. "Are you sure *you* don't want to go audition for a soap opera?"

And then radio station Star 98.7 FM shut us up and proved my point. I winced as I recognized the mellow opening chords of Sting's "Fields of Gold."

"Sorry." She punched at the buttons. Beyoncé wailed through the stereo speakers, but the damage was already done. "I don't suppose there's any chance you didn't hear that?"

I didn't say anything for a few minutes. Just listened to the upbeat pop now ping-ponging around the car and rained silent curses upon Sting and his damnable sappy love songs.

You'll remember me when the west wind moves . . .

I remembered him all the time. And I hated it. I hated that the wounds Dennis left could be ripped freshly open even in the sealed safety of Cesca's car. I hated that radios were still allowed to play the song that we were supposed to dance to at our wedding.

He didn't even have to be present to hurt me. Star 98.7 could smite me in his stead.

I sighed. "What do I have to do to get that song banned worldwide? Can we start a petition or something?"

My roommate had the trapped, frozen look that I had grown accustomed to seeing on the faces of my family and friends over the last semester. The I-don't-know-what-to-say-please-don't-freak-out look.

"Oh, *relax*," I told her. "I'm not going to bust out crying."

She removed the Tootsie Pop from her mouth. "I think *I* might cry. I'm so sorry, Gwen."

I snorted. "Why are you sorry? You're not the one who got engaged to a mind-changing toadass."

"I know, but . . . Jesus, you know?" She really did look a little weepy. "I mean, this time last year you were asking me to find a reading for the ceremony and now . . ."

"Cesca. Seriously. Stop with these *Steel Magnolia* lines. You're killing me." I took a moment to compose myself. "I'm good. I'm over it."

"That's what you keep saying."

"And it's true!" I insisted. "I admit, I had some temporary setbacks. But it's all for the best. I'm moving on. I've found a new man who's way better than Dennis. Even though he hasn't called yet. Now pass the Sweetarts and let's go do some Pilates. A fie on exes everywhere."

She suddenly became fascinated with the exit sign for the 10 Freeway. "Speaking of exes . . ."

I leaned over and killed the music.

We spent a long, silent minute listening to the hiss of the air conditioner and the rumble of the Mustang idling next to us.

"I, uh, I'm thinking about calling Mike."

"What? Why?" I demanded, sounding just a tad more like General Schwarzkopf than I'd meant to.

"Well, he's been leaving all these messages on my voice mail, begging me to call him back." She turned the radio back on.

"Again, I must ask why you would consider doing such a thing." I eased into my calmest therapist's tone. "Perhaps the plate-smashing marathon of last month's breakup has slipped your mind, but as the woman who had to sweep up the kitchen floor and go buy new dishes at Costco not three weeks ago, let me refresh your memory."

"Actually, I already called him."

"No. You. Didn't."

"We're getting together Friday night." She jabbed her index finger toward me. "And I don't want to hear it from you."

"What happened to not speaking the man's name in our house? What happened to him being dead to you?"

"We're just getting together as friends," she said, her face scarlet.

"But *why?* You gave me specific instructions to tackle you to the ground and tie you up until you regained your sanity if I ever caught you trying to call him!"

"Well, it looks like *somebody* didn't do a very good job with the tackling, doesn't it?"

"Cesca . . ."

She sighed. "He still has some stuff of mine, and I . . . need it back."

"Like what? The final ragged shreds of your dignity and

good sense? You told me yourself—the man has a copy of every Warrant album ever made. And he treats you like shit. Why on earth would a smart woman like you go back for more?"

This pushed her over the edge. She whipped around in her seat, nearly swerving into the Mustang. "You know, Gwen, you're pretty opinionated for someone who's still hanging on to her ex-wedding dress."

3

Once we resumed speaking to each other after a grueling Pilates session with Polo, who, I had to admit, was unspeakably fine), Cesca managed to overcome her initial disapproval and devoted the rest of the week to helping me prep for my Friday night date with Alex.

"Ooh, dinner *and* the Lakers! That's like fifth date material." The merciless teasing progressed to psychological torture on Thursday evening. "You better watch out, 'cause the next step is picking out engagement rings, moving to Colorado, and popping out triplets!"

"I so regret ever telling you about that." I frowned at the conservative taupe blazer and skirt I'd worn to work that day. "Now shut up and help me figure out what I'm going to wear."

She clasped her hands under her chin and struck a 1950s yearbook pose. "Are you two going someplace *nice* for dinner?"

I stared at my low-heeled pumps. "La Guancia."

Her eyes doubled in size. "You don't mean La Guancia on Melrose with the four-month wait for reservations and the snottiest maître d' this side of Paris?"

"That's the one."

"Wow! This guy must have *beaucoup* bucks!"

I couldn't help but think about the ostentatious watch. "I guess."

She tilted her head to one side and summed up what we now knew about my new prospect. "Rich and handsome . . . and he likes to flaunt it on first dates. Hmm. Perhaps he's compensating for other, you know, *shortcomings?*"

"Hey now, be fair. Our first date was technically the coffee shop. Right after he ambushed me on Le Conte Avenue in the middle of a temper tantrum."

"How romantic." She grinned. "Well, I'll just have to scope this guy out for myself and see if he's good enough for your little rebound fling. When do I get to meet him?"

I gritted my teeth and ignored the "rebound" gambit. "How about Friday night?"

"No can do. I'm seeing Mike, remember?" She put her hands on her hips. "He is so funny. He said the most hilarious thing—"

I knew it! "So you're definitely getting back together with him? The man who believes cannabis is a food group?"

She froze, her smile too wide. "Uh. No."

"Liar."

"I'm not!" She succumbed to a sudden coughing fit. "I told you—we're just hanging out. As friends. Completely platonic."

"And you say *I* pile on the denial?"

"You do. Laker girl."

I looked at her. "Five bucks says you get back together."

"Deal." We shook on it.

So now Cesca was off gallivanting with the last Warrant fan on the planet, and I was faced with a closet full of clothes, none of which were worthy of La Guancia.

I closed my eyes and tried to imagine an appropriate ensemble for dinner at L.A.'s hottest new restaurant. And what came to mind was the clingy white dress Harmony had worn. Of course, you had to have a body like Harmony's and a face like Harmony's and charisma like Harmony's to pull that off. Not to mention a bloated budget for deceptively simple, expertly cut designer clothes.

I sighed and flopped down on my unmade twin bed (my old queen-size had been shipped off to Goodwill because, seriously, who wanted to sleep in a bed that had been slept in by someone who slept with Lisa?). The truth of the matter was that nothing in my wardrobe was going to be acceptable because I didn't want to dress like myself tonight. I wanted to dress up like Harmony. I wanted to *be* Harmony.

But time was a-wastin'. So I heaved a mighty sigh, yanked open the closet door, and came face-to-face yet again with the plastic-shrouded confection of silk, lace, and curdled dreams.

"I have *got* to get rid of this thing," I reminded myself, shoving the wedding dress out of the way and pawing past the muted Ann Taylor career separates.

Might as well face facts. Any attempt to compete with Harmony in the hoochie department would be pathetic and futile. So I settled on fitted black pants, a white tank top, and a leather jacket. This outfit would actually be perfect for a basketball game, which, in Los Angeles, is the type of event to which everyone brings a Hermès bag and binoculars to spot courtside celebrities. You can get glasses of decent Pinot Noir at the concession stands.

By the time Alex picked me up at six, I had applied powder, lipstick, and mascara, wiped it all off, reapplied it, and given myself a stern lecture. Why ruin the whole evening obsessing over his goddess-on-a-mountaintop ex? I might not be Carmen Electra, but I looked pretty damn good for an academic.

The tricky part would be pretending I'd never met "H. St. James" or her troubled child. According to legal guidelines, it would be unethical for me to discuss any of my clients with anyone other than my supervisor. It made me feel weird— cagey, like I had some huge advantage over Alex because I'd gotten a glimpse into his romantic archives. And I couldn't help but wonder: had Alex and Harmony dated before or after Leo was born, and if it was after, how had Alex adjusted to the role of surrogate father figure? Was Leo, in fact, responsible for sparking Alex's obsession with stay-at-home moms and tobogganing?

Thanks a lot, kid.

Alex showed up, right on time, in a dark blue Audi sedan.

The kind of car I could never drive because I would be constantly terrified of scratching it, denting it, or basically touching
it in any way. You needed a sense of casual fatalism to drive a car
like that. An ability to accept the impermanence of material
objects. And also a job that paid a lot better than a clinical
internship.

While I was philosophizing about his choice of wheels, Alex,
who had apparently memorized the complete works of Miss
Manners, actually got out of the driver's seat to open the car
door for me. He looked dashing yet low-key in khakis and a
black merino wool sweater.

"Hi," I said.

"Hi," he replied, and before I had time to step back and take
a thorough analytical reading of my reaction to seeing him
again, he had wrapped his hand tightly around mine and ushered me into the passenger seat.

Golden early-evening sunlight pooled in the soft tan leather
interior. The seat felt warm against my back, and while he
walked around to the driver's seat, I curled the hand he'd held
into my jacket pocket. The stereo was turned down, way
down, but I could discern the faint strains of . . . the Beach
Boys? In a clinic trustee's car? Where was the requisite Waspy
compilation of Gershwin and Holst? The fanatical devotion to
talk radio?

He slammed the door and buckled up. I smiled over at him
and finally started to relax. "'Good Vibrations'?"

He grinned. "Best pop song ever made."

I shook my head as we pulled away from the curb. "Somehow, I didn't picture you as the 'Surfin' U.S.A.' type. Aren't you a little young for the Beach Boys?"

"Can't help it. That's what happens when you're born in Malibu. I started surfing out at the Point when I was six."

"Six? As in six years old?"

"Sure. I was constantly pestering the older kids in the neighborhood, nagging them to teach me. I had a single mom—my biological father was generous with money, but he didn't want to be involved in my life. I ran her ragged, so eventually she gave in and bought me a board one summer just to get me out of her hair." He shrugged. "Gotta love the Beach Boys."

"*That's* your sad story of childhood woe and single motherhood? Growing up in Malibu, shredding waves with the Sheen brothers between margaritas?"

He rolled his eyes. "It wasn't quite like that."

I settled back into my seat as we turned onto Wilshire. "How was it?"

"Well, actually, I went to boarding school in New Hampshire."

"So, instead of surfing with the Sheens, you were snowboarding with guys with names like Ephriam Pennington the Third?" But I could see how that would be a lonely childhood—no siblings and a party-girl parent who packed you off to boarding school the moment you could tie your own shoes.

"Well . . . yeah." He laughed. "God, I sound like such a snob."

"Yes, you do," I said cheerfully. "Got any other tragic secrets to share? Was your 'single mom' actually in line to the throne of England?"

"You know, I'm picking up on your sarcasm. Let's get back to the topic at hand. What about you? Do you surf?"

I laughed. "I grew up in the Chicago suburbs. Landlocked flatlands. We didn't even have hills to sled on."

"Chicago." He nodded. "That explains the accent."

"I don't have an accent."

"Yes, you do. You sound . . . honest."

"What's up with you Californians and my alleged accent?" I demanded. "My friends out here listen to my mom talk for two seconds, and immediately ask what country she's from."

"What country *is* she from?"

"Iowa."

"Well, there you go." He tapped the steering wheel in time to "Surfing Safari." "I can't believe you've never been surfing. You'd love it. Clears your head. But you know, it's one of the most difficult sports out there."

I rolled my eyes. "How hard can it be if Keanu Reeves and Patrick Swayze can do it?"

"You a big *Point Break* fan? Wow, I've finally found my soul mate."

"*Now* who's being sarcastic?"

By the time we had arrived at the restaurant, we found ourselves in accord on several critical issues: the best donuts in L.A. (Bob's), the best place to go for brunch when hungover (The Griddle Café), and the best thing about sleeping alone (me:

don't have to listen to anyone snoring, him: don't have to listen to anyone's complaints about the snoring).

I really did like him. Rebound or no rebound, I wanted to know him better. And maybe occasionally kiss him. With tongue. And assorted other body parts. But all that didn't matter just now, because we were having *fun,* something I hadn't really done since the infamous nonwedding and all that preceded it.

But once Alex surrendered his car keys to a stern-faced valet, fun time was over. The restaurant, with all its muted lighting and carefully crafted ambiance, did not lend itself to frivolous discussions about snoring. Rather, this was the sort of joint where one could only discuss Eastern mysticism or high-stakes contract negotiations whilst craning one's neck to see if Steven Spielberg and Kate Capshaw had just arrived at the bar. Decor by International House of Chiffon, hostess by Mattel.

He pulled out my chair at a cozy little table in the back.

"Thank you," I murmured, trying not to disturb the amorous couple locking lips at the next table.

"You're welcome." We sat down and cleared our throats and glanced around in stilted silence until the willowy brunette waitress asked if we'd like to order an appetizer.

The twosome next to us stopped canoodling and glared at us as we scanned a menu and ordered white asparagus tips.

The waitress sashayed off. The canoodlers went back to business, pausing to seethe whenever Alex and I dared to speak above a whisper.

Service was agonizingly slow. At eight o'clock, we were

stranded with our empty appetizer plate and the rapidly fading hope of ever submitting a dinner order.

"Damn." He checked his watch and frowned. "We're going to miss tip-off."

I took a sip of water, considered chewing the ice to vex the canoodlers. "That's okay. I gotta tell you, I'm not the biggest basketball fan. I mean, it's *okay*, but my roommate Cesca is a rabid Lakers fanatic."

"Well . . . do you want to forget the game and do something else?"

The couple next door both turned their blond heads to scowl at the ear-splitting racket we were creating.

"Not unless you do," I whispered.

He nodded emphatically. "I definitely do."

I folded up my napkin. "Then let's forget this whole thing and go get some French fries."

His eyes lit up. "French fries. And red meat?"

"Sure. And let's throw in some cigarettes and booze while we're at it."

Thus, we ended up at Jerry's Famous Deli in Westwood, dipping fries in ketchup and reveling in our grease-laden bourgeois tackiness.

"Thanks for dinner. This is great." I bit into my grilled cheese sandwich. Heaven.

He finished a bite of meat loaf. "I keep forgetting there's a world outside corporate finance and overhyped bistros."

I shook my head. "You need to get out more. Or stay in

more. There's this thing called pizza delivery. God invented it just for people like you."

"Yeah, maybe." He grinned, hanging his head. "I have a DVD player I've never even used. I bought it six months ago, and it's still in the box."

"Too busy trading stock tips with old Ephriam Pennington the Third?"

"The stock market is more interesting than you might think. Especially in this economy."

"Well, there you go—you could order a pizza, take your DVD player out of the box, and watch *Wall Street*."

"How obsessed with capitalism do you think I am? Please. Do *you* kick back and watch *Analyze This* in *your* spare time?" He paused for a bite of meat loaf. "I did buy the whole first season of *Northern Exposure* on DVD, though. Did you ever watch that show?"

"I *loved* that show!" There was an energy in my voice that surprised me. I sounded almost happy.

Laughter bubbled up inside me, and we were off to the races.

"That episode where Maggie burns the house down!"

"The one where Joel goes on strike in the tent!"

"You don't want your pickles?"

"They're all yours." I shoved my plate toward him.

"How could I forget that I bought *Northern Exposure*?" He shook his head. "We should go watch it right now."

"Okay." I realized, even as I said it, that I was being snookered. But I did not care. I had gone three hours without once thinking about Lisa or Dennis or even Harmony, and that had to be worth something, right?

We managed to polish off the French fries sans cigarettes and booze, but I was feeling a little buzzed by the time we parked in front of Alex's Santa Monica condo. Because I was seriously considering sleeping with this guy.

This was not my usual style. I was very much a well-we've-been-together-for-three-months-shall-we-risk-it kind of gal.

At least, I used to be. But things had changed. No more three-month preludes to heartbreak. I was going to have to revise the rules of engagement (so to speak) in my postapocalyptic romantic landscape. I didn't want to waste the best years of my life mourning a man who didn't love me enough. The time had come to rejoin the ranks of desiring and desirable humans.

And I craved human contact. The simple solid warmth of another body pressed against mine. It had been so long since I'd had anything, a back rub, a somnolent embrace, *anything*. My emotional health had come down to this: get some action or get a cat. Given my dander allergies, the choice was clear.

This time I'd be smarter—I wouldn't load myself down with unrealistic expectations. None of this "*. . . but I'm in love*" crap. As long as we continued to skate on the surface, we'd be fine.

En route to his condo, he held about fifteen doors for me. The car door. The front door to his building's marble-coated lobby. The elevator door. And on and on.

As we left the public domain and entered the private, conversation dried up. Because frankly, his lifestyle intimidated the hell out of me. He lived in the architectural equivalent of a Patek Philippe watch: the type of building where you could march up to the doorman and demand a fresh bottle of imported water for your purebred bichon frise.

The spotless polish of the elevator mirror reflected a handsome, happy-looking couple. We could have posed for the Spiegel catalog, him tall, solid, and chiseled in merino and khakis, me small and streamlined in textured white and black. A perfect match made in marketing. Except for our eyes: his looked cautious, mine looked distant.

We just stood there, listening to the muffled dings ticking off the passing floors as the silence thickened between us.

I fiddled with my purse strap and tried to think of conversational gambits to throw out there. "So . . ."

He grinned. "Yeah."

"Is this a little awkward, or is it just me?"

The bell dinged again to announce our floor. We both startled.

"Oh, it's not just you."

We stepped into a high-ceilinged hallway with thick walls and deep beige carpet. A vase filled with dozens of artfully arranged white tulips rested on a mahogany table. A rail-thin woman with tight tan skin swished past us, a shark in black Gucci.

I shoved my hands in my pockets. "All right. Not to flaunt my suburban roots, but your building is scary."

He looked around as if noticing his surroundings for the

first time, then shrugged. "I guess it's a little pretentious, but it's a good investment."

"A good investment?" I gave him a look. "Whatever happened to warm and cozy? Or do we have to go to your Malibu beach house for warm and cozy?"

I waited.

"Alex. That's a joke."

He stared at the tulips, looking supremely uncomfortable.

"Oh my God." I collapsed against the hallway wall. "You do *not* have a Malibu beach house."

He jangled his keys. "It's small. Very small. I just thought, you know, talk about your good investments . . ."

"Oh my God. Who *are* you?"

He looked straight into my eyes. "I'm just a guy who can play the numbers well. I'm not out there saving lives. That's you."

"Are you kidding me with this?" I threw my hands up. "Well, I was going to seduce you with all my womanly wiles tonight, but now I can't."

Oops. Did I say that *out loud?*

He seemed stunned into speechlessness for a second, then rejoined the discussion with a vengeance. "You were? You can't?"

"I was! I can't!" I admitted all without a trace of shame. I was too aggravated to be demure. "Now you'll think I'm only after your fabulous Malibu investment property."

"No, I won't! I swear I won't!" He paused, then asked, not without some justification, "What *are* you after?"

I sighed. "I don't know. I should probably just go home now."

"Hold on." He practically tore a ligament blocking my path back to the elevator. "Slow down. We were having a good time."

"I agree." I sighed again. "But . . . remember the ex-fiancé? The cell phone in Le Conte Avenue? Well, my roommate keeps telling me that it's too soon to rush into another relationship, and she may have a point . . ."

He waited.

"I'm just so *tired* of being smart and safe and sidelined. And I like you. So, to be perfectly honest, I was considering throwing caution to the wind. And, you know, moving too fast." I studied the carpet. "Which is pretty presumptuous, considering, you know . . . I don't even know if you'd even be interested in something like that."

"Oh, I'm interested. But I do have one question."

"What?"

"Why are we having this discussion in my hallway?"

"No clue."

He opened the door to apartment 5C and ushered me into the darkness. As the closing door eclipsed the last sliver of the white light from the hall, I heard an undercurrent of deep, sexy laughter in his voice.

"So this 'moving too fast'—what exactly does that entail?"

I grinned. "Come here and I'll show you."

4

Plunged into darkness, my senses swirling, I tried to prepare for my new identity as a love-'em-and-leave-'em
vamp. A woman of freedom and sensual sophistication and—
God, was it ever dark in here.

His fingers brushed against mine and I did a little bunny
hop of surprise. *Nicely done, Gwen. Very seductive.* His warm,
minty breath—apparently, he had popped an Altoid on the ride
home—added to the heat in my cheeks.

I licked my lips and waited. No matter how wide I opened
my eyes, I couldn't see his face. There was nothing to focus on.

And then I felt his hand on my shoulder. His fingers slid
over the soft leather of my coat and on to the paper-thin skin at
the hollow between my collarbones. He slid his thumb beneath

my chin and applied gentle pressure until my face tilted back. I held my breath. I opened my mouth.

"Can we turn the light on?"

All the faint rustlings of cotton and leather stilled. The warm energy flowing around us evaporated into thin, cool air.

"What?" He said this practically into my mouth. I could feel the word hot against my lips. He was that close. I backed away and coughed.

"I just . . . sorry. I can't see."

He pulled away and flipped the light switch. Stark white fluorescence blazed down. I caught a glimpse of gleaming gray marble countertops and stainless steel kitchen fixtures at the end of the wide beige hall.

"Thanks." I closed my eyes against the blinding flood of brightness.

Alex, understandably, was now sounding confused. "Listen, maybe we should—"

I took a deep breath, stepped back up to the plate, and kissed him. Just wrapped myself around him like a reticulated python and went for it.

I kissed him to prove that I could still enjoy a kiss. I kissed him because I wanted to reawaken the graying, numb parts of my soul. But most of all, *worst* of all, I kissed him because somewhere tonight, Dennis was kissing Lisa the popcorn goddess and I refused to be the scorned woman who had to stay home listening to Alanis Morissette.

I was sick and tired of the constant undercurrents of regret and self-reproach that had washed through me every day since the man I loved explained that he could not love me back. My life had to get back on track, even if my heart could not.

For one breathtaking minute, everything fell into place. His hands slid around my waist. Deliberation flared into desire.

He was a great kisser, just the right mix of confidence and patience. And there was a subtle, mellow undertone, inexplicably reminiscent of red wine.

Oh *God*. I was comparing male saliva to Merlot. So much for staying emotionally distant.

Our hands were roaming all over each other. The heavy burdens of anger and suspicion I'd carried with me for the past six months fell away. I felt alive and impassioned in a way I hadn't since . . .

I shoved away from Alex's embrace and backed up to the wall, icy with sudden claustrophobia.

"I'm sorry. I can't do this. I thought I could, but I just . . . I can't. It's not you, it's me." I tugged down my shirt hem. "Or I guess, really, it's what I'm not."

He nodded cautiously. "And what are you not?"

"Ready for this stuff." I studied the slabs of gray slate tiling the floor. Then I rubbed my forehead, too embarrassed to look him in the eye. "I know you must be confused. I mean, here I am, hurling myself at you one second, and then going all frigid and Victorian. Giving psychologists a bad name. You're confused, right?"

"Yeah, I'm a little confused." But he did not sound even remotely hostile or annoyed.

"I'm just not ready to go down this road again. If I were, you would definitely be my first choice, but I . . ." I swallowed. "And you . . ."

"Shouldn't be kissing women I can't get serious with," he finished. "No matter how gorgeous and charming they are."

I crossed my arms. "There's no need to exaggerate."

"I'm not." He smiled.

"Well . . ." I broke eye contact but didn't know where to look and ended up scanning the room like a paranoid schizophrenic. "This is very bizarre. I'm sorry to be such a—"

"Don't be sorry. I'm the one who asked you up here with ulterior motives." When he grinned like that, he looked like a one-man travel brochure for Martha's Vineyard vacations. "But I know that you're not ready for anything serious. I'm not, either, unless—"

"Unless you find that paragon of womanhood who wants to settle down back at the ranch. Which isn't me." I sighed. "I know. But it's a shame."

"A *damn* shame." He led me down the hall to the kitchen, opened the stainless steel refrigerator, and grabbed two bottles of water. "What if we just take it slow?"

I raised an eyebrow. "Meaning . . . ?"

"Exactly what I said. We'll take it slow, see how it goes. Hang until we figure out what we want to do."

"Hang?"

"Yeah. Like basketball. When you're taking it to the hoop for the dunk. You hang."

"Uh-huh." Maybe I *should* give him Cesca's number. "And

may I assume that 'hanging' does not involve hasty commitment or false promises?"

"You may."

I tucked my hair behind my ear, blushing as I remembered the searing sweetness of that kiss. "Then I guess you can put me down for some hanging. What harm could it do?" I sighed, straightening the straps of my tank top. "But, God, sometimes I wish I could just approach the physical stuff like a guy."

"And how is that?"

"Like an alley cat in heat."

"That's nice." He collected two tumblers from the cabinet and placed them on the counter next to the water bottles.

"I don't hear any angry denials."

He poured the water and handed me a glass. "You know, some men are capable of thinking beyond their . . . testosterone."

I laughed. "Name *one.*"

"Well." He stalled by taking a looong sip of water. "The pope, probably."

"Eighty-five, bound by holy writ, and arthritic. You can do better."

"How about . . . Henry David Thoreau?"

"A recluse who composed lengthy odes to bean fields?"

"You asked for examples. Those are my examples. Life is short—do you really want to keep arguing about wussy men or do you want to watch some *Northern Exposure?*"

I checked the chrome-rimmed clock over the sink. Eleven-thirty. "I should be getting home soon, but I can stick around for the first episode."

"Fair enough." He topped off my water and led me to the buttery black leather sofa in the next room.

Four hours later, both of us were drowsing in front of the TV, empty shells of our former selves, unable to tear ourselves away. This was what happened when people who were too busy to watch television finally got some free time, a DVD player, and a remote. Total OD.

"I'm leaving after this one, I swear to God," I said after episode two.

We decided to order pizza halfway through episode three.

"I should really get you home," Alex said as the credits rolled after episode five.

We looked at each other. "Just one more."

I yawned.

"We can stop anytime we want to. We don't have a problem."

The piercing shafts of late morning sunlight finally woke me. Even before I opened my eyes, I knew I wasn't in my own bed. For one thing, I knew how to close the curtains, and for another, my bed didn't reek of pizza and leather.

I shoved my hair off my forehead and rubbed my forehead as I waited for total recall, which materialized about a fifth of a second later.

Yes, I was still in Alex's living room. Sprawled out on his

insanely expensive sofa, which I had, in all probability, drooled on. My sassy little outfit now felt constricting and vaguely damp.

I groaned and opened my eyes to find that I was curled up under the ugliest blanket in the Western Hemisphere. Thin and soft, it was emblazoned with bold black and white horizontal stripes. The visual effect was positively dizzying. Perhaps he had stolen it directly from Sing Sing.

Rolling my head toward the TV of My Undoing, I spied the note folded on the dark wood coffee table. I recognized the decisive handwriting on the yellow Post-it as Alex's.

Out hunting and gathering. Back momentarily.

Great. He had already seen me in all my slumbering, open-mouthed, mascara-smeared splendor.

It would not do to have him come back and find me still sprawled out with ratty hair and bleary eyes. Time for a little damage control in the bathroom.

The guest bathroom had precisely the tidy, empty feel one might expect in an apartment inhabited by a lone workaholic who buys a to-die-for condo for the investment value and then hires a cleaning service. The white porcelain gleamed, the gray towels were folded in thirds over sleek steel rods, and a pile of untouched blue soap shells nested in a hammered silver bowl by the sink. Attractive yet simple. Unlike, say, the reflection in the mirror.

I tried to console myself with the thought that the sadist

who'd decorated this place had made a pact with the devil of fluorescent lighting, but the fact was, I looked like hell. Apparently, the creators of the *Northern Exposure* DVD had left off the yellow warning sticker reading: "Be advised: viewing contents all in one sitting will result in looking like anemic junkie." My hair hung in limp brown hanks. The left half of my face was creased and blotchy from the sofa cushions. And even the aforementioned mascara smears couldn't hide the purple bags under my eyes. My clothes hadn't fared much better. The tank top was twisted and wrinkled—a trampled white flag of surrender.

Who would have thought that my long and colorful dating career would come to this? All the agony of the morning after without any of the ecstasy of the night before.

I did what I could with the available tools (cold water, soap, and the unopened packages under the sink containing toothbrushes, dental floss, and toothpaste) and was scrounging around for any variation of Vaseline or moisturizer when I heard the front door open.

When I peeked out into the foyer, I saw Alex heading toward the kitchen, loaded down with several white plastic grocery sacks and one brown paper shopping bag. He was decked out yet again in khakis, accompanied today by a black polo shirt and—wait a second, was he *whistling?* Had I just unwittingly spent the night under the roof of an inveterate *morning person?* God forbid.

Three minutes later, I finally accepted the fact that splashing water on my cheeks was not going to magically transform me into a dewy-eyed Estée Lauder model. And the rich scent of freshly brewed coffee beckoned me to the kitchen.

He hadn't exaggerated with that "hunting and gathering" comment. He was unpacking strawberries, bagels, cream cheese, croissants, and orange juice from the grocery bags and systematically arranging everything on the marble counter.

I observed from the doorway for a few seconds, shifting my weight from foot to foot and trying to find the right words to announce my presence. Finally, he looked up and smiled. The muscles in my neck and shoulders unknotted.

"Hi."

"Hi."

"I'm making breakfast, or trying to," he said. "I don't usually cook, but how hard can it be to toast a bagel?"

"Famous last words."

"Coffee?"

"Sure. Or, actually, do you have any Diet Coke?"

He gave me a look. "I'm a straight male, living by myself in an apartment that I still haven't gotten around to buying curtains for. What do you think the odds are of opening that refrigerator and finding 'diet' anything?"

"It was worth a shot."

He handed me a big blue mug brimming with coffee and leaned back against the counter. "Isn't it a little early for soda?"

"It's never too early for Diet Coke."

"I'll keep that in mind. How'd you sleep?"

"Um." I tried not to blush. "Great. How about you?"

"Sorry about that blanket. It's beat-up, I know. I have a

bunch of other sheets and stuff, but I don't actually know where. That was the only thing I could find on short notice."

"It's very penitentiary chic."

He nodded toward the shopping bag. "I got that for you. I thought you might want to change."

"There's clothes in here?" I pulled back a corner of the brown paper, consumed with curiosity yet terrified to see what the man who had purchased that migraine-inducing high-contrast blanket would consider appropriate breakfast attire.

I sifted through some yellow tissue paper and pulled out a very simple, very modest, and very (expensively) well-cut white shift dress embroidered with pale blue flowers. As I unfolded the soft cotton, I realized that this was exactly the kind of thing a man with hopelessly retro ideals about courtship would choose. A modest, girly, A-line frock Tricia Nixon might have worn while shopping for poodle skirts and pinwheels.

The dress reminded me once again that he and I were on opposite ends of the spectrum, romantically speaking. When he looked at me, he wasn't seeing the woman I really was, he was seeing the woman he wanted me to be—fresh, unguarded, capable of great feats of nurturing and baking. My mind flashed for a moment to Harmony. Now there was a babe who could pull off this dress. Remembering her casual charm, flawless face, and Aphrodite curves, I wanted to wail in despair. Why could I never snag these men *before* their exes ruined them for all other women?

I turned to him and smiled. "This is beautiful. But honestly, you didn't have to. I mean . . ."

He held up a hand to curb my protests. "I kept you up until four in the morning and you had to sleep on a couch with no pajamas. It was the least I could do." He took a sip of coffee. "Go try it on."

I *did* want to get out of my sleep-rumpled clothes. And he *had* gone to a lot of trouble. So I headed back to the bathroom for the moment of truth. Men buying clothes for women was always a dicey proposition. Too small a size = big trouble. Too large a size = end of world. As I struggled out of my pants, I wondered what all this meant—the cell phone, the dress, Alex's impossible dreams of a perfect wife and his paradoxical attraction to unsuitable, gun-shy me.

Only one thing was certain: this was not going to end well.

But we sure would have fun in the meantime.

I zipped up the dress and admired myself in the mirror. The material swished down to my knees, the embroidery was delicate and light. It fit, almost. The only problem was the bodice, which was a little baggy. I realized with a sinking heart that, based on all available evidence, he was used to women who had more on top than I.

Harmony and Alex. What a weird combination. Like pairing a macrobiotic papaya frappe with a steak.

I returned to the kitchen, tugging at the dress bodice the whole way, and presented myself.

He grinned. "It fits. You look great."

"Thank you." I forced myself to stop fidgeting. "I have to tell you, I'm impressed. Where did you find this?"

"There's a little clothing store on the way to the farmers'

market. I'd never gone in before, but I figured you'd need something to wear."

My eyes widened. "Wow. That's so nice of you. No one's ever—I mean, you really shouldn't have."

We stared at each other through the coffee steam. I was suddenly very aware of the thin translucence of the dress. He wasn't saying anything. I wasn't saying anything. Was he thinking about the kiss? Because that would . . . be . . . trouble. Yes. Sultry, wine-flavored trouble.

I shifted my focus to my chipped pink pedicure. "Well. Thanks."

He picked up the cordless phone and offered it to me. "If you want to—"

"No, I better just—"

"I'll take you home."

"My roommate will think—"

"I'm sure she won't."

"So I'll just grab my purse and . . . okay."

"Okay."

He parked the car in front of my apartment building, strode around to the passenger side, and opened my door for me. As he extended a hand to help me out, I couldn't suppress a smile. "They really drilled the whole door-holding routine into you back east, didn't they?"

"That's nothing. You should see me RSVP."

"Oh, stop—I may swoon." I grabbed my purse with both hands, zipping and unzipping the front pouch. "Well, okay. Bye."

He stopped my retreat with a firm hand on my waist. "You look so sexy in that dress. Come here a second."

When he kissed me, I kissed him back. I couldn't stop myself. My mind had denied my body last night, but the body was staging a comeback this morning.

Last night's sudden, startling heat hadn't been a fluke—it flared right up between us again. This time felt safer—we were in broad daylight, fully dressed, apt to be separated by a carload of frat boys yelling "Get a room!" at any moment. No danger that my libido would entirely overrule my good sense.

And right on cue, a Jeep teeming with scruffy hooligans slowed down long enough for the occupants to hoot, holler, and wrest Alex and I apart.

"Damn," he muttered as I pulled away.

"You are a *freakishly* good kisser." I sighed and headed for the apartment building foyer, stammering and tripping over the curb in the process. "I should go in before this turns into a Hugh Grant comedy."

He started in with the obligatory male postdate party line. "I'll—"

"*Don't* tell me you're going to call me," I warned.

"Okay." He leaned back against the car door. "I won't tell you. I'll just call."

I smiled and rolled my eyes, but I believed him. My love life was turning around. I was dating a guy who could figure out my dress size and my secret weakness for grilled cheese.

In yo *face,* Dennis.

*   *   *

I expected Cesca to pounce and interrogate me the instant I walked through the door. But the apartment was quiet. Too quiet. This, combined with the fact that she had arranged to meet Mike last night, did not bode well.

I heard a steamy hiss as the bathroom shower turned on, then Cesca's voice echoing off the tiled walls.

"American wo-maaan . . . Stay away from meee-ee . . ."

She did not sound heartbroken and bereaved. In fact, she sounded delighted. Ebullient. She sounded like a woman who just spent the night in the throes of—

"Yo. G-dog. What up?" Mike Jessup shuffled into view, wearing scuffed Adidas slides and Cesca's purple bathrobe. He held a bottle of Corona in one hand. Apparently, he had tried to grow a goatee since I last saw him—the soft blond fuzz clung to his chin in sparse patches.

"Mike. We meet again."

"Hells, yeah." He pulled a pack of Newports from the robe's pocket. "You know. Me and C. met up last night, and then before you know it, we were back here, and it was—"

"I got it, I got it." I glanced at the cigarette in his hand. "Could you please not smoke that inside? I'm allergic."

"A little asthmatic distress going on? That's cool." He fished out a lighter. "I remember—you've got the whole control freak thing happening, right?"

"That's me." I nodded.

"Yeah, you shoulda seen your face after C. and me broke

those plates. You were *pissed*." He returned his focus to the Newports. "What about when you're not here? Can I smoke inside
then?"

This startled me. "How often are you planning to be over
here?"

"All the time. Me and C. are back together. Back for good."

"I see. Will you please excuse me for a moment?" I headed
for the bathroom and pounded on the door.

"Come in," Cesca singsonged.

So I barged on in. "Francesca DiSanto."

"Oh, look who finally came home! Did your big date go
into triple overtime?"

"Don't you 'triple overtime' me. I want some answers."

Long pause on the other side of the curtain. "About what?"

"Why don't you tell me?"

Big sigh. "I suppose you're wondering about Mike."

"I am, yes. The last time I checked, he was fleeing from the
pottery shards and I was forbidden to speak his name."

She turned off the shower. "Oh. That. Well, that was all just
an unfortunate misunderstanding."

"I see." I could hear the faucet dripping into the drain.

"I can feel your disapproval radiating through the shower
curtain. Don't get all prim and proper on me. I can't explain it,
Gwen. He just makes me so happy."

I gagged. "Do you want me to yak right now?"

"That's not very sensitive of you."

"Come on! The guy is out there right now having beer and
nicotine for breakfast."

"You're just mad because he used to steal your Diet Coke out of the fridge."

"For your information, I had forgotten all about that," I said. "Although, yeah, it was pretty annoying now that you mention it. But it's not about the soda and you know it. It's about the fact that he treated you like crap."

My roommate poked her head out from behind the curtain and glared at me through the soapy rivulets trickling down from her hair. "You are not my keeper. If you are really my friend, you will respect my choice. So. Now will you tell me about your date?"

I put my hands on my hips. "You're sabotaging yourself with him and you know it. Honestly? I think you date guys like him to keep yourself from getting into a real relationship. How can you be so smart and so dumb at the same time? It's like you deliberately hold yourself back."

She jerked her head back into the shower. "It's none of your business. Lock up your Diet Coke, chickie! And by the way, nice dress. You auditioning for *Our Town?*" She turned the water back on, full blast.

I slammed the bathroom door behind me and marched back into the kitchen, where Mike greeted me with, "Hey, G-dog, if you and C. ever decide you want to shower, you know, *together,* I'm down with that."

I opened my mouth, then decided it wasn't worth it and stormed into my bedroom. I was already in enough trouble with "C." Heaven forbid I offend her precious Prince Charming.

As it turned out, Cesca took care of that herself. I heard her emerge from the bathroom and join Mike in the kitchen, where their soft murmuring escalated to a screaming match in ten minutes flat. I didn't know what the argument was about, but they both seemed quite adamant in their positions.

"If I could kill you right now, I would!"

"Nice talk from a psychologist!"

"I'm not a psychologist yet, you scum-sucking freak! Get out before I do something we'll both regret! And gimme my robe back!"

Slam. Exit Mike.

For now.

5

My Monday morning interview with Harmony St. James got off to a deceptively good start. She showed up almost on time (I accepted her excuse about jam-packed freeways with a polite smile and no comment), ready to take on the world.

"Hi, Dr. Traynor," she said, gliding into my office in a cloud of gentle grace and jasmine perfume. "Check it out—I'm ready to roll up my sleeves and get to work! Ask me anything!"

I did check her out, suffering a crushing loss of self-esteem in the process. She was resplendent in fawn-colored sandals with four-inch heels and straps that snaked halfway up her calves, a tight white miniskirt, a black silk sweater that dipped off one tan shoulder, and huge black pearl earrings that probably cost more than my entire year's fellowship.

She curled up in the blue armchair near my desk and tossed her purse to the floor. "So where do we start, Dr. Traynor?"

"Oh, call me Gwen." I uncapped my pen, flipped to a fresh page in my notepad, and reminded myself that even though I didn't look like one of Charlie's Angels, I had other skills. Or something. "I haven't technically finished my Ph.D. yet, and there's no need for formality."

"Okay. Gwen." She leaned forward, practically resting her chin on my desk. "Do you want to hear about my mother? My childhood? My dreams? You know, I have the craziest dreams, but they're all in black and white, never in color, what do you think—"

"Why don't we start with your son?" I suggested.

"Oh." She looked a little disappointed. "Okay."

"As Leo's mom, you're going to have to do a lot to help his therapy along. After all, I'll only see him for an hour or so each week. You have him every day."

She nodded, furrowing her brow in concentration.

"So it's important that you and I agree on a course of action, and that we work together. You cannot reinforce bad behavior when Leo's at home, or let him get away with breaking the rules because you feel guilty. I know he's probably very difficult to deal with right now, I know you feel sorry for him, but you've got to hang in there. It may be a while before he shows any improvement—at least four or five months."

"Four or five *months?*" She repeated, dismayed. "I screwed him up that bad already? He's only in preschool!"

"You didn't 'screw him up,' Ms. St. James," I soothed, glossing over the fact that lots of clinical studies linked childhood depression to a chaotic home life and inconsistent parenting. "But you can help him feel better. Let's start with when you first noticed changes in behavior. Children his age often start showing signs of depression after the loss of a parent or a symbolic object—a security blanket, something like that. Has there been any sudden loss like that in the past few months?"

Harmony twisted up her lips and thought. "Well, his dog died last month."

I checked my notes from Leo's last session. "Jellybean?"

"Yeah. He really loved Jellybean, so his poor little heart was broken. And then—oh! I know! My mom was living at my place for about nine months, and then she moved out a few weeks ago. At the beginning of June."

"So Leo was used to living with his grandmother?"

"Yeah, but she met this old rich guy who was here on vacation, and it was love at first sight. He's just crazy about her, and he bought her this huge diamond from Harry Winston. So she moved out to Hawaii with him. They're getting married."

"I see." I jotted 'flighty grandma' in my notes, not really surprised by this information. Chaos and impulsivity tended to cycle down through generations.

"So then I hired Nell from the best nanny agency in town—I checked all her references, I really did—but Leo hasn't, you know, bonded with her very much."

"Mm-hmmm." I scribbled notes down in my yellow legal pad.

"And then I told him a few weeks ago that we might be moving to New York City if I get this part I'm auditioning for on a prime-time sitcom, which would be huge for my career. And he threw a fit and said he hated New York and he hated me. In that order." She lowered her voice and confided, "The casting director just called my agent yesterday and said it's down to me or Alicia Silverstone."

I tried not to be derailed by the gratuitous name-dropping. "And what about Leo's father?"

She gave me a sunny, carefree smile. "What about him?"

"Is he involved in Leo's life?"

She shook her head. "Nope."

"Well . . ." How to put this delicately? "Has he *ever* been involved in Leo's life?"

"Nope."

"Look, I know these are very personal questions. I'm just trying to get a clearer picture of your home life and the family structure."

"Oh, no problem whatsoever." She flicked a strand of dark hair back over her shoulder. "Grover—he's my spiritual adviser at Synchrona—says that it's very important to be honest. Honest with myself, honest with him, honest with, you know, the *universe*."

I blinked. "Synchrona?"

"That's my spiritual group. They're based in West Hollywood, and they've been written up in the *Los Angeles Times, Us Weekly* and *InStyle,* even the *Wall Street Journal.*" Her blue eyes widened. "They're very into family values and morals."

I think I had read that *L.A. Times* article, and if I was not very much mistaken, the word *cult* had been bandied about.

"Um. Great." I forced myself to shut my mouth and not write "pseudo-religious wackjob" in my notes. "So what is *your* relationship with Leo's father?"

"I don't have one. He was just this guy I dated for a while, and then we broke up." She shrugged. "That's it."

"He didn't want to be involved in his son's life?" I asked, thinking about how painful it must be for a little boy to feel rejected by his father.

"He might have, but . . ."

I looked up from my pad. "But *what?*"

"Well . . . I never exactly told him I was pregnant." She giggled and covered her mouth like a schoolgirl caught passing notes.

The first black stirrings of suspicion uncurled in my stomach.

"Really." I paused to take a sip of coffee and choose my next words very carefully. "And, uh . . . did the two of you have a serious relationship? Prior to the breakup?"

Her forehead wrinkled up. "I guess so. We were going out for a while, and then he just broke up with me for no reason." She paused, looking guilty. "Well, I'm being honest, right? *Honestly,* I borrowed his credit card—this was before *Twilight's Tempest* was the ratings success it is now—and went a little overboard at Fred Segal. It was the semiannual sale on Melrose. You know how it is. And then I was furious with him after he broke up with me, and then by the time Leo was born, I was dating his friend, and I don't know . . . I just never got around to telling him. It would've been awkward."

The room was so quiet, I could hear the seconds tick by on the wall clock across the room.

She finally opened her mouth again to break the silence. "You know, it's possible that his friend told him about the baby after I dumped him, but I doubt it. He was pretty mad at him."

I crossed my fingers and prayed that I was not about to hear what I thought I was about to hear. "Who was mad at whom?"

"The father—Alex C.—was mad at his friend—Alex S.— after Alex S. and I hooked up."

Oh no. *Nonononono.*

"Alex C. and Alex S." I pretended to jot this down and surrendered the entire right side of my brain to hyperventilating panic.

"I know. I seem to have a thing for guys named Alex." She adjusted her skirt hem. "I've dated like ten of them. Except for the guy I just broke up with. He was a Paul."

"But back to Leo's father—I'm sorry, what did you say his name was, again?" I gave up subtle nudges in favor of arm-breaking shoves for information.

"Alex Coughlin." She smiled sweetly.

I clutched my pen so hard my knuckles went white. Luckily, she was off and running with her reminiscences and didn't even notice my dismay.

"The other guy, his friend that I dated, was Alex Spears." She paused to adjust her earring. "But, anyway, I couldn't tell Alex C. that he was the dad because first of all, he had changed his phone number so I would stop calling him to apologize, and second of all, he would've freaked out. He had a thing about single moms."

"Did he?" I choked out.

"Yeah." She leaned in and lowered her voice. "See, he never had a dad. Well, I mean, there was some rich guy who had an affair with his mom, and when she got pregnant with Alex, he gave her this huge trust fund to keep her quiet. But his mom was a little bit like, the light's on at Motel Six, but the guest has checked out, you know? So he grew up in boarding schools like you see in those old Shirley Temple movies. He had this gigantic hang-up about single parents. He would've been a pain in the ass about my pregnancy." She deepened her tone and did what I had to admit was a pretty good imitation of Alex. *"No child of mine is going to start his life without a father."* She shrugged. "And now that I'm at Synchrona, Grover says I should free my soul of deceit and earthly encumbrances, but I don't even know how to find the guy anymore."

I tried to close my mouth and look professionally detached. "Have you been *looking* for him?"

"Only a little bit. I checked the phone book. He wasn't listed. But I didn't call his office or anything."

There was nothing left to do but repeat the stock therapist response. "I see."

"But now that my pookie's depressed and my mom can't take care of him, I've been thinking." She raised one blood-red nail to her lips. "Maybe I should search a little harder for Alex C."

She fixed those clear blue eyes on me. "What do *you* think I should do, Gwen?"

I arrived at my adviser's office breathless and sweaty. But the door was closed, which meant one of two things: either he was off-site or he was conducting some private administrative meeting in there, the interruption of which would result in my instantaneous death.

"Is Dr. Cortez here today?" I asked his secretary, peering over the stacks of manila folders and pink phone messages piled on her desk.

"No." She didn't take her eyes off the invoice sheet in front of her. "He's at a conference in San Francisco for the next two days. Why?"

"I guess I have what you might call an ethical dilemma. I wanted to ask his advice."

"Dr. Vaughn is here today. You could talk to her."

Heather Vaughn, one of Dr. Cortez's postdocs, was a fussy, dour-faced woman who wore her glasses on a chain around her neck and loved to start her sentences with phrases like "I'm reminded of what Immanuel Kant said about consciousness . . ."

"Thanks anyway." I headed for the nearest exit. As I burst into the blazing midmorning sun, I checked my watch and realized that I had only five minutes until my next appointment.

Five minutes to get hold of someone—anyone—who could tell me what the hell I should do about Harmony's little secret.

No doubt about it: this was a thorny dilemma. She had disclosed information in the privacy of my office during a therapy session, which meant that I was legally bound to keep it in confidence. Except I was also required by law to disclose information about abuse or neglect of children. Did depriving Leo of his father constitute neglect? And did depriving Alex of the chance to claim his child constitute, I don't know, cruel and unusual punishment?

But wait. Maybe Leo wasn't really his child at all. Maybe Harmony had just gotten all those besotted Alexes confused. It could happen, right? I was due for some good luck in the romance department, dammit!

I didn't even try to fool myself into thinking that I could retain a rational and unbiased perspective. Alex and I . . . I wasn't sure exactly what we had going on, but it was definitely something sexual. Something promising. Until now.

Of course, Harmony had no reason to suspect that I had recently spent the night canoodling with her ex in his curtainless condominium. And Alex would definitely flip his shit if he knew that his ex and I had sat down and dissected his childhood.

Then there was Leo. Poor little Leo. Regardless of the consequences, my first obligation was to protect him and his best interests. I had made a professional commitment to that end, but more importantly, Alex—his *father*, dear God—would want it that way. I'd only known him a week, and I was certain of that. So. What to do?

I had a slow, sinking feeling that I knew the answer to that question.

I took a seat on a wrought-iron bench under a palm tree and

dug my new cell phone out of my bag. This time, the batteries were all charged up and ready to go. Cesca picked up on the third ring, sounding groggy and irritable. Clearly, someone had headed back to bed after breakfast this morning.

"'Lo?"

"It's me," I said. "I need help."

I heard the rustling of bedclothes on the other end of the line. "What now?"

"I have an ethical question."

She groaned. "If this is about another rebound guy, I'm hanging up."

"No, it's . . . remember when I told you that one of my new clients' mom was Alex's ex-girlfriend?"

A big yawn. "Yeah."

"I met with her today, and she told me something that . . . well, I'm not sure what the rules of confidentiality are in this case."

Long pause on her side. Then: "Gwen. You know I love you, but you are seriously going to The Bad Place with this whole Harmony thing. Now that you know for sure that she used to date your new boyfriend or *whatever* he is, you can't work with her anyway. Just refer her aerobicized Carmen Electra ass to somebody else. Let Heather deal with her; that'll serve her right for messing with your man."

"Well, obviously now that I'm sure it's his ex I'm going to refer her," I said impatiently. "But it's too late to unask the questions I already asked. And this morning she told me something that I think Alex really needs to know."

Another long pause.

"I'm not overreacting, Cesca. This is a *big deal*. It is life-altering."

She sighed. "Are we talking about child abuse?"

"Not exactly."

"A murder confession?"

"No."

"Then you know what the rules are. I don't see what's to discuss."

"Believe me, there's plenty to discuss."

"Is Harmony actually a man?"

"Cesca—"

"Does she have a horrible STD that she secretly gave to Alex?"

"No."

"Then I can't imagine what could be so earth-shattering. Besides, you're screwed either way. If you tell Alex, Harmony can sue the clinic up the ying-yang, and if you don't, you're going to feel weird and guilty about it forever." She yawned. "Good luck with that."

"Thanks. You're a big help."

"I live to serve."

My call-waiting beeped. "I gotta go. I've got another call."

"It's probably the *National Enquirer* wanting an exclusive. True Confessions of a Serial-Dating She-male, starring Harmony St. James."

"You're going to hell, you know." I hung up on her and clicked over to the other line. "This is Gwen."

"Hey, Gwen. This is Alex."

I clamped a hand around the wooden slats of the bench seat. "Oh. Hi?"

"You sound shocked. Are you really that amazed that I called?"

"No, no, I . . ." I took a deep breath. "Listen, Alex, this really isn't a great time to talk. I'm late for a session."

"That's fine." His voice sounded crisp and untroubled. "I just called to ask if you'd like to grab dinner tonight. And to tell you to keep Saturday morning free."

"Saturday?" I reached for my planner, then threw it back into my bag. Who knew what we'd all be doing on Saturday? He'd probably be embroiled in a custody bloodbath with Harmony by then.

"Yeah. We're going surfing."

Oh God. Surfing. He was thinking about surfing, and I was thinking about how to tell him that—surprise!—he was the father of an emotionally disturbed preschooler. *Why* hadn't I just gone to law school like my parents had wanted me to?

"Gwen? Hello?"

"Yeah. I'm here."

"So I'll pick you up tonight around eight?"

"That might present a problem on several levels," I finally said. "And you know, you might want to keep your weekend open, just in case something comes up."

A brief pause ensued. "Do you not want to see me again?"

"Of course I do!"

"Do you have to work?"

"Well . . . no."

"So what's the problem?"

I sighed. "There is no problem. Yet."

"Your optimism is inspirational. Do you want to hang out tonight, or not?"

"I do," I hedged. "But it's been a crazy morning, and—"

"Then we're going. Nothing fancy, very low-key." He clicked off the line. I stared at the phone, my mind racing. The dull twinges of an emergent headache crept into my temples.

But something else was seeping into my soul. Something sour and small. Fear? Envy? The sudden certainty that once Alex found out that Harmony was raising his child, he'd want to reconcile with her and live happily ever after? Sure, they'd broken up, and sure, she was pretty scary with all that Synchrona claptrap, but she had a body that put Halle Berry to shame. And she held the ultimate trump card—a tow-headed little boy with a Fider-Man wardrobe and Alex's thoughtful brown eyes.

I am still not totally positive how this happened (I suspect my weakness for classically handsome men who plied me with French fries may have been involved), but I ended up going to dinner with Alex on Monday night, despite my trepidation. Then a movie on Thursday. Then a retro snogging session in his car when he dropped me off in Westwood. On at least ten different occasions throughout the week, I wanted to tell him about Harmony and Leo, but here is what came out instead:

"I'd love to go out again this weekend."

"Get out! *Bull Durham* is one of my top five favorite movies too!"

"So what exactly does NASDAQ stand for?"

Etc. It was bad. I led the double life of a very dysfunctional superhero. By day, I left frantic messages on Harmony's voice mail, begging her to call me back. By night, I hit the town with Alex, then came home, went to bed, and woke up at 4 A.M. in a cold sweat.

I worried about what would happen when Alex found out about Leo. I worried about how I was going to explain all this to Dr. Cortez. But mostly, I worried about the way I had started to feel about Alex.

I liked him. A lot. And not in a I'm-so-desperate-for-validation-won't-you-pretty-please-be-my-rebound-man kind of way. It was more of a let's-stay-up-all-night-engaged-in-unspeakable-acts-of-passion kind of way. My hormones, which didn't know any better, kept insisting that this was The Guy. Mr. White Knight himself.

"Haven't I learned anything?" I wailed to Cesca on Friday morning, my lips still swollen from all the kissing the night before.

"Apparently not." She grinned. "But it sounds like it's gonna be hot. Bring him back alive."

Harmony's next scheduled appointment was Monday at noon.

That turned out to be twelve hours too late.

I spent the weekend with Alex, promising myself that any minute now, I would tell him the truth, the whole truth, and nothing but the truth, so help me God.

Any minute now.

He took me to the international surf museum in Huntington Beach. He took me to Carmine's II Café. And on Sunday night, he took me to bed.

I was asking for it, really, wearing the crisp white *Our Town* dress to dinner. I might as well have hung a PROPERTY OF ALEX COUGHLIN sign around my neck, and I knew it. But I headed out into the night with only a tiny black purse and an over-abundance of bravado.

He played to all my weaknesses. With his blue button-down shirt, gray slacks, and a woodsy trace of cologne, he could've been the spokesman for Give Men Another Chance International.

He arrived at my apartment looking even more healthy and tan than usual. "I went surfing this morning up in Malibu," he explained. "The waves were brutally good."

I laughed. "Were they, like, totally tubular?"

"Get in the car, woman."

And we were off.

We ate ravioli and calamari in the dusky candlelight while our feet and calves tangled together under our tiny table for two. A buzz of lust and tension swelled up between us, but the catalyst fueling the crescendo was hope. I felt lucky. Lucky to be here, drinking and laughing with a man who could discuss the fall of the deutsche mark, brutally good waves, and his best childhood pal (a golden retriever named Beauford) in the same evening.

The odds of finding a man like this in Los Angeles were roughly the same as that of finding a black cat in the Black Forest during an eclipse of the moon. Statistically speaking, Alex was impossible. And yet, here he was, eyeing the neckline of the *Our Town* dress and plying me with simple carbohydrates.

We had it all: throaty laughter, lingering glances, repartee that we considered witty. It was practically an ABBA song brought to life. Well, except for the whole Leo thing. Still had to deal with that.

I procrastinated through dessert, through Asti Spumante, through fifteen minutes of light traffic on Westwood Boulevard.

Finally, when we pulled up in front of my building, I cleared my throat. No more idle chatter about NASDAQ. Time to come clean and turn this budding fairy-tale romance into a sick and twisted farce.

I stared straight ahead into the thin yellow glow cast by streetlights. I licked my lips.

He watched me licking my lips.

"Okay." My hands twisted together in my lap. "I have to tell you something."

His voice was thick and low. "Am I going to like it?"

"Well . . . you'll have to be the judge of that." I finally looked at him and tried to smile. "Things have gotten sort of complicated. Since last week."

"Really." He stroked my bottom lip with his thumb.

I tilted my face away, determined to deliver the bad news before I lost all control and attacked him like a puma from the trees. "Yeah. I'm having a good time with you—a *really* good time—but I think we may have something of a situation on our hands. And I don't know what to do." I took a deep breath. "Alex, I—"

"Me too." He kissed me, soft and slow.

I pulled back a fraction of an inch. "Hang on. I have to tell you something."

He brushed his lips across mine. My palm slid down his chest, coming to rest just above his belt buckle.

"Tell me later."

The man made a compelling argument.

I swallowed. "You say that now, but—"

He kissed me again.

"Wait," I breathed.

He eased his fingertips under the hem of my dress. "No?"

Tell him. Lower your pulse rate, open your yap, and tell him that you met Harmony. It'll take forty seconds. Twenty if you cut to the chase.

I opened my mouth. When I met his eyes, they were reflecting emotions I didn't recognize. Something deeper than what I'd had with Dennis.

Something I was about to give up by telling secrets in a flagrant breach of ethics. Something I was about to give up in punishment for sins I didn't commit.

So I did something I'd never done in my entire dating career. I shut my mouth, I shut my eyes, and I opened my soul to him. Tomorrow would have to take care of itself.

It was good. Eyes-rolling-back-in-head, involuntary-spasming good. My sweet little twin bed was utterly defiled. And afterward, he stood up, put his boxers back on, and ventured out to the kitchen to bring me a Diet Coke. Then he settled down on the minuscule mattress, engulfed me in both arms, and went to sleep without a single complaint about the fact that his feet were dangling in midair.

What a catch.

My alarm clock woke us on Monday morning. I tensed as soon as I hit the snooze button and tried to sit up, reeling with the horrifying morning-after questions. What if he was repulsed by my stale Diet Coke breath? Worse, what if he realized he was way out of my league?

He stirred and pulled me closer to him, squinting at the luminous digital dial. "What time . . . oh God, I've got an early meeting today."

I gave him a light jab with my elbow. "Why didn't you tell me? I would've set the alarm."

He rubbed his stubbly cheek against my neck. "The sunlight usually wakes me up."

"A plan foiled by the fact that I actually have curtains."

We ended up showering together "to save time." As I brushed my teeth and dried my hair, I realized that the reason I felt so wired this morning was that I was now both hopeful *and* scared. Hopeful that my night with Alex might turn into something real, scared that we were doomed by circumstances beyond our control.

But.

Maybe not telling him was the best thing I could do. Maybe we could make this work. Maybe Harmony had gotten confused, and Leo wasn't even remotely related to Alex.

Or *maybe* I had just hopped on the fast track to doom and

damnation by withholding information that would instantly change every aspect of his existence.

When we emerged, fully dressed, we ran smack into Cesca and Mike at the breakfast table. By all appearances, they were back on again. Clad in guilty grins and strategically arranged bath towels, they had bogarted the last of the orange juice. As the males sized each other up, Cesca raised her eyebrows at Alex and mouthed, "Cute."

"I know," I mouthed back.

"Top o' the morning to ya," Mike drawled, lighting up a Newport as part of this complete breakfast.

I managed a half-hearted smile. Cesca was decidedly less tolerant. She whirled on her stool and fixed him with an icy glare.

"There is nothing worse than a fake brogue before I've had my coffee."

"Except *nagging*," Mike countered, dragging on his cigarette. He nodded at Alex. "Women, eh?"

Cesca's face turned a dull red. "Way to put the 'duh' in dumb-ass."

"Whatever. Nagger."

I grabbed Alex's hand and tugged him toward the door. "Let's get out of here before the flatware starts flying."

We escaped down the hall as the volume racheted up in the kitchen.

"So what did you want to tell me last night?" he asked.

I coughed. "Um, it's about your ex-girlfriend. Harmony."

"Harmony." He eyes narrowed. "What about her?"

"Well, I saw her . . . in a magazine, obviously . . ." Yeah, obviously. It's not like she'd shown up in my freaking *office* or anything. "She's really beautiful, isn't she?"

Understanding dawned in his eyes. "I know where you're going with this."

I shook my head. "I really don't think you do."

"Gwen." He closed both hands around my shoulders. "I know you're gun-shy about this type of thing, but I will make you a promise here and now. I'm not like that guy who left you at the altar. I will never go back to Harmony."

I winced. "But . . ."

"*Never*. Understand?" He squeezed my shoulders again. "That whole thing was a mistake, it's in my past, and that's where it's going to stay."

I tried to smile.

"You are the one I want. I will never go back to her. She's my worst nightmare." He smiled back and traced my cheekbone with his index finger. "Now. I have to get home to change for work, but I will call you later."

Before leaving, he gave me a chaste little kiss on the cheek. The morning after, in Mayberry.

I kept smiling until he disappeared around the corner. Then I slammed the door, snatched my cell phone, and dialed up Alex's worst nightmare.

7

I spent the next hour and a half forcing myself to concentrate on seven-year-old Lucy Spitz, a sweet little girl with thick red braids and a serious attention deficit problem, and prided myself on keeping my personal and professional problems separate, if only for a clinical hour.

True, I wasn't sleeping with Lucy's dad while simultaneously trying to talk her mom into revealing the truth about her child's illegitimate parentage, but I'd take my victories where I could find them.

At the end of the session, I headed out to the waiting room and started to give Mrs. Spitz the update on Lucy.

"Luce and I had a great time today—"

"Oh, Gwen, there you are! Thank God!" Harmony St. James

lunged up from the chair beside the magazine rack. "I've been waiting for you."

I blinked. "Harmony. Hi. You're early."

She wrapped her hand around my wrist. "Don't worry. I know you're insanely busy, but this'll only take a second."

Mrs. Spitz and Lucy gaped.

"Mommy, is that Catherine Zeta-Jones?" Lucy asked.

Harmony blushed and fluttered. "Oh no, honey! I'm not Catherine Zeta-Jones." She beamed at Mrs. Spitz. "I get that all the time."

Mrs. Spitz turned to me with one eyebrow raised.

"Okay. Harmony, you'll have to hang on a few minutes because I need to talk to my current clients."

"But I'm supposed to be on the set by noon! And you said you needed to talk to me! I'll be done in five minutes, I promise." She started tugging me back toward my office.

"Can't we just reschedule the appointment?" I asked.

"We may as well just do it now, as long as I'm out here. Don't worry, I'll talk fast!"

I looked at Mrs. Spitz, who looked at Lucy, who still hadn't closed her mouth.

"Go ahead." Mrs. Spitz waved us away. "We'll talk next week at the regular time."

I shook my head. "But it's very important that you—"

"Oh, thank you!" Harmony covered her heart with both hands and whirled around to face Mrs. Spitz. "Thank you so much!"

Mrs. Spitz shrugged. "If it's an emergency . . ."

"Oh, it is! It is!" Harmony gushed right over my objections. "I'm going to be sending you good karma for this. Good, powerful, *Synchrona* karma!"

At the word *Synchrona*, Mrs. Spitz nodded nervously and hustled her daughter out of there.

Harmony blew past me and powered down the hallway, which left me no choice but to lecture the back of her head.

"Harmony, I understand that you want to speak with me, but I insist that you respect the rights of my other clients. When I ask you to wait, it's for a good reason."

We stopped in front of the office while I unlocked the door.

"Oh, I know. It's terrible of me to just barge in like this." She widened her enormous blue eyes. "But after we talked last time about Leo and Alex C., I got to thinking, and well . . ."

My hand froze on the doorknob. As I waited for details, I forgot to inhale, exhale, or relax my forehead, which had suddenly gone all wrinkly in the manner of a Shar-Pei.

"Yesss?" I finally prompted.

"I talked to my spiritual adviser this weekend and I asked him what I should do and what would be best for Leo."

I gave in to my irritation for a moment. "In the future, when you have questions about Leo's mental health, please remember that he does have a *psychologist*—"

"Oh, I know, and you guys are great." She seemed to feel a bit sorry for me. "But you just can't understand life's complexities the way Synchrona can. I mean, Synchrona is really based on science, while psychology . . . well, you know . . ."

Deep breath in. Deep breath out.

She patted my arm. "Anyway, Grover—my adviser—felt the same way you did. He said I should tell Alex C. the truth. Because family security is very important to kids Leo's age."

"That's true."

"And he said a father has a right to know about his own son."

Odd how when *I* said something, it went in one ear and out the other, but when Grover said the exact same words, it was like Moses had just carried them down from the Mount.

"So I have to call Alex C." She nodded solemnly. "But I need you to help me."

I paused. "And how would you like me to do that?"

"I need you to be here to support me while I call and tell him."

I collapsed against my office door, which swung inward, freeing me up to fall on my ass. When I picked myself up, Harmony had fixed me with an expectant gaze.

"Harmony, before you say anything else, you should know that I'm in the process of referring you and Leo to another therapist here."

"But I *like* you!"

I tried not to feel flattered. "It's not really a choice. I have a conflict of interest."

"What's the problem?" She didn't seem nervous or defensive, just curious.

I cleared my throat. "Remember Alex C.?"

"Of course!"

"Well, I sort of . . . know him." In the biblical sense.

94

She did a double take worthy of any soap opera. "You do not!"

I hung my head. "I do."

"Well, that's perfect!" She smiled. She actually smiled. This, to her, was good news. "Then you know his number?"

"Yes, but—"

"Great! That'll save me one boring 411 call. And—bonus!— you can calm him down if he gets all angry and, you know, *guy* on me!"

"I really don't think—"

"Oh, thank God for Grover. He always shows me the right path. This is such a miracle." She bent over, disappearing from my line of vision while she rummaged through her Louis Vuitton bag, and reemerged clutching a purple candle and matches in one hand and a small glass pyramid in the other.

"Okay. Just give me a minute to get centered." She lit the candle, wafted some lavender-scented smoke my way, then closed her eyes, clutching the little pyramid in both hands.

I coughed. "You're not really supposed to light candles in here."

"*Shhhh.*" Her palm swooped down inches from my face and then back up over hers. "Can you hear that?"

I listened. I heard some little kid caterwauling in the waiting room, but nothing else. "Hear what?"

"The earth. Turning. Connecting." Her eyes popped open, white and blank like something right out of *The Exorcist*. "*Embracing.*"

"Uh . . ."

"I have courage because I am a strong and worthwhile person," she chanted, turning the pyramid over and over with her fingers. "I have courage because I am a strong and worthwhile person."

So beautiful yet so mental. Ain't it always the way?

Then the humming started. After which followed more deep cleansing breaths and positive affirmations. "My spirit is pure, my path is clear. I follow the path of Synchrona to live my best life."

I couldn't decide whether to call Oprah's copyright lawyers or write her up as my next case study. I had no idea how long this would go on, but just before I started checking my email, she seized the phone on my desk and turned back to me.

"I'm ready. What's his number?"

There are moments of grave doubts and regret in a therapist's life (not to mention a new girlfriend's life), and this was one of them. But after a slight hesitation, I surrendered Alex's work number, my reasoning being that she could have easily obtained this information from someone else, so it wasn't as if I was giving away state secrets.

She dialed, waited, and then adopted a very brusque, clipped voice. "Hello, this is Harmony St. James calling for Mr. Alex Coughlin." She pursed her lips, shook her head impatiently. "Well, I understand that, but I must insist that you pull him out of the meeting immediately. This is urgent!"

She covered the receiver with one hand and winked at me. "Do I do a great businesswoman or what?"

"I'm blown away," I said, slumping back into my chair.

She turned her attention back to the phone and continued lambasting the secretary. "Young lady, you get Mr. Coughlin on the line right now, or I'll have you fired!"

I started waving my hands frantically, but the damage was already done. She winked again. "Want me to put it on speaker-phone?"

"Oh my God, *no!*"

"Okay, okay, here he comes." She tossed her long curls over her shoulders and took a deep breath. "Alex? Hi. It's Harmony . . . Yes, *that* Harmony. No, don't hang up. Guess where I am!"

She paused for a moment, scrunching up her nose. "No . . . no . . . oh, knock it off, Alex." She gave me a thumbs-up. "I'll tell you—I'm in Gwen Traynor's office!"

For the next thirty seconds, Harmony had to hold the phone about a foot away from her ear. I could hear Alex from all the way across the desk. He didn't sound happy.

Finally, she tried to regain control of the situation. "But that's not even the big surprise . . . Well, I'm never going to tell you if you're going to be like that . . . You say that now, but believe me, you'll be sorry if I *don't* tell you . . . Say you're sorry . . . No, say you're sorry . . ." She stamped one stiletto-clad foot on the carpet. Apparently Synchrona serenity was a very transient state.

She tried to hand the phone over to me. "He wants to talk to you."

I cowered in my chair. "I really don't think that's a good idea."

She beseeched me with her eyes. "You tell him about *L-e-o*."

I dropped the cool therapist façade. "Are you insane? *I'm* not telling him! You tell him!"

She exhaled loudly, then pressed the receiver back against her ear. "Oh, fine. Alex? You still there? Well, here's the surprise. Sit down . . . Okay, fine, don't sit down. My news is"—she closed her eyes and went for broke—"I have a son, he's four years old, his name is Leo, and guess what, you're actually his father and I just wanted to tell you that so okay bye."

She slammed the phone down and turned to me with a relieved smile. "Well, it sure felt good to get that out in the open."

"What did he say?"

"Oh, he'll be right over."

Fifteen minutes later, my office turned into a free-for-all. Can open. Worms everywhere.

Alex stormed in with both hands balled into fists and immediately headed for Harmony, who was still curled up in the blue armchair.

"I just walked out of a meeting with my most important client. This had better not be some childish prank." His voice was quiet and controlled, but the harsh lines in his face betrayed his fury. The good-natured closet surfer I'd met last week had vanished completely.

She leapt to her feet and came out swinging. "Oh, you are such an *Aries!*"

"I'm going to be a hell of a lot more than that in a second. I do not want you anywhere near my girlfriend. Why are you in Gwen's office?"

Harmony widened her stance and planted her heels in the carpet. "Gwen is my son's therapist! Actually, strike that, she's *our* son's therapist!"

Alex took a step back to absorb the one-two punch. "My son." He shook his head. "My son needs a therapist? Already? He's not even five—what did you *do* to him?"

"Nothing! He's depressed. It's not my fault. FYI, depression is a biochemical thing. So maybe it's *your* genes that did it."

Alex turned to me. "Is that true?"

"Well, the research is kind of mixed on that," I hedged. "The causal factors are very complicated. There are at least two distinct types of depression . . ."

But neither one was listening anymore. They were too busy circling each other like rabid wolverines.

"I didn't think you were capable of this, Harmony."

"Of what? Having a baby or dialing a phone?"

"Gwen, how long have you known about this?" he asked.

I feigned momentary amnesia. "Uh . . ."

His eyes narrowed. "How. Long. Have. You. Known."

I stared at my hands and muttered, "A few days."

"A *few days?*" He whirled around, headed for the door, whirled back around, and got right up in my face. "All this time—last night—you were lying to me?"

I backed up to the bookcase. "I didn't lie, technically. I didn't know what to do, because—"

"Save it." He cut me off with a glare and commenced pacing

the room, clenching and unclenching his fists. "So you've met him. You met my . . . Leo?" He turned back to Harmony. "What the hell possessed you to name a helpless infant Leo?"

"He is a Leo," she informed him coolly. "He turns five next month. And Leo is the most powerful, charismatic sign in the zodiac."

The vein pulsing in his forehead looked ready to pop at any second. "The zodiac. Don't tell me you're still into all that crap."

"It is not crap! If you weren't so locked into the . . . the rigid linearity of Western thought, maybe you'd start to appreciate the mystical forces at work in your life."

His jaw dropped. "'The rigid linearity of Western thought'? Where'd you get that one?"

"Don't patronize me. I'll have you know that my life coach at Synchrona thinks I'm very—"

He stopped pacing. "Did you say Synchrona?"

She nodded. "That's right."

"You're raising my son in a *cult?*" His face went from crimson to purple.

"It is not a cult! It's a group of enlightened philosophers who—"

"Christ almighty. You're raising my son in a fucking cult." He shucked off his charcoal gray suit jacket and threw it down on the desk. "My son. My son. This has got to—" He paused and narrowed his eyes. "Wait a minute. How can you be so sure he's my son?"

Harmony gasped. "How dare you?" She reached up to slap

him, stopping inches short of his jaw when he froze her with a look of pure, cold fury.

"How do we even know this kid is mine?"

"Because I was sleeping with you when I stopped having my periods, that's why!"

"You were sleeping with Alex Spears before we broke up."

"I was not." Her hand curled by her collarbone in a pose of Victorian indignation. "I told you, the whole boxers-in-the-bathtub thing was all a tragic misunderstanding! What kind of girl do you think I am?"

He smiled wryly and let that question pass. "So you'd agree to a paternity test?"

"Fine." She folded her arms. "If you're going to be that way, fine."

"I'm definitely going to be that way. I'm not as stupid as I used to be."

"Whatever." For all of her bluster, Harmony still looked to Alex for her cues. "And then, when the test shows that you're the dad—which it *definitely will,* by the way—then what?"

"We'll cross that bridge when we come to it." He started rolling up his shirtsleeves, practically yanking off the cuff buttons in the process. "In the meantime, why don't you keep the kid away from the big vats of Kool-Aid down at the temple, just in case?"

She snatched up her little glass pyramid and threw it at his head, missing by a good three feet and cracking my office window.

I took a deep breath and plunged into the fray. "Let's all calm down for a second here. Maybe we should just—"

He cut me off. "You stay out of this. You've done more than enough already."

But Harmony tilted her head and smiled. "I think I know what to do. It's a little drastic, but hear me out." She took a deep breath. "It's too soon to get engaged, of course, but I think we should start living together."

Deafening silence on all sides.

I glanced at Alex, who had gone in the space of two seconds from tie-loosening rage to ashen-faced shock.

"*What?*"

She collapsed into a chair and tucked one leg underneath her. "Let's give it a try. You can move in, but I don't want to get engaged yet. I mean, obviously we still have some issues to work out."

"Some *issues?*" He exhaled in a burst of sudden, choking laughter. "*Some* issues? Woman, are you high on drugs right now?"

I rounded on Harmony. "Yeah, really. What is in that candle?"

She reached out to squeeze my hand. "I'm sorry, Gwen. This is a horrible thing to say to the new girlfriend, but you two will have to break up. Alex and I have a child together."

"*Maybe,*" he emphasized.

"We do," she assured him. "I'm sure, and after we get the tests done, you'll be sure too."

"But . . . I'm confused." And the prize for the understatement of the year goes to Gwen Traynor. "How does that lead to cohabitation and a diamond ring?"

"Well, one of the things they teach us at Synchrona—one of the things I've been struggling with—is that family connections are important." Her eyes glazed over. "Family paves the path to serenity."

Alex appeared torn between killing himself and killing her.

"So?" he prompted.

"So Leo needs a mother and a father. Grover is always saying that, but I ignored him because I was afraid to track you down. Now that I've told you, though, I feel better. I feel cleansed. Ready to move up to the next level." She nodded. "You were right all along. Family truly is the most important thing. That's what keeps us centered. And our little boy is depressed. He needs us, Alex. He needs us both."

He sat down on the edge of my desk. "This is crazy. I'm not having this conversation. And do you know why? Because it's *fucking crazy.*"

"We have to do what's best for our child." She opened her arms in a sweeping, Earth Goddess relevé. "Step outside your little box, Alex. Take a look at the big picture. The universe."

Alex took two steps over, placing himself directly between me and his ex. "The universe."

"Uh-huh."

"The big picture."

"Exactly."

He squared his shoulders. "Okay. Just so we're clear here, let me describe what I see as the big picture. You call my office out of the blue, threaten to fire my assistant, and pull me out of a critical quarterly meeting. You then proceed to announce that you have a four-year-old son, whom you purport to be mine. You do all this while sitting in my new girlfriend's office, and your announcement of motherhood is followed immediately by a demand for reconciliation and marriage. Is this an accurate portrayal of events thus far?"

She peeked around his gray wool pants and waggled her eyebrows at me. "He was on the debate team in college. Can you tell?"

He did not take the bait. "It's a yes or no question, Harmony. Is this an accurate portrayal of events?"

"He should have been a litigator," she informed me. "I kept telling him."

He crossed his arms and waited.

Finally, she let out a loud, impatient sigh. "Well, I guess you *could* see it that way, but you don't have to be so melodramatic. My God."

"*I* don't have to be so melodramatic?" His short, sarcastic laugh was sounding as bitter as mine these days.

She crammed her aromatherapy candle back into her purse. "Don't patronize me. I'm trying to move forward with a positive solution, and you're just being mean."

"Forgive me if I'm not ready to 'move forward with a solution' just yet. I'm still stuck in the 'when did my life turn into an issue of the *National Enquirer*' phase. And as for living together . . ." The debate club steam ran out as he grappled with this prospect. "That is the most . . . you are just . . ."

She slung her purse over her shoulder and got to her feet. "Kids complicate everything, don't they? It's been my problem for almost five years, and guess what, Alex? Now it's your problem too. The whole time we were dating, you never shut up about how much you wanted the perfect wife and the perfect family, and you were going to be the perfect dad. Well, guess what, big guy? Your wish is granted!"

The path to serenity had taken a detour. But even now, with wild eyes and a ferocious scowl, Harmony looked glamorous and perfectly coiffed. Her gold and black curls flowed back, Wonder Woman style, as she took him apart.

"You always had something to prove, didn't you? Blah blah blah, children's charity; blah blah blah, ranch in Colorado. You just wanted to think that you could be a better father than your dad. Well, now's your chance. Before you make fun of the Synchrona morals, why don't you look at your own? Are you going to put up or shut up?"

"Do not bring my father into this."

My eyes widened at the sharp steel in his voice.

"What are you going to do? Abandon your child like your dad did, or act like a man and take care of your family?" She pivoted and marched to the door. "I'll see you at home."

Slam.

We stood there, silent, for a few seconds. Then I opened my big mouth. "Listen. Alex. I know you're angry with me right now, but you have to understand—"

"I'm leaving." He picked up his jacket and headed for the door without a backward glance.

I nodded. "Okay, but if you want to talk about it—"

"With you? No thanks." He paused but didn't turn around.

"I expect this kind of crap from Harmony, but you . . . How *dare* you keep this from me?"

Suddenly, all my ethical hand-wringing over the past two weeks now seemed ridiculous. Cruel, even. I had let this go way too far. He had every right to his anger.

What do you say to a man whose emotional life is imploding before your eyes?

"I'm sorry," I whispered.

"You should be." He opened the door.

"But what happens now?"

Another slam of the door was the only reply.

"Holy cow. She said *what* about *what* and then *what?*" Cesca folded another red licorice whip into her mouth and chewed vigorously.

"You heard me." I stopped StairMastering long enough to wipe the beaded sweat off my forehead. "And will you lay off the licorice? We're supposed to be working out."

"I am working out." She pointed to the "calories burned" counter on her machine. "I'm working out so hard I need to refuel. Hence, the Twizzlers. Don't get pissy with me just because your new boyfriend's a deadbeat dad."

I took a swig from my water bottle and cranked the Stair-Master back up to hellish levels. "He didn't even know his kid existed until this morning."

"You have no idea how tempted I am to say something about rebound men. And also that I told you so."

"Fight that temptation," I advised. "I'm in no mood."

"Fair enough." She continued to refuel. "So Harmony actually said that she wanted to start living with him?"

"Yeah. She wants to start talking marriage."

"That's, like, the most psychotic thing I've ever heard in my life."

"I know."

"And *why* would she do that? I thought you said they can't stand each other."

"They can't. For now."

She narrowed her eyes and jabbed her index finger at me. "Oh, for God's sake. Do not get sucked into some paranoid fantasy world where all exes live happily ever after in a delightful Nora Ephron comedy."

"Is it really so paranoid?" I jabbed my index finger back at her.

"Yes."

"*Is it?* Look at Lisa and Dennis."

"Yeah, look at them." She dispensed with the candy and increased her stair-climbing pace to a sprint. "Two superficial morons with bad taste in art. You have to get past this, Gwen. Not every guy you date is going to run back to his ex-girlfriend."

"So, according to you, I'm deluded to even imagine that just because his ex showed up in my office, announced she bore his child, and asked him to live with her as a prelude to sending out wedding invitations, they *might* be thinking about getting back together? That's crazy talk, according to you?"

Since she couldn't refute this, she went on the defensive.

"Well, why do you care, anyway? Last I heard, you and Alex were just having fun and not getting attached."

"Last you heard," I muttered.

Cesca punched the "emergency stop" button on her Stair-Master. The she punched the "emergency stop" button on *my* StairMaster. I stumbled into the handrails, nearly breaking my femur in the process.

"Ow! Dammit, Cesca!"

"Tell me all, right now."

"Just because you grew up in a houseful of burly men doesn't mean you can—"

"I have ways of making you talk."

I threw up my hands. "Well, you know we slept together. And it was great, okay? And yes, it meant something to me and I'm a horrible cliché from the Lifetime channel, okay?"

"And . . ."

"And now it's over. He was really pissed that I didn't tell him about Harmony. He was *irate*." I swallowed hard and turned to grab my water bottle.

"Eh." She toweled off her StairMaster. "He'll get over it after he has some time to absorb the shock."

"I highly doubt that. He has major issues with paternal abandonment. He doesn't get along with his dad. I found out all the gory details when Harmony announced them at the top of her lungs."

"And this hurts your feelings because . . . ?"

"When I asked him before about his family, he barely said a word, but now it turns out that this . . . this hopped-up, incense-addled sex kitten knows all about him. He told her everything about his dad. Me—nothing. Her—everything. *And* it turns out he was on the debate team in college! I didn't know any of that stuff!"

She clamped a hand on my shoulder, the coach consoling the ousted quarterback. "Well. Isn't it better that this happened now, before you got even more involved? The whole deal sounds like more baggage than the LAX arrivals terminal."

"I guess." I sighed.

"And if that doesn't make you feel better, how about this: I have tickets to the Dodgers game tonight."

"My cup runneth over."

She frowned. "I was going to bring Mike, but I tell you, I have learned my lesson about that guy."

I collected my towel, water bottle, and gym bag. "Oh yeah?"

"Oh yeah." She crushed her candy wrapper into a tiny ball for emphasis. "We are through, for good this time. I am never speaking to that jackass again. I don't care how many times he calls."

"Okay."

"I mean it! I don't care how many bouquets he sends over."

"Okay."

"And if I ever start talking about getting back together with him, I want you to haul off and slap me across the face. For real this time."

"Okay."

"Gwen. Are you even listening to me at all?"

"Of course I am," I lied. "Listen, let's go get a Jamba Juice or something."

As Cesca began to catalog Mike's many flaws, I smiled vacantly and nodded. Ordinarily, I would have been happy to join in, but today, Mike's transgressions didn't seem all that bad. So he broke a few plates. People had done a *lot* worse. Naming no names.

One of the first things we'd learned about couples and family counseling is that the opposite of love isn't hatred. It's utter indifference. Where there's strong emotion of any kind, there's a chance for passion and reconciliation. And the brawl I'd just witnessed between Alex and Harmony had been anything but indifferent.

They knew just how to press each other's buttons. And now she was ready to talk cohabitation. A hop, skip, and a jump away from taking stock of the linen closet and registering for new sheets, towels, and mystical scented candles.

To think that I'd been paranoid about *Alex* wanting to track down his former flame. I'd had the wrong ex all along.

9

Alex waited until Friday afternoon to call. Four long days after the showdown in my office. Four days of obsessively checking my e-mail and voice mail, bringing the cordless phone into the bathroom while I showered, and poring over research articles about the pros and cons of single parenthood. Every time the phone rang, I lunged for it.

And the phone rang a lot, because Mike had waged a massive campaign to win Cesca back. But as she refused to speak to him, I had been appointed screener.

The typical conversation went a little something like this:

Me: Hello?
Mike: Is C. there?

Me: Hmm. Let me check. [offer receiver to Cesca, who'd ward it off with the hand gestures of an air traffic controller clearing a 747 for takeoff] Nope, not here. Sorry.

Mike: Well, you better tell her to call me when she gets home. I've been sending her flowers all week, and she still needs to give me my lucky boxers back.

Me: Is that Whitesnake I hear in the background?

[Click. Dial tone.]

We had these lovely little chats at least three times a day, and when I wasn't on the phone, I was bonding with the FTD guy, who daily dropped off bouquets for "Lady C."

I myself received nothing. No calls. Definitely no flowers. Every afternoon when I walked to The Bomb Shelter to grab a cup of coffee I scanned the crowd for a familiar face, but Alex was never there. Of course. He was off with his brand-new insta-family, probably having carefree picnics on a red gingham blanket by the shore. Looking for shells and allowing himself to be buried in the sand. Buying everyone ice cream cones and saying things like, "Golly, that's swell."

But I did see Dennis. Wednesday afternoon, in the library of science and medicine. I ducked and hid behind a copy machine. A proud moment for ex-girlfriends everywhere.

By Wednesday evening, the heady scent of irises and daisies began to overpower the acrid undertone of romantic disappointment in our apartment.

"I know he's a little weird at first," Cesca said, reading the card on the latest arrangement of flowers, "but he had a very dysfunctional childhood. You just haven't seen his sensitive side. And he does have good taste, doesn't he? Look at these colors! He remembered about irises—Laker purple, my favorite."

By Thursday, her defenses were dangerously weakened. "I mean, it's pretty sweet of him to send me all these flowers. It must be expensive, especially since he doesn't have a job right now."

And then Friday afternoon. Waterloo. We were camped out on the sofa, staring at the TV in a postworkout stupor and munching our way through a giant bag of Swedish Fish.

"Gwen?"

"Yeah."

"How bad would it be if I decided to give Mike one more shot?"

I sighed. "I'm supposed to reach over and slap you right now."

"Yeah, yeah, yeah. But you know. He's a hard habit to break."

"Listen to yourself. Men who make you quote Peter Cetera are not good for you."

She slumped lower into the cushion. "Nobody's perfect, you know. I'm not. *You're* not."

"True." I didn't take my eyes off the Dodgers game. "But that's not the issue here."

She put both feet up on the coffee table. Loudly. "Don't patronize me. I'm just asking—"

"And I'm just telling." I selected an orange Swedish Fish and popped it into my mouth. "You don't have to listen."

"You got that straight," she huffed. "Know what? I don't care. Next time he calls, I'm answering."

I shrugged. "Okay."

She gasped. "And you're going to *let* me? What kind of friend are you? You know how toxic he is."

I stared at her. "But you just *said*—"

"I know, but—" The phone rang.

We looked at the receiver. We looked at each other.

The phone rang again.

Cesca sighed. "What can I say? I'm a fool for a man who still lives at home and gets tattoos when he's bored." She snatched up the phone. "Hellooo?"

Her eyes widened. "Oh, hi, Alex. Yeah, she's right here. Hang on."

She passed the phone over to me, hissing, "It's Alex, it's Alex."

"I gathered," I hissed back. Then I took a deep breath and turned away from my roommate. "Hello?"

"Hi, Gwen. It's Alex."

"So I hear." I headed for my bedroom, where I could escape Cesca's blatant eavesdropping. "How've you . . . you know, *been?*"

Furious? Vengeful? Looking into getting me fired?

But when he spoke again, he didn't sound angry, just tense. "Between the new son and the crazed drama queen demanding I move into her house, how do you think I've been?"

I paced the perimeter of my bed. "My money's on 'not good.'"

"Not to mention all the lawyers."

I paused. "Lawyers?"

"Yeah." I could practically hear his tightly wound nerves twanging over the phone line. "In the space of four days, I've become the best client at the law firm we retain. Custody issues. Trust funds."

"Any word on the DNA test yet?" A girl could always hope.

His grim sigh was answer enough. "Yeah. I don't know who my lawyers had to bribe down at the lab, but they rushed the results. It's official—I'm the father."

Another long moment of silence.

I closed my eyes, cleared my throat, and tried again. "So. About Harmony. I just wanted to say that . . . I know I should have told you . . ."

"We're not having this discussion over the phone." And then his tone got even tenser, if such a thing were possible. "I want to see you tomorrow."

When I reopened my eyes, I was staring directly at the closet door, which was ajar. I could see the Wedding Dress of Doom, gleaming away under the clear plastic casing. "Oh boy."

"Tomorrow morning?"

"Why bother waiting?" I wedged the phone between my ear and shoulder and threw both hands up. "You can just break up with me right now. You don't have to wait to do it to my face. Etiquette be damned."

He paused. "Why do you think I'm breaking up with you?"

"Well . . . because . . ." I blinked. "Is this a trick question?"

"Are you always this defensive?"

I mulled this over for a few seconds. "Yeah, pretty much."

"Good to know. But let's not jump the gun here."

"So you still want to—"

"We'll deal with all that later," he said brusquely. "Right now I just need to know . . . Well, I wanted to ask you . . ." For the first time since I'd met him, he seemed hesitant.

"Yes?"

"You've been introduced to Leo, right?"

"Yes."

He cleared his throat. "Well, I haven't. But Harmony has arranged a meeting tomorrow morning, and I think it might be a good idea to have you there."

I dropped the phone on the bed, then snatched it back up. "No, it wouldn't."

"You're his psychologist."

"Not anymore! I transferred his case to another clinician."

"I don't have a lot of experience with kids." There was a dark undercurrent of panic in his voice. "I know things are complicated between us right now. But I would really appreciate it if you could come with me."

Need. That was what I heard in his voice. He needed me. Not because I was an irresistible femme fatale, not because I was a rock of support in uncertain times, but because I could run interference with a four-year-old.

And I owed him, big-time.

How touching.

"Oh, all right."

"You'll come?" His voice flooded with relief.

"If you insist. I'll see you tomorrow morning."

"And Gwen."

"Yes?"

"Don't jump to conclusions. I'm *not* getting back together with Harmony."

"But she said—"

"She says a lot of things. Believe me, it's not gonna happen."

"Uh-huh." I tried to sound convinced.

"No way, no day." He paused again. "Listen, about Leo—do you think I should get him a present?"

I sat down on the edge of the twin-size mattress that had cradled our sleeping bodies just last week. "That might be a good idea."

"Any suggestions?"

I grinned. "Think Spider-Man."

10

As it turned out, Harmony welcomed my presence at the father-son reunion. According to Alex, who had spoken to his ex "too many times" since Monday, the illustrious Ms. St. James had a few things she wanted to discuss with me.

"Should I be frightened?" I asked when he picked me up on Saturday morning.

"Probably." He made no move to touch or kiss me when he opened the passenger-side door, but he didn't seem hostile, either. Just frustrated and exhausted.

"Are you nervous about meeting Leo?"

"I don't know." He started the car and turned the radio up, drowning out any attempts at further conversation.

The sky was heavy with thick gray clouds. When we pulled

into the Santa Monica Beach parking lot at nine-thirty I tugged at the sleeves of my black hooded sweatshirt. "Here we go."

He slammed the driver's side door. "Here we go. And Gwen?"

"Yeah?"

"I shouldn't have been so . . . curt with you this week. In your office."

"Don't worry about it. I completely understand—I'd be outraged with me too."

This elicited a small smile. "I'm not *outraged* with you. Anymore." He looked like he had more to say, but he stopped himself and leaned in, giving me a quick buss on the cheek. Then, before I could reciprocate, he had shoved his hands into his pockets and started walking toward the ocean.

Harmony had suggested that we all meet by the Ferris wheel at the Santa Monica Pier. Her reasoning seemed to be that the cotton candy, flashing lights, and mimes on the boardwalk would distract Leo from the built-in trauma of the whole experience.

Foolproof, right?

Alex took my hand as we neared the sand. I squeezed his fingers. He squeezed back. Neither of us said a word.

Screeching gulls wheeled overhead. At this hour, the sand was nearly deserted except for the occasional jogger and one daring child who, wearing a hooded coat and no pants, darted in and out of the icy surf, laughing uproariously.

I smiled and pointed. "Obviously a midwestern child."

Alex did a double take. "Where are that kid's parents?"

I pointed to a pair of nontanned, nonblond adults huddling

under a blanket and waving at the child. "Right there. See? Midwesterners."

He shook his head. "Do you know how cold that water is right now?"

"That's why he's wearing a coat."

"I wouldn't go surfing in this weather without a full wet suit," he said. "And no child of mine—"

He broke off and let go of my hand. "But of course, I have no idea what my child has been doing for the last four years."

I reached out for his hand. "Hey."

He pulled away. "Those Synchrona maniacs probably encourage nudist wading. The colder, the better."

"Come on. Harmony loves Leo," I said. "She's a little, you know, *nontraditional,* but she tries to be a good mom."

He stopped walking and turned to me. "How many times have you met Harmony? Once? Twice?"

"Twice."

"Twice," he repeated. "I almost married the woman. I know she's very charming at first. But, trust me, there is no telling what she would or wouldn't do."

I didn't break eye contact. "She loves Leo. She really wants the best for him."

He shrugged. "Yeah. She loved me too. She tends to get love confused with self-interest." He turned back to the concrete path that led up to the pier. "Let's do this."

Leo apparently felt that his first meeting with his father called for full Spider-Man regalia. When Harmony finally showed up at the Ferris wheel, twenty minutes late, the child by her side was a human billboard for all things arachnoid. Hat, sweatshirt, sneakers—all red, blue, and webbed. He looked smaller than ever, somehow.

He smiled shyly when he saw me. "Hi, Miss Gwen."

"Hi!" Harmony shoved her gold-rimmed Chanel sunglasses up into her tawny hair. "Sorry we're late, but the 10 was totally backed up."

Leo peered up at his mother from beneath the baseball cap brim. "Mommy, you said we're late 'cause you lost your lipstick."

"Well, whatever. There was traffic too." She gave me a cute little squinchy-nosed face. "Kids."

Both of us turned to Alex, who was staring at Leo with his mouth open and his hands behind his back. I waited for him to comment, but nothing seemed to be forthcoming. Either he was bonding with his offspring or he had gone completely catatonic.

Harmony followed my gaze over to Alex. She grinned and framed Leo's shoulders with both hands. "So? What do you think?"

No response from Alex. Definitely catatonic.

I rubbed my fingertips across the soft cotton shirt covering his shoulder blades. "Hey. How you doing over there?"

Harmony gave up on both of us and turned to the only socially competent member of the party.

"Pookie, this is your dad." She patted his head. "Remember how we talked about meeting Dad?"

"Yeah." For the first time since I'd met him, Leo took his hat off. He kept it clenched in one hand as he crossed his arms over his chest and sized up Alex. "Are you my mommy's new boyfriend?"

Alex's mouth snapped shut. He looked at Harmony. "Am I what?"

Leo sighed and rephrased the question, speaking slower this time. "Are you going out with my mommy?"

Harmony's giggle had an edge of desperation. "Pookie, no. We talked about this, remember? This isn't Mommy's boyfriend. This is your daddy."

The little boy stuck out his lip. "You told me I didn't have a daddy."

Alex looked at Harmony with eyes like obsidian.

"Silly! I never told you that," she trilled, a bit hysterical now.

Leo nodded earnestly at his mother. "Yes, you did." He leaned way back, looked Alex right in the eyes, and put his cap back on. "Mommy says you're going to marry her. And come to live with us."

Alex stopped breathing. I heard his air passage empty out in a strangled choke.

Leo kept staring. "So, are you?"

Alex turned to Harmony. "May I speak with you for a moment. *Alone?*"

She winced. "Now?"

"Now." He wrapped his hand around her elbow and dragged her toward the railing several yards away.

I figured that as long as I was going to get left out of the grown-up discussion, I might as well make myself comfy at the kids' table. I sat down on the wooden slats of the pier. "So. Leo. What's new?"

He pointed to the Ferris wheel. "My mommy's gonna take me on the rides today. The big ones. Scary ones."

"Oh yeah?" I patted the floor next to me, and he collapsed in a cross-legged heap.

"Yeah. She promised. And we's going to get cotton candy. As soon as I meet my dad."

"Well . . ." I pointed over to Alex, who was muttering in low, black tones. "There he is."

"Uh-huh." Leo seemed unimpressed. "He's tall. But not as tall as Fider-Man."

"You know what?" I bumped gently against him with my shoulder. "I know your dad. He's nice. Really nice."

His eyes were big as dinner plates. "Do you think he'll be nice to my mom?"

"Um . . ." I glanced over at Alex and Harmony, both of whom were gesticulating wildly and snarling. The wind changed direction, blowing small snatches of conversation our way.

"How many men have you paraded through your house in front of him?"

"My personal life is none of your business."

"Apparently it is, if you're trying to coerce me into moving in with you. I can't believe you told him that. What the hell were you thinking? You are so incredibly—"

"Shut up! Just shut up! You're gearing up to spend your next life as a frog."

I gave Leo my best fake grin, which of course he saw right through.

"They don't like each other," he announced.

"Well . . ." I nudged at a candy bar wrapper with my sandal toe. "I know he'll like *you*."

The dinner-plate eyes widened to serving platters. "Why will he?"

"He's going to love you, Leo. You're his son, and dads love their sons."

"He has to?"

"He *wants* to," I assured him. "He's very, very lucky to get a little boy like you for his son."

He twisted up his mouth and looked over at Alex and Harmony, who were still knee-deep in the world's hissiest hissy fit. "Mommy says I have to be nice to him."

"She's right. You'll be nice to him, and he'll be nice to you."

He drummed his heels against the wooden planks. "She says we're going to be a family now."

"Oh really?" I was not going to pump an innocent preschooler for juicy details. I was *not* going to pump an innocent preschooler for juicy details.

As it turned out, I didn't have to. He was more than willing to spill his guts.

"And when my dad comes to live with us, he's gonna come to Synchrona too."

My eyebrows shot up. "He is?"

"Yep. 'Cause that's where dads go. Mommy said."

"Interesting." Before this day was over, we were going to

need a riot squad, a tranquilizer gun, and someone to buy the movie rights.

There was no point in trying to convince him that Alex and Harmony were old meditation buddies. Four-year-olds can scent emotional deception from fifty paces. So Leo and I broke off our conversation, stared intently at his parents, and waited for them to wrap up the brawl.

Harmony was mid-"you son of a—" when I cleared my throat.

She and Alex whipped their heads around to look at us.

"Hi. Remember us?" I tilted my chin down at Leo. "We're getting bored. And chilly. So could you guys table the discussion for now?"

Alex gave his ex a final glare. "We'll finish this later."

"Oh, I think we're done." She hoisted Leo up into her arms. "What do you want to do, Pookie?"

He tucked his face into her neck. "Ferris wheel."

She kissed the exposed patch of hair near his ear. "You want to go on the Ferris wheel?"

"Yuh-huh. With you and my dad."

Another long pause. The three adults all glanced around with shifty eyes. Leo didn't look at any of us.

Harmony shifted her hold on him. "You think me and Daddy should both come with you?"

"Yep. But not Miss Gwen. She's not in our family."

The kid who had been my best buddy not three minutes ago turned on me with the swift ferocity found only in hungry sharks and cranky preschoolers.

Alex came to my defense. His first verbal exchange with his only son went thusly:

"But you like Miss Gwen, don't you, Leo?"

"No. She's ugly."

Alex recoiled as if punched in the face.

Harmony gasped. "No, she's not." She gave me the patented eye-rolling smile of parental apology. "She's very pretty."

Leo shook his head, burying it farther into his mother's shirt. "She's a demon."

I bit back a bubble of laughter.

Alex crossed his arms and looked at Harmony, who said, "Don't blame me. I don't know where he picks these things up."

I held up my palm. "Relax, relax. I've been called worse."

My erstwhile boyfriend looked dismayed. "You have?"

"Sure. Preschoolers aren't exactly masters of understatement. It's no big deal. Seriously. I think he's just a little . . . over-wrought."

Alex nodded. Harmony seemed unconvinced.

"Really?"

"Of course. Very understandable. I mean . . ." What I meant, obviously, was *who wouldn't be overwrought with this freak show of a family*, but I kept this to myself. I got to my feet, brushed off my pants, and smiled in what I hoped was a non-chalant fashion. "Why don't you three go on the Ferris wheel? Give Leo a chance to talk to his dad?"

Harmony saw her opening. "Maybe I'll stay down here too. Let my little Pookie bond with Daddy?"

"Nooooo!" We all got a glimpse of Leo's tonsils.

"You should go," I told Harmony. "He'll be more comfortable if you're there."

If only we could say the same for "Daddy." Alex had lapsed into a long, heavy silence. He kept raising his right hand, almost touching his child, and then stuffing his fist back in his pocket.

Leo wiped the scowl off his face. "Okay. Let's go. Daddy."

And Alex just melted from the inside out. I could see it in his eyes—the resurrection of all the sitcom fantasies, complete with home-baked apple pie and impromptu baseball games in the meadow. He looked at Leo, and something steadfast and pure emerged from the confusion and animosity.

Father and son smiled at each other, and no kidding, the bright morning sun literally burst through the clouds. A vast patch of flawless blue spread out overhead.

I know. Total atmospheric overkill, but impressive nonetheless. I watched Alex's face, I felt the solar heat start to seep into my black sweatshirt, and I knew that, no matter what happened between him and me, I had done the right thing encouraging Harmony to call him.

His veneer of casual confidence relaxed into actual happiness.

"Okay." He offered his hand to Leo, who took it. "Three for the Ferris wheel."

"Aww." Harmony dug a Kleenex out of her purse, apparently forgetting that she had cursed this man to reincarnation as an amphibian a scant five minutes ago. "You guys are the cutest!"

"Come *on*, Mommy." A four-year-old waits for no woman.

Alex regarded me with the kind of adoration that I had tried to wrest out of Dennis for two fruitless years. "Thank you, Gwen."

Then he took off with his child and his ex-girlfriend, all of them chattering about Spider-Man and snakes.

I didn't want to watch him walk away from me without a backward glance. So I leaned over the railing and watched the tide pound against the pier's stout wooden pilings.

I told myself that I wasn't the pathetic, soon-to-be-ex girlfriend who refused to see the neon writing flashing on the wall. I told myself that brand-new relationships had weathered worse than this.

But I knew what was coming.

And sure enough, when Alex returned from the Ferris wheel, windblown and toting Leo's baseball cap, he stopped grinning and placed his hand over mine like an oncologist who's about to break the bad, inoperable news.

"Gwen."

I knew that tone. "Oh no."

He furrowed his brow. "I think I'm going to have to get back together with Harmony."

11

Picture me saying, "*What?!?*" And then picture me saying it about five hundred more times while internally rattling off the F-word, and you have a pretty good idea of my reaction.

When I finally pulled it together enough to say something other than "what" I segued right over into disbelief and hostile recriminations.

"But you said . . ." I took a deep breath and tried to remain rational. "You said, and I quote, that there was no way, no day . . ."

"Gwen, okay. Come here." He tried to put his arms around me, but I wrenched away.

"Do *not* touch me," I spat. "Oh, wait, it's too late for that, isn't it? I cannot believe you"—I glanced over at Leo, who was pointing out sailboats to Harmony ten feet away—"trifled with me like that, and now . . ."

Pieces of my heart that had just started to heal split wide open again, and I started to cry, thus completing my total humiliation.

He stopped trying to comfort me but positioned his body so that my escape route was blocked. "I did not trifle with you. Last weekend meant something to me."

"So much that you just have to run back to Harmony?" I shook my head and swiped at my eyes with the backs of my hands. "You know, it's bad enough that you're treating me like a one-night stand. Did you have to lie this morning too?"

He sighed. "I didn't know."

"You didn't know *what?*"

"I didn't know what it would be like to actually meet my child. And now that I have, I just think that—"

"You dragged me out here just so you could dump me in front of your ex-girlfriend! That is beyond sick." Then a horrible thought occurred. "Is this supposed to be some kind of revenge for not telling you about Leo? Because if it is—"

"Gwen, are you listening?"

I shoved my hair back with both hands and seethed. "Yes."

"I didn't lie to you."

"Really? Then riddle me this, Batman—how exactly does promising not to go back to an ex-girlfriend, then going back to said ex *not* constitute lying?"

His put a hand on my arm. "I didn't have all the information. Harmony is threatening to move to New York and take Leo with her if I don't—"

"Batman?" Leo suddenly materialized between us, glancing from my face to Alex's. His mouth was open in a round little O.

We both stared down at him. "I'm sorry, what?"

Leo poked my kneecap. "You said something about Batman."

I shrugged away from Alex's hand. "Oh. Yeah, I did say 'Batman,' but I was just—"

"Are we going to see Batman?" His eyes lit up. "I know! Let's go home and watch Fider-Man."

I arched an eyebrow at Alex. "I think that's a fine idea. Why don't you go home? It'll give you a chance to bond with your bride-to-be. And P.S.: enjoy the Synchrona initiation rites. I hear they're into nude wading."

I pivoted on my heel and strode toward the sand. Fast, but not so fast that he couldn't have caught up if he'd tried.

Behind me, I heard Leo yelling, "Mommy! Guess what? My dad's going to watch Fider-Man with me!"

I found a taxi idling near the hotel next to the pier, yanked the door open, and flung myself inside. As the driver pulled away from the curb, I risked a look back at the beach. I didn't see Alex anywhere.

"Man alive. Sit down. Have another Sweetart. Actually, here, just take them all." Cesca pushed the foil roll of candy across the kitchen counter.

I lowered my head until my forehead thunked against the cool beige Formica. "I'm way beyond Sweetarts."

"Hang on. I have Oreos."

I shook my head. "Do you have any of Mike's cigarettes laying around?"

"Ugh. No. We broke up again. And you don't smoke."

"I'm starting right now."

"No, you're not. The man's not worth it. If you made it through the breakup with Dennis, you can make it through this. Besides, you can't afford cigarettes on your fellowship stipend." She aimed the remote control at the TV, clicked off ESPN, and plopped down on the stool next to me.

My sigh echoed off the white walls. "I should have known. He's exactly the same as Dennis."

She looked dubious. "Well, let's not get carried away here."

"They're like two wretched peas in a pod. And I should have known. The first time I ever met him, he told me flat out that he had a history of leaving his fiancées. Just like Dennis."

"Okay, *once* does not constitute a history. Besides, he left Harmony because she's a complete nut job."

"Well, what do you think Dennis is telling Lisa about me right now?" I countered. "'*That Gwen chick was so mental. Pass the popcorn.*'" I sat up and pounded a fist on the countertop. "How could I miss all the red flags?"

"I love you so much that I'm not even going to say I told you so." She ripped open the bag of Oreos. "Although, in his defense—"

"Why the hell would you defend him?" I demanded. "He wooed me like there was no tomorrow, and now he's ditching me for a woman who named her firstborn after an astrological sign. He loved me, he lied to me, he left me, and now I'm all awash in oxytocin with no place to go . . ."

Cesca nodded at the neuroscience texts stacked on our bookshelf. "The bonding hormone. I *aced* neuropsych."

". . . So don't you dare defend him," I finished. "He's a relationship kamikaze, same as Dennis. And the worst thing is that I didn't see it coming. Again. I am such an idiot."

She brandished a cookie like a professor's pointer. "Not quite. If you compare the two cases, I think you'll agree that there are slight but significant differences."

"Oh boy." I sat back and waited for the lecture. "This should be good."

She got to her feet and began pacing. "First of all, motive. Alex wasn't planning to break up with you. He's responding to circumstances outside his control." She gave me a look. "Circumstances that *you* knew about and *he* didn't."

"Oh my God. How many times do I have to explain this? There's this little thing called professional *ethics*."

"And yet you slept with him."

"Well . . ." I grabbed a cookie. "There's another little thing called 'he's hot.'"

She shook her head. "There are those who might say that you and Harmony ambushed him and forced him to make a decision under duress. And lest we forget, Harmony is really the driving force here. She's the one who brought up getting back together. He's just trying to be a good father. You know men. You confuse 'em, they panic. Much like possum."

I stared at her for a moment. "That's a lovely little analysis, but I don't buy it. I see it more like this: Dennis left me for a buxom ex-girlfriend on a moment's notice. Ditto Alex. End of story."

"So you're just writing him off?"

"Yep."

She raised her eyebrows. "Don't you think that's a bit harsh?"

"Don't you think seducing me and then throwing me over for a soap opera actress who used to do commercials for Bally Health Clubs is a bit harsh?"

Cesca looked impressed. "Did she really?"

"Yes. Now do you understand what I'm up against?"

She whistled long and low. "I always thought the women in those ads were computer-generated to taunt normal people like us. Anyway, I know you feel miserable right now, but at least you can take comfort in the fact that he probably does too."

"No, he doesn't. And, anyway, I don't want him to be miserable," I said, realizing that this, incredibly, was the truth. "I just want him to come crawling back, shower me with European chocolates and pricey jewels, then sweep me off my feet."

She laughed. "Stop your lies. Of course you want him to be miserable. He deserves a little pain and suffering."

"I thought you were on his side."

"I said you shouldn't write him off *forever.* I didn't say he should get off scot-free." She smirked. "But he'll get his. You said yourself he's looking to settle down with a latter day Donna Reed who can bake a mean strudel."

I sighed. "Yeah. So?"

"So Harmony's not exactly in the running for homemaker of the year. Why was he dating a woman like her in the first place?"

"Why was he dating a woman like *me?* I'm not exactly Martha Stewart material, myself."

"I have a theory about this."

"Enough with the theories!" I groaned. "Can't we just agree he's a tool and move on?"

"Alex dates women like you and Harmony because you're the opposite of his ideal woman."

"Thanks."

"It's true." She nodded. "What he says he wants and what he actually wants are on opposite ends of the spectrum. He says he wants June Cleaver, but then he dates a drama queen and a die-hard career woman."

"But why would he do that?"

She shrugged. "You'd have to ask him. Maybe he's afraid of intimacy. Maybe he's afraid that if he *does* find the perfect woman and settle down, he'll screw it up."

"He screwed it up regardless," I pointed out.

"True." She rubbed her chin thoughtfully. "Did his parents have a good marriage while his dad was still around?"

"I told you, his dad wasn't around. At all."

"Well, there ya go. Commitment problems."

"Commitment problems. *Real* original." I changed the subject. "So what happened with Mike this time?"

"Get this: he told me I couldn't have granola for breakfast because it was too fattening."

"But you're a stick," I pointed out.

"I know!" She bared her teeth in a primal scowl. "He was just doing it to be a controlling jackass. Do I say anything about the fact that his entire diet consists of nicotine, bacon cheese-burgers, and caffeine? Nooo. But—"

The phone rang, cutting her rant short. Both of us looked at it, then started backing away from the counter.

"I'm not getting that," I announced. "And if it's him, I'm not here."

"You think I'm gonna pick it up?" she whispered, eyeing the receiver as if it were a ticking explosive. "What if it's the controlling jackass wanting his Bon Jovi CD back? *You* get it."

In the end, of course, the machine clicked on, whereupon the caller hung up. Both of us feigned indifference.

"What kind of sorry excuse for a man can't even leave a message?" Cesca scoffed. "Really. How are we supposed to ignore them if they won't even use the answering machine for the purpose God intended? You know what would make us both feel better?"

"What?"

"Watching the NBA play-offs. They start tonight, and the Lakers are taking it to the top. I'm going to Maloney's to watch on the big screen. You should come. In fact, why wait? The highlights special is on right now." She vaulted over the back of our couch and grabbed the remote control.

"Suddenly life is worth living again." I rolled my eyes and headed for the bathroom. The time had come for a bubble bath, a big glass of wine, and the latest issue of *US Weekly*.

"Where are you going?" she called. "This is just getting good. Hey! What was that foul about? Ticky-tac! Ticky-tac!"

I shut the door firmly behind me and turned on the tiny water-resistant radio we kept on the bathroom counter. Cesca's indignant critique of the referee was replaced by the sounds of

Norah Jones and the latest puff piece on Reese Witherspoon. What better way to numb the heartache? I'd soak for an hour, then head to the lab and spend the rest of the weekend crunching data for my dissertation. Much more productive than crying, eating four pounds of M&M's, and watching Bally commercials with morbid fascination.

I turned on the hot water, knelt on the tile floor, and rummaged through the cabinet under the sink. We'd stashed some vanilla bubble bath in here somewhere.

But wait. What was this tucked behind the extra rolls of toilet paper?

I studied the purple and white box, then sat down on the floor. What on earth had been going on around here while I was lost in my little whirlwind romance?

Tweezing the incriminating box between my thumb and index finger, I nudged the door open with my toes and marched to the living room, where my roommate was still happily savaging the televised referees.

I cleared my throat and tossed the box onto the couch. "Cesca? Do you have something you want to talk about?"

She shrunk back from the package emblazoned with the letters E.P.T. "No."

"So you didn't hide this in the bathroom?" I sat down next to her and held her gaze.

"Not really." She shrugged. "Why do you ask?"

"Because I'm sure I would remember buying this. So if I didn't put it there and you didn't put it there, I guess the magic fertility fairies paid us a little visit in the night."

She clicked off the TV. "It wasn't supposed to be under the sink. I meant to move it to my bedroom."

"Why?"

She crossed her arms. "So that you wouldn't find it and make me have this exact conversation! But the second I got back from the drugstore, you and Alex came barging in, so I tossed it in there . . ."

"Well." I tried to figure out what to say. "What's going on? Are you okay?"

"Yeah. I mean, I'm fine, I just might also be . . ." She lifted her chin toward the box and let the *P*-word go unsaid.

"I'd offer you a nice stiff drink, but I guess that's out."

"Do not even joke about that." But she smiled a twisted little smile. "I'm not *that* late. Well, I'm a little late. Well, late enough to buy that, but you never know, right?"

My eyes widened by about two inches. "When are you going to do the test?"

"Soon." She tucked her feet under her and burrowed back into the cushions. "I keep putting it off. But I know I have to do it. Very soon."

"Are you scared?" I watched the tough tomboy expression drop onto her face and hastened to add, "*I* would definitely be scared."

"I don't know. I mean, this won't even be for sure, right? What's the false positive rate on this thing?"

I peered at the back of the package. "Don't know. I think you can get false negatives, but not false positives."

"Yeah, well, I'd like to see the data on that. Do they have an informational website?"

Just two behavioral science researchers having a chat about life and love in the big city.

"I mean, I could be late for any number of reasons, right? Stress. Or hormones. Or stress. Right?"

"Absolutely." I nodded.

"I didn't skip any pills this month . . . well, okay, maybe one . . . but it was all because I was frantically cramming for those damn qualifying exams. And according to the little pill pamphlet, that shouldn't even matter. I mean, who misses their period because they're actually *pregnant?* Practically no one, right?"

"Practically no one," I echoed, trying not to think about Harmony. Mike's next girlfriend might be in for a big surprise. Maybe this would be a growing trend in suburban family life: SUVs and Stealth Children.

"Okay then." She turned the game back on.

"But just to be sure, let's go ahead and do the test," I urged. "Just for the hell of it."

She looked at me. "Who is this 'we'? Read the directions, Gwen. It's a one-woman job."

I rolled my eyes. "Okay, *you* go do the test."

"I will. In a minute." We remained crouched on the sofa, coiled with tension, watching Kobe scream at the ref. Finally, she turned to me and said, in a pleasant conversational tone, "You know what would solve all our problems?"

I could think of a lot of possible answers to this question, none of them legal. "What?"

"We need to go blond."

12

Never let it be said that I didn't try to stop her.

"Cesca," I said, "Stop."

But she was insistent. "Yeah! Blond is what we need. It's the perfect breakup cure."

"And you're basing this on what?"

"Senior year of high school. Broke up with Brad Fiorelli right before the prom. He was cheating on me with this useless piece of fluff named Annalee Feyer. She was the kind of girl who worried she wouldn't make it into a college sorority because she couldn't speak Greek. But then I showed up in that high school gym looking like Madonna on the *True Blue* album cover, and let me tell you, my dance card was full. *And* I got accepted to Northwestern that day. So there you go."

I eyed her shiny black hair and olive skin but kept my mouth shut. This was a woman facing the specter of parenthood with Mike Jessup. If she needed a little peroxide to get her through it, who was I to stand in her way?

Besides, any protests would fall on deaf ears. She was like a rat on crack once she got going with these things.

"You're going to look like Marilyn Monroe, and I'll . . ." Her jaw dropped open as genius struck. "You know what? Maybe I'll streak my hair gold like you said Harmony does."

"*Et tu,* Francesca?" I clutched my chest. *"Et tu?"*

"Oh, relax." She rushed to the computer tucked away in the corner of the living room. "What we need to do is find a picture of Harmony online. And then I'll be able to tell if it's the right look for me. Because you said she's gorgeous, right? Men falling all over themselves?"

I clenched my fists. "That's right."

She fired up the modem, then double-clicked her way into the World Wide Web to search for "*Twilight's Tempest* Cast Members." We watched, she in anticipation and I in horror, as a full-color picture of Harmony St. James filled up the screen, inch by inch.

The flawless tan skin. The enormous blue eyes. The sultry red lips.

Cesca sat back in her chair. "Day-um. She is a vixen and a half!"

"That's it; I'm killing myself." I turned and headed for the front door.

"No, no, I just meant her hair!" She raced after me. "I was looking at her *hair.*"

"Oh please. Stop your lies."

"I just meant . . ." She blinked at the computer screen, mesmerized the same way I had been when I first saw Harmony. "Between her and Alex, that Leo must be one good-looking kid. Anyway . . . *God,* her hair looks great. Do you think if we called her, she'd tell us where she gets her hair done?"

"No." I glared at her. "First of all, her monthly highlights probably cost more than our annual income. Second of all, I just got dumped for her, so no, I'm not really in the mood to ring her up and ask for a favor. Got it?"

"I know, I know. It's just . . . I *so* want my hair to look like that."

"Don't we all. But I guarantee, in order to get it you have to hand over your 401(k) to a Swedish guy with a purple shirt and an eating disorder. And we don't have 401(k)'s." I closed the browser window. Harmony vanished. "Listen, Cesca, stop the madness." I pointed to the bathroom. "Get in there and let's find out what we're dealing with."

"Or . . . let's hit the drugstore and pick up some L'Oréal. I can dye hair better than any Swede breathing. I know exactly what to do."

"You grew up in a houseful of men," I pointed out. "How do you know exactly what to do?"

"I *read.* Let's go."

She glanced at the E.P.T. box and shuddered. And because I too was in the throes of postbreakup insanity, I gave in and let her do it. I told myself that I would be blond and fabulous. That would show him.

*   *   *

Four hours, half a bottle of shampoo, and several panic attacks later, I had to face the awful truth: this was a disaster on par with *Gigli's* opening weekend.

But at least we were no longer discussing unplanned pregnancies.

"I hate you," I told Cesca.

"I hate myself," she said. "How did this happen?"

I narrowed my eyes. "Cast your mind back. You, Little Miss Displacement Activity, assured me that you were practically Paul Mitchell with the hair dye. And now look at me. *Look* at me!"

I tugged at my hair, which had assumed the texture and color of saffron linguini.

She grimaced. "You, uh, look good."

"Really. As good as you?"

"Listen, streaking is a very complicated technique. I might have been a little overconfident. I admit it."

She looked like Pepe LePew on acid. Her cute little pixie 'do was shot through with thick neon orange stripes. About as subtle as a Lil' Kim outfit.

"Wasn't the point of this to make us *more* attractive?"

She hung her head. "We'll have to cover all the mirrors until it grows out."

"But what about the clinic? What about my clients? I'm going to have to shave my head and buy a wig."

Her face lit up. "I have a brilliant idea."

"Keep it to yourself. I'm still dealing with the fallout from your last brilliant idea." I dropped my forehead into my hands.

Not only was my hair as coarse as raffia, but the "Golden Oasis" color Cesca had selected for me clashed horribly with my skin tone. I looked like I was in the final stages of tuberculosis. How was I going to explain this to Dr. Cortez? And what if—oh God—I ran into Dennis like this? What if I ran into *Alex?*

"Here is what we have to do." She gave me an assessing look. "You're not gonna like it, but desperate times call for desperate measures."

"I'm already opposed to this plan."

"We need somebody to do damage control. Somebody really good. There's no way around it. We're gonna have to call Harmony. I know you don't want to, but it's the only way. Her hairstylist clearly knows how to do the gold streaky thing. Maybe she can get us in for an emergency appointment."

I recovered the power of speech. "Have you lost your mind? Why don't we just sell our souls to the fucking *devil?*"

She straightened her shoulders and sniffed, "There's no call for such language. It's just an idea."

"A *bad* idea."

"Well, do you have anything better? Because I don't know about you, but I am not going out in public like this. The new trainee down at Fantastic Sam's is not going to be able to fix this. We need the big guns." She paused, then played her trump card. "And I must add, you are never going to get Alex back looking like that."

I closed my eyes. Inhale. Exhale. "Cesca. Ignoring for the moment the fact that this is *all your fault,* I don't want Alex back."

"Fine. Lie to yourself. I don't care. But *I'm* never going to get another date looking like Pat Benatar's color-blind twin, so give me Harmony's number."

"This is funny to you? You've ruined our hair—not to mention the bathroom tile—and you're pregnant, and you find this amusing?"

"I'm late, not pregnant," she corrected me. "Now cough up her number."

Without another word, I whipped out my cell phone and scrolled through the stored contacts until I reached St. James. I hit the talk button and handed it over to my turncoat roommate.

Cesca cleared her throat and put on her Upbeat Therapist Voice. "Hello? Is this Harmony? Yes, hi, this is Cesca DiSanto. I'm a friend of Gwen Traynor, and I am so sorry to bother you on a Sunday, but I have a quick question—what? Yes, she is. Hang on a sec."

Cesca raised her eyebrows and passed the phone over. "She wants to talk to you."

"Did I mention that I hate you?" But I accepted the phone. "Hello?"

"Gwen? Hi!" Harmony sounded exuberant. Doubtlessly because she and Alex had just finished a daylong marathon of passionate makeup sex. "How are you, *chérie?*"

I put her name on the growing list of people I despised. "Never been better. How're you?"

"Great! I'm making an apple pie! From scratch!"

I almost dropped the phone. "Excuse me?"

"Pie! I'm getting in touch with my inner homemaker." There was a long pause, then: "Ouch! Damn! How the hell are you supposed to get these seeds out? Is that a worm? Oh, gross . . ."

I rolled my eyes. "Aw. Isn't that sweet?"

"Do you know anything about pie crusts? Because I followed the recipe—well, except for all the butter and white flour, obviously—and it doesn't look anything like the picture in the cookbook."

"Pie is not my area of expertise," I told her.

"Anyway, it's great that you called. I just wanted to talk to you about yesterday. I know you and Alex were kind of involved, and—"

"I don't want to talk about it. My roommate, Cesca, is the one who would like to speak with you. She needs some help with her—"

"Hey, do you guys want to come over for dinner? I'm trying to do the Domestic Goddess thing today because, well, you know Alex, and believe me, I need to get back on his good side. He has been in such a mood today. His aura is, like, pitch-black. He isn't here right now, but he'll be back soon, and Leo and I are making a pizza for dinner. Carb-free, of course. We'd love to have you guys over."

Cesca winced when she saw my expression. I wasn't sure what Harmony was envisioning, but I wanted no part of her twisted *menage à* pizza scenario. I tried to remain cordial.

"Why would I want to go over there and have dinner with a former client, my ex-boyfriend, and the woman he left me for?"

"Well, you *did* call me," she said cheerfully. "And Leo'd be delighted to see you. He keeps asking when we're going to hang out with you again."

So the four-year-old I'd met twice missed me, and the thirty-five-year-old I'd slept with did not. Perfect.

I cleared my throat. "I'm going to have to pass on dinner. We're kind of having a hair emergency."

"Oh no!" She gasped. "That is the worst! I completely feel your pain. Once, when my regular stylist was in London, his assistant did my hair for the Daytime Emmys, and he gave me bangs and went bonkers with the mousse. Those vicious bastards on *E!* said I looked like the ambassador to New Jersey." She harrumphed at the memory. "What happened to you guys?"

She did not seem to understand that she and I were sworn enemies, not shopping buddies. She had stolen my man and disgraced the good name of postmodern feminism by baking a pie under false pretenses. How dare she be so . . . *nice?* It was a slap in the face!

I drummed my fingers on the countertop. "Let's just say we tried to turn our bathroom into a beauty parlor and mistakes were made."

There was a moment of silence. Then: "You . . . you . . . dye from a box? Oh, you poor things!"

I gritted my teeth. "We don't need your pity, thank you very much. Just a recommendation for a good stylist who's available on Sundays. Cesca wanted her hair to look like yours, so—"

"Oh, that is so sweet! Tell her I'm flattered."

I closed my eyes and imagined her Bel Air bungalow burning down in one raging, carb-free conflagration.

"Don't you worry. I've got my stylist's home number on speed dial. Matthieu is, like, a *genius.* I'll send him right over. Where do you live?"

"Slow down. I don't know if we can afford genius. How much does this guy charge?"

"Not that much. A couple hundred per hour, I guess. And he is worth every single penny."

"A couple hundred what? *Dollars?*"

Her voice was a verbal shrug. "Yeah."

I shook my head at Cesca, who pulled a face. "Well, thanks, but no thanks. I guess we'll just go Sinead O'Connor for a few months."

"Don't be ridiculous, *chérie.* It's on me."

I slapped my palm down onto the counter. Cesca jumped. "No!"

I heard pots and pans banging around. "Why not? You're my Pookie's therapist. It's the least I can—"

"I don't want your charity, all right? And I'm not Leo's therapist anymore." I took a deep breath, the pit of my stomach knotting, and addressed the real issue. "I know what happened with Alex isn't a big deal to you—I'm sure you have ex-fiancés move in with you all the time—but it *is* a big deal to me. A very big deal."

She paused. "He was never my fiancé. Where did you get that idea?"

Oops. Apparently, Alex C. hadn't had time to discuss his marital intentions before Alex S. came onto the scene.

I backpedaled at Olympic speeds. "Uh, since you mentioned getting engaged the other day, I just assumed . . ."

Her tone was warm and gentle. "Gwen. I know this is a big deal to you. I know Alex is all in love with you—"

I snorted. "Right. That's why he's moving in with you."

"Come on. He's moving in because he wants to be a good father to Leo." She broke off for a moment. "Hang on, is that— oh, phooey, I burned the pizza. The soy cheese is all black. Anyway. He's trying to be the father he never had. You know men and their dads. Issues up the wazoo. It's not like he and I are wild about each other." She lowered her voice. "In fact, we sometimes have trouble getting along."

I feigned shock. "Get out."

"It's true! I mean, we don't fight in front of you, of course . . ."

I laughed out loud. I couldn't help it.

". . . But believe me, we've had a few battles. He's a very negative personality. It's not like I wouldn't rather be dating Vin Diesel—and believe me, he's asked—but it's time we all grew up and created a whole, holistic family. A *Synchrona* family. If I want to achieve inner synchronicity, I have to start aligning my head values with my heart values."

My depression boiled into rage. Alex had given me up for a one-woman anthology of New Age platitudes?

Well. I didn't need a man who would do that. As my mother would say, he could go pound sand. I was well rid of him.

I'd learned my lesson. Men with values = certain chaos and rejection. Back to the usual shifty-eyed louts.

"So anyway, don't worry your brilliant little head about Matthieu. He'll be right over. Uh-oh. I think the apple pie is collapsing in there. I gotta go. Hey, Alex just walked in the door. Do you want to talk to him?"

"No." I gave her my address, hung up, threw the phone into the mass of sofa cushions, and hauled our one stainless steel pot out of the cabinet.

"What's going on?" Cesca asked.

"She has my dream man, she doesn't even want him, and somewhere out there Vin Diesel is pining away, all for the sake of an insipid Rodeo Drive cult," I said. "Thus, I am going to prepare and consume an entire box of macaroni and cheese. Don't try to stop me."

"Make me a box too." She cleared her throat. "What about our hair?"

"Matthieu will be right over."

Her eyes lit up. "Matthieu?"

"From Harmony's glam squad. Congratulations—your hair is going to be soap opera ready."

"I'll settle for going out in public without frightening small children." She frowned as I filled the pot with tap water. "How much is this going to cost?"

I smiled grimly. "Just my dignity. Harmony's taking care of it. Which is the least she can do, considering." I shook the blue macaroni boxes like maracas. "Now are you taking that pregnancy test, or what?"

She turned her back, pretending to search for a spoon. "Later."

*　　　*　　　*

Matthieu, a ponytailed strand of a man draped in black Versace, took one look at our apartment, blanched, and announced, "I cannot vork in these conditions." Apparently, he broke out in hives anywhere south of Sunset Boulevard.

He squired us to his glass-and-mirror studio in Beverly Hills, gave us a stern reprimand about the perils of home hair treatments, and set to work with honey conditioning cremes, vegetable-based neutralizers and, yes, Evian rinses. All the stuff you read about in *Star* while rolling your eyes.

He dealt with Cesca first, declaring her entire head "a state ov emergency" and then, while she was flipping through *Vanity Fair* under the hair dryer, he set to work on me.

"Gwendolyn, love." He frowned at me in the mirror and sifted through my hair, examining the body and texture. "Are you Irish?"

I blinked. "Half Irish. How did you know?"

He nodded and reached for his cigarettes. "You haff Irish hair. I see red undertones at the roots. Why would you dye your hair such a color as this?" He seemed personally wounded. "You should be ash-blond. Platinum."

I shrugged one shoulder under my voluminous black smock. "It used to be dark brown. Cesca seemed to think I should be golden blond."

He sniffed. "Francesca. What does she know? You girls are psychologists, yes? You stick to what is inside the head, and let me deal with the outside. This color." He grimaced. "It makes you look diseased."

"I know."

"Did this happen because ov a man?"

"How'd you guess?"

He patted my arm. "Don't vorry. We make him sorry. I make you look like Cameron Diaz."

I smiled and chugged a spare bottle of Evian. "Go for it. It's time for a change. The bigger, the better."

13

The end result came a lot closer to Jennie Garth than Cameron Diaz, but it was still a big improvement over the T.B. convalescent look. Matthieu had made swift work of my half-Irish hair, shearing off a good six inches and lightening the color to a luminous flaxen.

When I woke up Monday morning and headed to the bathroom to get ready for work, an intoxicating mix of unexpected confidence and daring washed over me.

My Inner Blonde was emerging.

As I scrambled to find something to wear to the clinic, I had to fight the urge to wear that modest black blazer without a shirt underneath. The sight of the wedding dress in my closet elicited nothing but a supercilious smirk.

Being blond, it seemed, was a natural mood enhancer. For the first time since I'd hightailed it from the Santa Monica Pier, I felt optimistic. Cheery, even. The glass was half full, dammit!

And I wasn't the only one.

"You really need bright red lipstick to go with that hair," Cesca commented as I headed out the door.

"I work in a clinic for preschoolers, not a bordello," I reminded her. "Don't you think red lipstick is a little much before cocktail hour?"

"Then magenta." She tossed me a little black M.A.C. tube. "Here, borrow mine. I'll wear red. It goes, don't you think?"

She raked her fingers through her perfectly streaked tousle of black waves. The leather jacket she'd paired with jeans and a white T-shirt completed the rebel intelligentsia ensemble. She looked ready for action. Like a sexy biker elf.

"You going to class or a party backstage?" I asked.

"My affective disorders seminar. There's a cute guy from the cognitive program who sits across the table." She winked. "And don't worry about . . . you know. I'll take care of it when I get home."

She was referring, of course, to the pregnancy test, which remained unopened under our bathroom sink. Last time I had asked about this, her only response had been: "Why menstruate when I can procrastinate?" Which I took as my cue to stop asking.

"Whatever." I grabbed my keys. "Ces. Look at us."

She grinned. "Isn't it great? I told you!"

"But where will this madness end? Can cosmetic surgery be far behind?"

"As soon as I can afford it," she vowed, raising her index and middle fingers in a V. "Peace out."

The whole blond power thing was more than just my imagination. A stubble-faced giant of an undergrad held the apartment building door for me. My five-year-old Saturn magically transformed into the Party Mobile. Today, I had the courage to sing along with the radio at the top of my lungs, which drowned out the slight squeak I'd started to hear whenever I braked. At the intersection of Hilgard and Le Conte (the very intersection where scant weeks ago I'd had the Vera Wang–induced meltdown) a silver Porsche pulled up alongside my car and the aspiring film producer behind the wheel interrupted his cell phone conversation, lowered his shades and winked. Somehow, now that I had sassy platinum hair, this no longer seemed like a clichéd and sexist affront. He was merely affirming the fact that, thanks to Matthieu's artistic genius, I had got it goin' on.

When I trotted out of the parking garage, drivers—*Los Angeles drivers*—stopped to let me cross the street. No stop light or riot police or anything.

I strutted through the clinic doors, ready to conquer.

Julie, the clinic secretary, darted out of her cubicle and blocked my path. "Gwen, I have a . . ." Her jaw dropped as she stared at my head. "Your hair."

She didn't look stunned by my beauty. She just looked stunned.

I managed not to squirm under her scrutiny. "A quick little makeover. Do you like it?"

"Yes, actually. You look great. It's just . . . not like you."

I smiled and brushed soft blond waves behind my ear. "Cesca's idea. I just hope it doesn't freak the kids out too much."

"Cesca. That explains it. Anyway, I have a message for you. An Alex Coughlin called for you."

I tried to freeze my facial muscles into a mask of indifference, but my lips and eyelids twitched madly. "Did he?"

"Yes. He said he'll meet you at twelve-thirty for coffee at Café Chou. He says it's urgent." I could tell she was dying to ask what this was all about, but I wasn't about to volunteer anything.

"Hmmm," I said. "Interesting."

She raised her eyebrows. "So shall I confirm for twelve-thirty?"

I shrugged. "Sure. Go ahead. Thanks."

When twelve-thirty arrived, of course, I was safely barricaded in my office, sucking down my third Diet Coke of the day. It wasn't that I was nervous about confronting Alex. No. It was that I was nervous *and* pissed off.

Why should I have to have coffee with him? To make him feel better? The faithless, lying lout. We'd shared a night of scorching passion, not to mention a day at the International Surfing Museum. We'd shared an undeniable pheromone connection and a common desire to flee the pretentious for the pedestrian. He'd traced the contours of my body with his tongue. But apparently none of that mattered to him.

So why should I come running at his every command? The

brunette Gwen Traynor might be pliable and empathetic, but the blond Gwen refused to put up with this crap.

The new Gwen would: (1) stop being such a simp when it came to men; (2) burn that insidious wedding dress and toast marshmallows over the flames to make three-thousand-dollar s'mores; (3) get her ass in gear, finish her stupid dissertation, and then move to a city far away where none of her exes were flaunting their lithe, alterna-artistic wives in her face. I was thinking London, Rome, or Chattanooga (they'd never think to look for me there).

You'll notice that the plan outlined above did not include having coffee with Alex Coughlin and humiliating myself.

But then someone knocked on the door.

I tried to ignore the sharp raps, but he was insistent.

"I know you're in there." His voice was muffled, but I recognized his tone. It was the buy-sell-you're-fired tone. All impatient productivity.

This, of course, enraged me. I was not some bothersome merger to be dealt with and filed away. I was not a woman to be trifled with. Not anymore. I too had become a force of nature—a blond beast created in the image of Harmony St. James.

So I marched across the office, flung open the door, and greeted Alex Coughlin with a white-hot glare.

"May I help you?!" I was so close I could smell the starch in his white-collared shirt.

He took a step back, at which point I got a good look at his total dishevelment.

His body was all buttoned up in Saville Row and knotted with a shantung silk tie, but his face looked ragged and uneven. His eyes were ringed in purple circles of fatigue. Lines I hadn't noticed before strained his forehead and lips. A dark crescent of stubble lined the part of his jawline he'd forgotten to shave.

He looked like I'd felt for the past three days. Embattled and exhausted by emotional jet lag. My heart started to open up despite my best efforts to hold on to my self-righteous rage.

This sordid situation wasn't entirely his fault. Why should I punish him for trying to be a good man, a good father in a society so full of fractured families that child psychologists had to turn away clients?

But then I remembered: he could just be overtired from wedding planning with his once-and-future wife candidate. The one he'd sworn he wouldn't leave me for.

I folded my arms and waited for him to speak up. Which he finally did, after loosening his tie, shoving both hands in his pockets, and kicking at the doorframe in some masculine evolutionary-throwback move.

"Gwen."

"That's my name, don't wear it out." A little retro slang went a long way, and I instantly felt cheered. "What is it you want?"

"You're . . ." He continued to stare. "You're blond."

"That's right." I fluffed my new lioness mane.

Long pause.

"Listen, I'm a busy woman, so if you're done here . . ." I turned on my heel and headed back inside my office.

He caught my wrist in a gentle but firm clasp. "You were

supposed to meet me at Café Chou half an hour ago."

I whirled around to face him and snatched my hand away. "Let's get something straight. I'm not your girlfriend. I'm not your fuck buddy. I'm just the runner-up in the 'Who wants to live with a waffling weasel' pageant. So I don't have to meet you anywhere, ever."

I could see him struggling to temper his frustration with cool rationality. "That is completely—" He broke off in mid-sentence, still gazing at my head. "You're *blond.*"

"Yes, I believe we covered that." I raised my eyebrows. "Got any new ones?"

"How did you . . . ?"

"It's called hair dye," I explained. *"Chéri."*

His jaw dropped at the *chéri.* "Oh my God. This is Harmony's doing."

"Don't blame her. I simply asked her for a salon referral and took it from there. And if you think this is bad, you should see Cesca."

"It's not bad. It's . . ." He swallowed hard. "You look like . . . you look like a man-eater."

I rocked back on my heels and smiled. "You say that like it's a bad thing."

"But you aren't the blonde type."

"Au contraire. My new stylist, Matthieu, said my complexion is ideally suited for a shimmery platinum."

"Damn that Matthieu." He gritted his teeth.

"Why? I assumed you'd like it. You don't seem to have any objections to *Harmony's* hair."

He exhaled sharply. "I see. That's what this is about."

I held up a hand. "No. Not everything is about you and Harmony. This is about me." *And Cesca. And E.P.T.* "In therapy circles, this is what's known as 'moving on,' my friend."

"You need to be blond to move on?"

"What do you care? It's not like you'll ever be seeing me again."

He shut the office door. "That's what I wanted to talk to you about."

"Hey!" I protested as he leaned back against the doorframe. "This is coercion! Ambush! Harassment!"

"Give me a break." He tugged at his tie and unbuttoned the top of his collar.

My eyes narrowed. I clutched the lapels of my blazer together.

"Blond. Jesus Christ." He finally dragged his gaze away from my hair and announced, "I've come to talk about what happened this weekend."

"There's nothing to talk about. You're history, I'm blond, end of story."

"Gwen—"

"Have a nice life with your gorgeous wife."

"Gwen—"

But I was on a roll. "It was fun while it lasted, but that's the way the cookie crumbles."

The corners of his eyes crinkled when he smiled. "'The way the cookie crumbles'?"

I sighed. "What do you want? I'm from Illinois." But his smile drained the fight out of me. I sat down on the edge of the desk and shrugged. "I don't know what else to say here."

"You don't have to say anything." He rested his hand next to mine on the desk. "I wanted to explain about this weekend. And to figure out where we go from here."

I shook my head. "If you think I'm having an affair with a guy who left me for a client, you've been watching too much *Twilight's Tempest*."

His eyes narrowed. "I don't want to have an affair with you."

"Good." I tried not to feel insulted.

"I don't believe in affairs. Especially not when children are involved."

"There's a shocker."

"I know you're upset. You have every right to be. I know we can't be . . . involved anymore."

"Then why are you here?"

He squared his shoulders. "I wanted—I was hoping we could still be friends."

I had to laugh. "You want to be *friends?*"

He nodded earnestly. "What happened with Harmony and Leo doesn't change my feelings for you. But I can't choose a two-week relationship over my son. And even though we can't be . . . you know . . . there's no reason we have to stop talking altogether."

I shook my head. "Slow down. Before we get all caught up in some tortured *The Sun Also Rises* scenario, you should know something."

"What's that?"

"I don't want to be friends."

He looked down, and when he glanced up again, his eyes were shuttered and dark.

"The whole friends deal would work out great for you," I pointed out. "You'd get to live in the Apple Pie Utopia with a cute kid and a hottie wife. Plus, you'd get the also-ran gal to buddy up with for surfing and *Northern Exposure*. But what would *I* get?"

"We'd still get to see each other. Not romantically, but . . ."

"We'd see each other when you're not busy with your family. Alex, you dumped me for an ex-girlfriend you claim you can't respect. Friends don't do that to each other." I leaned back against my desk. "I understand why you're doing this. I'd probably do the same thing in your place. You've got your priorities straight; a child *does* take priority over a two-week romance. Especially in a situation like Leo's, where there's no stability at home."

"She was threatening to take him to *New York* if I didn't give reconciliation a shot!" He was officially down to his last nerve. "How am I supposed to bond with my son from three thousand miles away? *What was I supposed to do?*"

"You did the right thing," I repeated.

The muscle in his jaw twitched. "But you can't forgive me."

I tried to explain. "It's not a question of forgiving you. It's a question of protecting myself. I can't just settle for second place."

"You're not second place."

"Of course, I am." I turned away from him. "And you're right, I am angry, but on some level I understand that this isn't your fault. We just had really, really bad timing."

"You can say that again."

"You're being honorable. You're trying to be a good dad so that Leo doesn't have to have a million psycho stepfathers. But yeah, I'm still upset because . . ."

"Because I made a promise I couldn't keep and you got hurt."

I waited for him to break down and confide that he too had been hurt. But he was not following the script.

"Your intentions are good." I threw up my hands. "And you aren't to blame for what Harmony did. But how am I supposed to trust you and pretend our little fling—or whatever the hell it was—never happened? I can't turn my feelings on and off like a faucet."

"So that's it?"

"Yeah." I studied the carpet. "I guess so."

"You'd rather have nothing than friendship?"

I crossed my arms. "It's not really about my preferences. We're out of options here, don't you think?"

He nodded.

I sighed again. "But I can tell you something that might make you feel better."

"What's that?"

"Whenever men ask me for parenting advice—which happens more often than you might expect; just last week my dentist asked me how to explain death to his six-year-old—I always tell them the same thing."

"Which is?"

"Which is, the best thing you can do for your children is to love their mother. So there you go. You, me, and Harmony all agree."

"Christ."

"My sentiments exactly. And I think the easiest thing for us—for me, anyway—would be to make a clean break. Why make things harder than they already are?"

"But—"

"No. I have to move on." The last of my anger slumped into sadness. "I don't *want* to move on, but I have to."

He gestured to my hair. "Hence, the blond."

We looked at each other and broke into wide, double-edged grins. The sort of panicked hilarity that precedes emotional free fall.

"So just let it go. Let it go." My smiled wilted. I took a deep breath. "Let me go."

But he didn't. He came closer. I turned my face away as he caught a lock of my hair between his thumb and forefinger, studying the pale shades of blond in the afternoon sunlight.

I waited, motionless, listening to the gentle whirr of the air conditioner.

When I finally turned back to him, he moved his fingers from my hair to my cheek. And I knew, raging physical chemistry or no raging physical chemistry, this would be the last time he touched me this way.

"I don't want to let you go," he said.

"Me either." I laced my fingers through his. He tugged me even closer. And our "good-bye" turned out to be a whole lot more than a peck on the cheek and a friendly handshake.

*   *   *

I'm proud to say that at least we managed to hold back long enough to lock the office door. After all, there were children wandering around. But once that dead bolt clicked and the window blinds closed, there was no turning back.

And it turned out that blondes, in addition to having more fun, also have fewer inhibitions.

"This is a big mistake," I murmured, fumbling with his belt buckle.

"Huge," he murmured back, popping a button off my blouse.

"Nothing good can come of it." I sighed as he swept me off my feet, winced as he pushed me back against the desktop—and my stapler.

"I wouldn't say *nothing*." He reached behind me and shoved the rest of my desk accessories onto the carpet. After which both of us stopped talking and tried to find what we needed. A strong, bittersweet release.

We didn't say much afterward. No holding, no talking, no rash and empty promises. We just picked up our clothes, buttoned up our shirts, and struggled back into our workday roles. He started to retrieve the piles of books and folders we'd tossed to the floor, but I stopped him.

"Don't," I said. "You have to go."

"I don't want to let you go," he repeated.

"But you will."

And he did. He let himself out without another word.

I turned the lights off, curled up in my chair, and put my head down on the desktop that was still warm from our bodies.

I didn't see how this day could get any worse.

Then Cesca called with the big news.

14

"Gwen! Thank God you're there!" My roommate sounded like she'd just sprinted all the way from Sacramento. "Guess what?"

I tried to manufacture some semblance of enthusiasm. "What?"

"Guess!" she insisted.

"Um . . . Alex came over to my office and offered to be friends, I told him to go to hell and right before we vowed never to see each other again, we ended up having sweaty, animal sex on my desk?"

I could practically hear her jaw hitting the floor on the other end of the line.

"You did *not!*" she yelled.

"Oh, but we did."

She whistled. "Damn, that hair dye oughta come with a warning label."

"Yes, I blame the peroxide. Slutty women everywhere ought to band together and file suit against L'Oréal."

"'Slutty'? Please. You're practically Sandra Dee."

"Until now." I sighed ruefully as I pondered my tawdry desktop escapade. "Anyway, didn't you have some news?"

"Oh yeah." She waited a beat. "About our dirty little secret under the bathroom sink."

"The pink-lined oracle has spoken?" I crossed my fingers, bit my lip, and held my breath.

"My uterus has spoken," she corrected. "The red seas have parted." Her voice radiated relief.

"Woo hoo! How do you feel?"

"Like a convict who's been paroled from the Mike Jessup Maximum-Security Prison. The grass is green! The sky is blue! And there are some mighty good-lookin' men on the outside!"

"Good for you." Now that the crisis point had passed, I was shifting back to droopy-eyed depression.

"Yeah. That was a close one. Can you imagine?" Her voice hushed in horror. "I could be carrying the spawn of Mike Jessup. Thank God my reproductive organs thwarted his fiendish sperm."

"Your womb must be very selective."

"Strictly A list. Invitation only."

"Well, now that you're in the clear, what are you going to do?"

"I can tell you what I'm *not* going to do: I am not going to call Mike Jessup." She laughed guiltily. "Well. I'm not going to call him *again,* anyway."

"Cesca!"

"What? I had to tell him about the pregnancy scare!"

"*After* you started your period?"

She sniffed haughtily. "A father has a right to know."

"That's the most pathetic rationalization I've ever heard," I scoffed.

"I'd hang up on you if I weren't so elated."

"*I'd* hang up on *you* if I weren't so miserable."

Our friendship truly was a beautiful thing.

By Friday afternoon, I was so distracted and sleep-deprived from the big breakup that I decided to stop pretending to work and just pack it in early.

Alex and I had stuck to our promise and avoided all contact since our little indiscretion on Monday, but that didn't mean I wasn't thinking about him. Obsessively.

So I went home around three-thirty, changed into the white tank top and red track pants that always served me so well in times of emotional distress, and had just collapsed into bed when the doorbell rang.

If you live in L.A., an unexpected doorbell chime before 5 P.M. signifies one of the following: a religious fanatic determined to convert you, a bloodthirsty serial killer, or a high-priced call girl who got the wrong address. I wanted nothing to do with any of these options, so I burrowed my head deeper into the pillows and squeezed my eyes shut.

Ding dong.

Damn serial killers. I rolled over, pulled up the covers, and gritted my teeth.

Dingdongdingdongdingdongdingdong.

"Oh my God!" I bolted upright. "Knock it off!"

The doorbell just kept on ringing. The premed student who lived next to us started pounding on the paper-thin wall. I charged out into the hallway, ready to unleash my bottled-up wrath on a deserving target.

Please, God, let it be a representative for Synchrona.

I flung open the door without even bothering to peer through the peephole. *"What?"*

"Hi, Miss Gwen. Your hair's different. I don't like it."

My gaze dropped from eye level down to waist level, where Leo stared up at me. His customary Spider-Man cap had been replaced by a large construction-paper crown with the number 5 emblazoned on the front.

I squatted down to get a better look at him. "Leo?"

"Hi." He strolled right past me into the apartment. "Do you gots any Goldfish crackers?"

I closed and locked the door, then started after him. "Leo! How . . . what . . . how did you get here?"

He stood in the middle of the kitchen, gazing speculatively up at the counters and cabinets. When he heard the tension in my voice, his eyes widened. "Am I in trouble?"

"I don't know," I said truthfully. I knew that open-ended questions would get me nowhere, so I fell back on the trusty standby of preschool conversation: directives. "Tell me how you got here."

He sighed and let the small blue knapsack he was toting drop to the floor. "I took a limo."

I sat down on the beige linoleum next to him. "You took a limo? Really? Tell me where your mommy is."

"Home. Can I have a snack?"

"One second. Tell me where Al—your daddy is."

"At his job."

I decided to go for broke and venture into the realm of yes-no questions. "Did you tell them you were coming here?"

He tried to look sweet and innocent, but mischief danced in his eyes. "No."

"Then I have two questions for you." I got to my feet. "And I will get you a snack while I ask them."

"Do you have any cookies?"

"No," I lied. "It'll have to be fruit. Do you want grapes or apple slices?"

"Grapes."

"Grapes it is. Now how did you get here without Mommy or Daddy?"

"I called the car service."

I sat back down, amazed. "For real? You can dial a phone?"

"Sure." He helped himself to a grape. "I know our phone number, and Mommy's cell phone number, and I can use the special buttons on the phone to call the policemen and the fire engine and the ambulance and the car service."

Which of these things was not like the others? "You guys have car service on speed dial?"

"Yeah." He nodded proudly. "Mommy lets me call and talk to them when she's getting ready. And also, I can use the computer. I can even get level three on Rattler's Revenge."

"Very impressive."

"Yep."

"So they know who you are at the car place? And they picked you up without your mommy?"

"Yep."

On to burning question number two. "But how did you get my address?"

I was dying to know the answer to this because Cesca and I were unlisted for exactly this reason. Therapists, as a rule, take a very dim view of clients showing up at their residence midnap.

"I asked Nell." He stuffed three more grapes into his mouth, his cheeks ballooning like a chipmunk's.

I waited for him to finish chewing, reminding myself as I did that this entire conversation—this entire event—was impossible. Four-year-olds cannot make phone calls independently. Everyone knows that. Everyone.

"But your nanny doesn't know where I live either," I pointed out.

He grinned, displaying a mouthful of masticated grape pulp. "She got Mommy's re-keep."

"What's a re-keep?"

He pushed his crown back on his forehead and regarded me like I had the IQ of a slug. "You know, a *re-keep*. Like from the *store*."

And the light flickered on in my head. "You mean a receipt?"

"Yeah, a re-keep. From Matthieu. Do you know Matthieu?"

"Yes." I was about to ask how he knew Matthieu when I realized that a woman who let her child arrange her car service probably also let him go out club hopping with her hairdresser, her personal stylist, and her astrologer.

"Nell found Mommy's re-keep and I gave it to the man driving the limo."

"But why would Nell . . . you know what? Never mind." I decided to stick to the point. Such as it was. "So the limo driver brought you here? To an address you can't even read, scribbled on a piece of paper? And then let you walk in here alone?"

He grabbed another fistful of grapes. "Uh-huh."

I leaned back against the oven door. "What is the *matter* with people?"

"Do you want to hear a joke?"

"Um. Okay."

"Why did Tigger put his head in the toilet?"

I braced myself. "I don't know. Why?"

But he was giggling so hard he could barely get through the punchline. "Because . . . because he was . . . he was looking for *Pooh!*"

And as he collapsed into my lap, laughing hysterically and spewing grape seeds on my track pants, I started laughing too.

His crown fell off and rolled across the floor. When I glanced down at his face, he looked relaxed and happy. Like a healthy preschooler ought to look.

"So, um, Leo?"

"What?"

"Thank you for telling me how you got over here. I was worried that something bad might have happened."

"No." He shrugged, totally blasé.

"But your mommy and daddy don't know where you are. Don't you think they're worried about you right now?"

His mouth snapped shut and he sat up. "I don't wanna live with them anymore." He kicked out with one foot, catching the paper crown with the toe of his sneaker.

I stacked my hands under my chin and tried to stay neutral. "I bet it's hard to live at your house right now. With a new dad and everything."

"Yeah." He drummed his heels on the floor.

"But I bet he's nice to you."

He picked at the old linoleum curling up under the stove. "Yeah. He says he's gonna take me to Disneyland."

"Well. There you go. That'll be fun."

"Yeah. And last night, me and him got tacos. Mommy was mad. 'Cause red meat is bad." His eyes were huge and perfectly round. "Like, worse than *bread*. Worse than noodles, even!"

"Wow." I managed not to roll my eyes. "How could anything be worse than noodles?"

"They fight a lot." He lowered his voice to a whisper. "Quiet fights."

I raised my eyebrows. "Quiet fights?"

"Yep. When Mommy fights with Matthieu or her friends at work, they scream and yell. But my dad just whispers to her."

"Does she whisper back?"

"Yeah. And then she calls our car service and goes to work and doesn't come home until late, late, late." Tears welled up in his eyes. "Last night she didn't come back until I was sleeping. And I'm five."

This kid needed to work on his conversational segues.

"You're five?" I glanced at the paper crown with the big 5 sparkling on the front. "It's your birthday?"

"Yuh-huh." He was flat-out bawling now. "But I run away!"

Gasping for breath between sobs, he flung himself into my arms. Finally, when the outpour died down to a trickle, I said the only thing I could to coax a smile. I told a joke that I had heard from Timmy Komatsu, age eight, just last week.

"Hey, Leo, what's brown and sticky?"

He dragged the back of his hand across his nose. "What?"

"A stick!" I tried not to laugh too hard at my own joke.

He stared at me. You could practically hear crickets chirping in the kitchen.

I sighed and fell back on the tried-and-true.

"Okay, then . . . Why was the letter *O* in the toilet?"

His smile crept back into the corners of his mouth. "Why?"

"He was looking for *P*."

This, of course, killed.

I called Harmony to let her know where her child was, but her voice mail picked up immediately, which could only mean that her cell phone was turned off. I left a short message, then tried to contact Alex. Another dead-end voice mail box. And when I reached his office, the world's brusquest secretary informed me that he was out of the office at the moment. Which was just as well—to be totally honest, I didn't know what I'd say to him, anyway.

"All right, kiddo." I tugged on Leo's hand until he stood up. "Let's get you back home. Where do you live?"

He helped himself to the last grape. "The hills."

I smiled. "The hills" is L.A. slang for the Hollywood Hills or the West Hills, both of which are trendy neighborhoods jam-packed with celebrities and obscenely over-priced real estate. But the way Leo said it, you'd think it was a separate U.S. state.

"No, I mean what street do you live on?" I asked.

He retrieved his paper crown, dusted it off, and positioned it carefully on his head. "I dunno."

"Sure you know! Like I live on Goodhue Street. Where do you live?"

He twisted his mouth into a little moue. "I dunno." He spread his arms and ran to the living room. "Look at me! I'm Fider-Man!"

"Come on—you know how to speed-dial a car service, you can track down my apartment plus a driver to drop you at my doorstep, but you don't know your *own address?*"

"I don't know!" He was starting to sound a bit defensive. As, it must be admitted, was I.

"How did you even find me in this building?" I demanded.

He looked insulted. "I know numbers. I know letters too. 1B is easy."

"This is crazy," I muttered, trying to devise my next move.

"*You're* crazy," he countered, sticking his bottom lip out.

Ha. Crazy like a fox. I dialed up the clinic, got Harmony's address, and buckled Leo into the Saturn's backseat, quashing my knee-jerk anxiety at the distinct lack of car seats. Desperate times called for desperate measures (and strict adherence to all traffic laws). We were hillward bound.

15

Harmony's house was a little piece of Provence in the middle of the desert. Lots of white molding, trellises draped in pink roses, a marble fountain shaped like a koi in the center of the circular driveway. A small, shaded, expensive-looking home. I didn't see children's toys anywhere in the yard.

I couldn't envision Alex living here. How would he be able to fall asleep in a room that had not only curtains but also droll little shutters and window boxes? I'd bet good money that there wasn't a single roll of duct tape in the entire house.

We pulled into the driveway, heralded by the high-pitched squeal of my brakes—I was really going to have to get those checked out—and made our way across the brick paving to the doorstep.

Leo rang the bell, and as the opening bars of "Frère Jacques" echoed through the house's interior, I realized that I hadn't changed out of my napping outfit. Which meant, unfortunately, that I was still clad in the red track pants and the white tank top, both of which were now liberally dotted with Leo's mucus. Sigh.

A red-faced Nell let us in, obviously aware of what was about to hit the fan, because she scurried off without a word to find the lady of the house. Leo did not look sad to see her go. But his face lit up when his mother appeared at the end of the long white hall.

My heart sank as I looked at the woman my boyfriend now lived with. After a long day on the set, Harmony's answer to baggy red track pants was a slim-cut white silk kimono over form-fitting black leggings. And a Grace Kelly chignon. *And* lipstick.

"Hi, Mommy! I'm back!" Leo scampered across the marble floor into Harmony's arms.

"Hi, Pookie! Excellent hat!" She gave him a kiss on the cheek but looked confused. "Were you gone?"

I stepped into the high-ceilinged foyer. "Yes. He was. He showed up on my doorstep about an hour ago."

She seemed delighted to see me. "Ooh! Love your hair, Gwen! Isn't Matthieu a genius?"

"He's the Noam Chomsky of the salon. Listen, I'm not sure exactly what's going on with Leo—"

"Me either, but I'll tell you one thing." She placed her hands on her hips. "Nell is fired. For good this time. She's supposed to be watching him, and he shows up at *your* place? I am so sorry."

I fidgeted with the straps of my tank top. "I don't mind that he came over, but aren't you curious as to how he got there?"

She tucked an errant strand of gold-streaked hair behind her ear. "I'm guessing that he called my car service again. Kids! What are you gonna do?"

I frowned. "He's used your car service before?"

"Sure. Last month he went to the Beverly Center to look at the puppies in the pet store." She leaned closer. I caught the scent of jasmine. "It was right after Jellybean died. You know, I'm just making some green tea. You should stay and have a cup—you look like you could use the antioxidants."

Leo let go of Harmony's hand and grabbed mine. "Want to see my room?"

"You're okay with him using your car service? Unsupervised?" I tried to keep the sharp edge of judgment out of my voice.

"Well . . ." She smiled and shrugged helplessly. "What can I do? You're awfully clever, aren't you, Pookie?"

"Come on!" He tugged me toward the staircase. "I got lots of Fider-Man stuff. I got PlayStation and everything!"

"What a little gentleman!" She clapped her hands. "You go show Miss Gwen your room, and I'll finish up with the tea. We'll have a tea party, just like in *Alice in Wonderland!*"

"And cake later, for my birthday!" Leo closed his eyes in the rapture of it all.

"That's right. When Daddy gets home from work." She winked at me and murmured, "Sugar-free carrot cake. Organic. And by the way, Gwen . . . could you do me a colossal favor and not mention any of this to Alex?"

I narrowed my eyes. "Any of what?"

"Anything about, you know, Leo taking off with my car service. I don't want him to think I'm irresponsible."

I limited my response to: "But he already thinks that."

"Well, then, it's too late to change his mind, and there's no point giving him any more ammunition!" She headed back to the kitchen, humming.

Leo tugged me up the stairs and gave me the grand tour. The first room at the top of the stairs appeared to be a guest bedroom, full of overstuffed pillows and lacy duvets.

"This is where my grandma lived before she went to Hawaii with Grandpa Franz," he explained. "We might go visit her. On a plane."

The next door opened up to a room with muted olive walls, an arching skylight, and pictures of Harmony. Lots of pictures. Memorabilia too.

Some people had home offices. Others, shrines to themselves. I guess it was all a question of self-esteem, and by the looks of things, Harmony's was quite high.

There were black-and-white head shots in ebony-lacquered frames. Posed photos of the entire *Twilight's Tempest* cast. Various crystal and metal statues mounted on plaques—I assumed these were entertainment awards. And the far wall boasted a huge, sun-drenched image of Harmony, Leo, and a frisky beagle. Harmony and Leo were making eye contact, laughing. They looked bonded and peaceful, a postmillennium Madonna and child.

Leo pointed to the beagle in the picture. "That's Jellybean. He died."

I patted his hair. "I know, buddy. You told me." But I was focused on a small, faded glamour shot tucked between the doorjamb and the wall. The woman waving to the camera in a bathing suit and high heels was clearly Harmony St. James (minus the blond highlights), but the bottom of the photo had been embossed with gold lettering: LIZZIE LEKAUS, LOTT COUNTY.

I called Leo over to consult. "Who's Lizzie Lekaus?"

"Oh. That was my name before." Harmony charged through the door, physically wedging herself between me and the photo. She was carrying two cups and saucers. "Isn't this room ridiculous? One of my ex-boyfriends insisted on setting it up. I should have known he was the obsessive type." She puckered her lips. "Now who was that? Alex N.? Alex K.? Anyway, I'm planning to clear it all out and make a yoga studio."

I couldn't stop grinning. "Where's Lott County?"

"It's, um, in . . ." She succumbed to a convenient coughing fit.

"I beg your pardon?" I said sweetly. "It's where?"

"Wyoming."

"Wow. The wild west, huh?"

She took the picture down from the wall and tucked it behind an end table. "*Chérie.* Forget you ever saw that. Anyway—"

But I had to ask one more question. "So were you in a beauty pageant or something?"

She opened her mouth, then paused. "Yes. But I shouldn't really say anything else about that. I'll get in trouble with my publicist." She handed me a delicate china cup brimming with foul-smelling tea.

I sniffed at it, then took a sip, confirming my fears that it tasted as vile as it smelled, and decided to stop torturing Lizzie Lekaus.

"Okay, kiddo, let's see your room."

We trooped back into the hall, and Leo gestured to a closed door on the left. "That's where my daddy sleeps."

I glanced at Harmony's face. Her expression remained deliberately, carefully vague.

He pointed over to a doorway that opened into a separate bedroom bedecked in ice blue satin, black velvet, and clothes balled up on the floor. "And that's Mommy's room."

"I see." I looked to Harmony for more information, but she wasn't talking.

So Alex had given up me, Harmony had given up New York, and now, evidently, both of them had given up trying to share a bed. Maybe I wasn't the only one facing a long stretch of celibacy.

It pains me to admit that I was still wearing the white tank top and red track pants when Alex arrived, but Harmony had selfishly failed to offer to lend me one of her couture ensembles. Not that I would fit into them anyway. Apparently, Wyoming turned out some pretty svelte specimens.

It pains me still more to admit that the significance of my outfit was not lost on him. He walked through the front door at seven-fifteen and found me trying to flee while Leo begged me to stay for a piece of sugar-free birthday cake, but he exhibited no visible signs of surprise.

He merely took off his charcoal gray suit coat, hung it up in the guest closet in the front hall, and said, "Those pants look familiar. Corner of Hilgard and Le Conte, right? Good cell phone goes bad?"

Harmony swooped in between us and tried to give him a kiss on the cheek. She got his right ear. "What cell phone? I don't get it."

I took a step back. "Listen, I have to get going."

"I'll walk you to your car." He looked at me, obviously speculating about what I was doing here, and I wondered if he was thinking about the last time we'd seen each other. Naked.

As a rule, when one starts picturing one's host nude, it is time to depart.

I collected my purse and prepared to exit stage right. "My car's parked right outside."

"I noticed. I'll walk you out," he repeated. Then he knelt down to address Leo. "Hey, buddy. Happy birthday."

"I'm five!" Leo pointed to the number on his crown. "And Nell doesn't live here anymore."

He raised his eyebrows. "She doesn't?"

Harmony shook her head. "Well, you see, there were a few glitches, *very* minor glitches—"

"I runned away," Leo announced defiantly.

Alex turned to me. "And that's why you're here."

I nodded, studying the silvery veins in the white marble floor.

He stood up. "Okay. I'm walking Gwen to her car."

"I will tell you a joke when you get back," Leo announced. Then he pivoted and ran back to the kitchen without so much as a "bye" in my direction.

Alex opened the door for me. Of course. As I stepped into the cool green shade, I caught a whiff of his shirt-starch-meets-pine-sap scent. This, of course, triggered further recollections of the kissing, groping, et cetera on my desk.

Before we could close the door behind us, Harmony had one final request. "Al, as long as you're out there, could you do me a huge favor and go pick up some dinner? We have nothing in the kitchen, and since it's Leo's birthday, I told him we could get Koo Koo Roo."

"Got it." He shut the front door firmly behind him.

My tight little smile broke into a grin. "Al?"

He looked pained. "Please do not ever call me that."

I was relieved that at least they hadn't already adopted vomitous little pet names for one another. Which, when you thought about it, was quite petty. They lived together. They had a child together. It was only right that they *should* use vomitous little pet names.

But I was relieved just the same. File me under "petty and proud of it."

Since he was not my boyfriend anymore, and since I had declined all offers of platonic friendship, I was not entitled to ask questions like: "How's it going with you two? Headed down to Fred Leighton to look at five-carat rings yet?" Or: "Why do you sleep in separate bedrooms?" Or: "You do realize that Harmony is an *E! True Hollywood Story* waiting to happen, don't you?"

No, as the gracious ex-girlfriend, it was not my place to disparage the mother of his child. My only job was to get back to Westwood with my self-respect intact.

But he seemed to be hell-bent on having a chat. "So Leo ran away today."

I turned both palms toward him. "Listen, I probably shouldn't get involved."

"I come home from work and you're in the foyer. You're already involved." He waited until I made eye contact with him. "If you don't talk, I'll only have Harmony's version of events to go on."

I sighed, then launched into an abbreviated account of Leo's arrival at my apartment. He looked increasingly concerned with every word.

When I finished, he had one simple yet mind-boggling question: "So how do I fix this?"

I studied his face and realized how much he truly wanted to be a good father. This was more than a burden he took on because he *had* to. He *wanted* this family to work.

And so did I.

In theory.

I tried to explain. "You can't exactly 'fix' kids."

"No, I mean the situation. Why did he run away? What do I need to do that I'm not doing?"

"It's not that straightforward. And I really shouldn't be talking to you about this. I'm not Leo's therapist anymore. And we have—we *had*—a personal relationship."

He just looked at me, waiting.

I tossed my purse onto the Saturn's hood. "Oh, all right. Here's my pithy little kernel of wisdom. This one's free, but after this, it'll be two hundred dollars an hour."

His eyebrows shot up. "Two hundred an hour? Isn't that a bit steep?"

"Standard Malibu therapy rate," I assured him.

He was staring at me. "I still can't believe you're blond. You look so—"

"Don't start with that again. Remember what happened last time you got worked up about my hair?"

He shoved both hands in his pockets. "I know. That will never happen again."

"No, it will not. So let's not go down that road." I tried to clear my mind of salacious thoughts. "Now here's my advice: Leo's going through a lot of big life changes. He just found out he has a dad, who then suddenly moved into his house. His mother . . ." I paused in the name of diplomacy. "His mother is trying very hard to find spirituality. And you should be aware that he can pick up on any and all tensions between you and Harmony. Children are like bloodhounds when it comes to hostility. And deception."

He didn't say anything. I focused on the sun setting in the smoggy horizon and continued.

"He's getting ready to start kindergarten in a few weeks.

It's pretty overwhelming. So of course he's going to act out."

"But what can I do?" He had resumed the grave, founding-father expression.

Almost involuntarily, I reached out and placed my hand on his shoulder. It felt so good to touch him again that I left it there for a few seconds before forcing myself to pull away. "This isn't all your responsibility. The only thing you can do is try to create an atmosphere of harmony—of, I mean, serenity in the home. You know. Everybody get together, try to love one another right now."

He raised an eyebrow. "People pay two hundred dollars an hour for *that?*"

I laughed. "They do in Malibu."

"But you don't think next week will make things worse?"

I tilted my head to one side. "You've lost me. What happens next week?"

"Harmony didn't tell you?"

"No." I tried to decide if I really wanted to know the answer to this next question. "What didn't she tell me?"

"She'll be out of town next week. *Twilight's Tempest* is going on location in Mexico. Big kidnapping story line for sweeps or something. Anyway, she'll be away for six days."

"Which leaves you and Leo on your own," I concluded.

The faint creases in his forehead deepened. "She says this is the perfect chance for us to bond. But what am I going to do with him for six straight days? You can only go to Disneyland so many times. Even the zoo wears thin."

"Disneyland? The *zoo?*" I clicked my tongue. "Rookie. You

have to save the bells and whistles for special occasions. You take him to Disneyland on random Saturdays, what are you gonna have left to bribe him with?"

He shrugged. "Piano lessons?"

I pretended to wipe away a tear. "My heart goes out to you."

"So you think I should just take him back to my condo in Santa Monica and, you know, try to be dadlike?"

I hopped up on the trunk and dangled my sandals over the cobblestone driveway. "I'm not sure that's your best bet."

"No?"

"He's already going to be freaked enough that his mom left him with some tall, mysterious stranger who's supposed to be his father. If you change his living environment too, you're looking at six days of nonstop, code-red temper tantrums."

"Oh God. What have I gotten into? I don't know any of this stuff. Why the hell did I ever think I could be somebody's dad? I've probably already screwed the kid up for life." He shook his head. "I've been reading all these parenting manuals, but reading isn't the same as *doing*. Harmony lent me a book, the one by the nanny to the stars? Half of that stuff doesn't even make sense."

"Okay, okay, don't hyperventilate. Men less prepared than you manage to raise sons every day."

"Yeah, but they're not raising them with Harmony."

"True."

"Six days alone with Leo." He glanced back at the house, scowling. "That woman is delusional, always has been. No way is this going to work."

"You're doing great," I assured him.

Panic was setting in. "Don't give me that. I know how I'm doing: piss poor. You have to help me."

Uh-oh.

I reminded myself of my goal: get back to Westwood with my dignity intact. That did not include offering up free child care consulting services to the most drama-ridden family this side of V. C. Andrews. "You don't need my help," I said firmly. "You're here, you're interacting with him, you remembered his birthday. I bet you even got him a present."

He nodded. "Oh yeah. A mint condition, first edition Spider-Man comic book. From 1954. Signed by Stan Parker."

This didn't seem like the appropriate time to point out that Leo couldn't read. "Well, see? You put a lot of thought into that."

He looked at me. "But . . . ?"

I cleared my throat. "But nothing."

"Come on. You have something to say."

"I have nothing to say. I better be going." I tossed my hair like a Pantene ad to distract him and groped for another topic of discussion. "I just hope my car makes it down the hill."

Mission accomplished. He was instantly peering through the windshield at the dashboard. "What's wrong with it?"

"Nothing much." I dug my car keys out of my purse. "The brakes just started making this weird grinding noise when I stop."

From the expression on his face, you would have thought I'd just confessed to a seven-state killing spree. "You're driving around with *grinding brakes?* Don't you know what that means?"

I jammed my key in the door lock and twisted. "Uh . . . no?"

"Your brake pads are worn down."

"And that's bad?"

He started to illustrate his point with choppy hand gestures. "Okay, think of your brake pads as erasers. After too much use, the eraser wears down to—"

I waved this away. "I got it, I got it. I'll swing by the dealership next time I'm in Culver City and get it checked."

He looked like he was going to be sick. "You take your car to the *dealership* for repairs?"

"That's right." I opened the door and settled into the driver's seat. "Know what else? I use the cheapest, lowest-quality gas I can find. That should keep you awake all night. And anyway, how do you know it's the brake pads? You're a financial analyst. Or consultant. Whatever—something financial."

"Gwen. Brakes are serious business. Let me take care of this. We'll just—"

"No!" I fastened my seat belt with a click. "I'll get it taken care of. You're not my . . ."

"Your what?"

I swallowed and sat back against the seat. "My mechanic."

Our silent frustration pulsed through the car door, permeating steel and glass.

He set his jaw. "I'm going to give my repair guy a call. He'll fit you in tomorrow morning. Corner of Olympic and Westwood Blvd."

I was shaking my head before he finished his sentence. "You can't do that."

"I am doing it. Calling my mechanic isn't wrong. It's not as if—" He stopped to rake both hands through his hair. "Somebody has to take care of this."

"And it has to be me. You cannot take care of me anymore. Just worry about this." I gestured past the lawn to the cute little white house and all the chaos lurking inside it.

We stared at each other for a long, loaded minute before he spoke.

"I really—" And with that he shut his mouth, spun on his heel, and marched back to his family.

I watched him walk away from me again. Then I started the engine and gunned it for Westwood. Brake pads be damned.

He really *what?* Appreciated the parenting advice? Hated living with all those velvet throw pillows? Missed me the way I missed him?

The little coupe kept pace with my racing thoughts, and I noticed the flashing police lights in my rearview mirror halfway down Beverly Glen. After suffering a small stroke, I pulled over and started to rehearse my story.

I'm on my way to rescue orphans from a burning building . . .

But the burly cop who strutted up to my window with bulging pecs and mirrored sunglasses didn't look like much of an orphan sympathizer.

He had a surprisingly Matthew McConaughey voice for such a Schwarzenegger physique. "Ma'am, do you know why I pulled you over?"

When in doubt, lie like an Enron accountant. "No?"

And then he smiled, which made him look even more like a former *Baywatch* guest star. (Given the economic climate in L.A., this was an entirely feasible possibility.)

"Well, you might have been speeding a little. But that's not why I pulled you over."

Oh boy. Here we go again with the fucking brake pads. I fumbled with my wallet and handed over my driver's license with trembling hands.

He studied my photo. "Hey, you're not blond in this picture."

"I know. I just had it colored."

He adjusted his sunglasses. "Are you, um, single, Ms. Traynor?"

This surprised me so much, my heart stopped palpitating. "What?"

"Well . . ." He fiddled with my side mirror. "I noticed your hair when you rolled through that last stop sign. And I thought . . . well, I was wondering if I could maybe get your phone number."

16

"I have a date with a cop," I announced the minute I set foot in the apartment. "A cute one. Officer Paul Brenneman. He's totally ripped, but with an 'aw shucks' southern sensibility."

Cesca glanced up from the scientific journals piled on the kitchen table. "That sounds nice."

"Let's just hope he doesn't have any surprise illegitimate children, right?"

"Mmm," she murmured. "I'm sure he's wonderful."

Something was definitely awry here. "'That sounds nice'? You're sure he's wonderful? I came in here all ready for a filibuster on the perils of relationship vine-swinging."

"Oh, Gwen, I would never presume to meddle in your love life. You should do whatever makes you happy. Follow your heart."

"Oh no." I put one hand on my hip and pointed an accusatory finger at her. "You got back together with Mike, didn't you?"

Her only response was, "Love your outfit."

I glanced down at the track pants so red they put lobsters to shame. "I keep meaning to retire these."

"And yet, just like Michael Jordan, they keep coming back to torment the rest of us."

"It's laundry day. It was either this or pajama bottoms."

"You should have gone with the pajama bottoms, G-dog." The dreaded ex strolled out of our bathroom and collapsed into the chair next to Cesca.

I grabbed the kitchen counter for support. "How did *this* happen?"

"Don't make me paint you a picture, G." He chortled and held up a hand for a high-five. Cesca just sneered at him. *Follow your heart,* my ass.

I tried to suppress my own little sneer. "No, I mean, why are you here? In my apartment?"

"Study buddy. Someone's got to quiz Lady C. on the"—he frowned down at the pile of index cars on the table—"on, you know, all this stuff about drugs."

I rounded on Cesca, but before I could demand answers, she said, "Good news" and handed me a check for $5,000.

Five thousand dollars from the account of Dr. Dennis

Schell. Made out to me. And this was no joke. I didn't recognize the new address printed in the upper left corner, but I knew that careless scrawl on the signature line.

I stared at my roommate. "What the hell?"

She dusted off her hands. "You're welcome. It was my pleasure."

Mike seemed torn between admiration and abject fear. "Don't screw with this girl. She'll mess you up."

"But how . . . ." I frowned as a series of increasingly sinister scenarios paraded through my mind. "Do I even want to know?"

"Oh, relax. I just ran into the jackass today at The Bomb Shelter, and he had that bottle-blond minx with him—what's her face, again?"

"Lisa. And less running down the bottle blondes, please."

She dismissed this with an airy wave of her hand. "*You* look good."

"Foxy." Mike fished a cigarette out of his pocket.

"Whereas this chick was the ne plus ultra of skank. Dark roots, split ends, a travesty. Matthieu would weep, absolutely weep." She offered me a Life Saver. "I can't believe he left you for . . . well, anyway, he had the audacity to say hello."

"So you mugged him?"

"Yeah, basically. I figured you could use a little pick-me-up to the tune of five G's."

"I definitely can. But am I now aiding and abetting a violent criminal?"

"Please. I just used a few little tricks my brothers taught me.

I can shake a fool down when necessary." She pointed a warning finger at Mike. "You remember that. Darling."

Mike stood perfectly still and exercised his right to remain silent.

"Anyway, I figured after all this crap with Alex and everything, you could use a little retail therapy." She beamed. "If you want to hit the Beverly Center this weekend, I'm available. Oh, and by the way, I told him you were engaged."

"You what?"

"Well, *practically* engaged. I told him you were seriously involved with this dark, handsome, filthy rich hunk. Hugh Jackman meets Bill Gates."

"Interesting. But if my fiancé's so rich, why do I need five thousand dollars?"

"It's not the money; it's the principle of the thing," she explained. "Breach of promise, restitution, all that. In fact, you were threatening legal action if he didn't cough it up."

"Was I?"

"Oh yes. You're quite litigious, as it turns out. And Chet is a partner at a very prestigious firm downtown."

I burst out laughing. *"Chet?"*

"Yes. Your promised husband."

"I would never marry someone named Chet."

"Of course you would. He's dreamy. Now, speaking of dreamy, tell me about this smooth-talking traffic cop."

Mike squinted at me. "Yo, didn't you just break up with that stockbroker?"

"Financial analyst," I corrected. "It's a long story, but yes, we've gone our separate ways."

"G-dog got the *moves*." He nodded approvingly. "Must be the new hair."

Cesca smacked him upside the head. "It is not the new hair, you moron. There's more to a woman than her looks. How superficial can you—"

"Actually, I think it *is* the hair." I recounted my conversation with L.A.'s finest.

Her jaw hung open. "He pulled you over for the express purpose of asking you out? Talk about abuse of power."

"Yeah, but he seemed nice. Shy, even. And very polite. Chet may have a little competition."

Mike pulled out his Newports, took one look at the pair of ferocious "no-smoking" glares, and beat a hasty retreat to Cesca's room.

I crossed the kitchen to see if Mike had left any of my Diet Cokes in the fridge. "So I agreed to have dinner with him. Why not? It's not like I have any better offers." I sat down next to her and poured a tall frosty glass of carbonated heaven. "Anyway. How was your day?"

"Long. Boring. Yours?"

"Well, let's see. Alex's son ran away from home today, showed up here, and I had to take him back to Harmony's."

"He showed up here?"

"Yeah."

"By himself?"

"Yeah."

"But isn't he four years old?"

"Five, actually, as of today. I know. I too was stunned and amazed. He's highly skilled for a preschooler."

"I'll say. So did you run into the big A. when you returned the kid to Harmony?"

I choked on my soda. "'The big A.'?"

She flushed. "Sorry. I've been hanging around with"—she jerked her head in the direction of her bedroom—"too much. As I was saying, did you run into *Alex?*"

"Yeah. But don't worry. Nothing happened."

"Nothing?" She raised an eyebrow.

"That's right! Nothing! We didn't do anything wrong, okay? I barely looked at him. I wouldn't even accept a mechanic referral from him. So don't give me that look! It's not my fault that they can't keep tabs on one lousy preschooler."

"Whoa." She pushed her chair back from the table. "The defense rests."

"Sorry." I rubbed my forehead. "I might be a tad oversensitive about this whole thing."

She slung an arm around my shoulder. "Well, onward and upward, right? When's the big date with Officer Studly?"

I smiled. "Next Friday."

"Well, if that doesn't work out, I could always introduce you to one of Mike's buddies. They're quite the motley crew."

"Mötley Crüe?" Mike ambled back into the kitchen. "You want me to bring *Decade of Decadence* next time I come over? It is the definitive metal album."

My roommate closed her eyes, praying for patience. "No. Please no. I was just telling Gwen about all your eligible bachelor friends."

"Hey! Yeah!" He took a swig off the bottle. "I should hook you up with Hooch. Hooch would *dig* the G-dog."

She dropped her head into her hands. "As God is my witness, I will never, ever miss another birth control pill."

Due to circumstances beyond my control, I never did go out with Officer Paul, *Baywatch* refugee. But this was not for lack of trying.

Here is a list of some things I did during my work week: mainlined caffeine; read roughly twenty-five journal articles on common ADHD diagnosis errors; worked with Lucy Spitz to develop her impulse control; crunched dissertation data and cursed when all my analyses refused to yield significant results; met with Dr. Cortez and tried to explain aforementioned nonsignificant results; went to the gym with Cesca, where we talked smack about our advisers behind their backs.

Here is a list of things I did *not* do during my work week: Obsess over Alex Coughlin. Think about Alex Coughlin. Remember who Alex Coughlin even was.

I purged all traces of Leo and Harmony from my office. I made a point of not asking Heather Vaughn how their therapy was progressing. I screened all my calls at home and at work, which turned out to be unnecessary because no one screenworthy called.

But there was nothing I could do about the fact that every

time I looked at my desk, memories of fervid, panting sex flooded my mind. I finally had to rearrange all the office furniture and spread paper and books over the desktop. This fooled my conscious mind, but not my body, which wanted more of what it could not have. I tried to convert my frustration with Alex into excitement about Paul, but even Cesca didn't buy into this act.

"You could at least *feign* enthusiasm," she scolded me on Friday evening as I dragged myself to the closet.

I gestured expansively at my wardrobe. "You see? I have nothing to wear. Nothing!"

"Just stay away from those hideous red track pants and you'll be fine." She threw herself down on my bed, ripped into a box of Good & Plenty, and propped her ankles up on my pillow.

"You look comfortable."

"Oh, I am." She began to pluck all the pink candies out of the box.

"Don't you have any plans tonight? Aren't you back together with the walking encyclopedia of eighties hair bands?"

"Eh." She shrugged. "We had a screaming match in the video store last night. He wanted to rent *Road House,* and when they didn't have it, he just went nuclear. So I tried to calm him down, but you know how that goes. Long story short, they revoked our membership card, and we're not allowed in there anymore."

I narrowed my eyes. "Who's 'we'?"

"You, me, and Mike."

"Why me?" I yelped. "I wasn't even there!"

"Yeah, but our card's in your name, and apparently you

attract a bad element. Anyway, it just reminded me how imma-
ture he is. You've been right all along; I just use him to keep
myself out of a functional—read 'scary'—relationship that
might actually go somewhere. It's got to stop. I'm meeting him
tonight to break up with him. For once and for all. After the
Lakers game, of course."

"Lie to yourself if you must, but don't lie to me." I turned
back to the closet and ran smack-dab into the wedding dress.
"Why? Why do I keep this thing here?"

"To torture yourself. To continue to accept blame for Dennis's faults. To subvert your own growth."

"Thank you, Dr. Obvious."

"No problem. Listen, if you don't want it, give it to me. I
think it's gorgeous."

I fingered the transparent plastic encasing the dress. "You're
breaking up with Mike, remember? No weddings for you. And
anyway, this thing's oozing bad karma. I'll donate it to Goodwill or sell it on eBay or something."

She peered into the Good & Plentys in search of more
pinks. "Donate it to the Cesca DiSanto Grant Foundation.
Make a difference in a starving student's life." She suddenly got
serious. "Come on, Gwen. Get it out of your closet. It's making
you guilty and crazy. Let me take care of it. That dress is worth
a lot of boxes of mac and cheese."

"I know. I just keep thinking that if I hang on to it, I can fix
whatever needs to be fixed. With me. Because on the day before
I was supposed to wear this thing, my whole life turned to shit."

She sat up and looked at me. "It wasn't you."

"I'd like to believe that, but now, with everything with Alex . . . it just seems to be a pattern with me."

"Give it to me," she repeated. "Get it out of your life."

When I handed Cesca the heavy pile of silk and lace, I let go of the last remnant of faith I had in fairy-tale endings.

She trundled it off to her room, and when she returned, she looked about a thousand times happier than I.

"All right, missy, out with the old, in with the new. What are you going to entice Officer Paul with?" She rummaged through the tailored shirts and cardigans until she spied my sequined black tank top. "Here we go! Wear it with my black stilettos and that little red skirt you bought at Anthropologie last year."

"I cannot wear that," I explained, "as I am not a prostitute."

"But you *are* a blonde. Live up to your reputation! Have more fun!"

"You're the devil," I told her.

"The devil doesn't lend you fabulous strappy sandals," she said. "Now loosen up and live a little. Don't worry, you'll be dead soon enough."

"Ah, I feel better already."

We ended up compromising—I agreed to wear high heels and too much eyeliner in exchange for the right to cover up my legs with slim black pants.

"I want to leave something to the imagination," I explained, dabbing on shimmery pink lip gloss.

"Yeah, yeah, you and Susan B. Anthony."

"Don't you have to go get ready for your main metal man? Drive him away for good?"

"Yeah. Lemme borrow that little red skirt."

I threw the mascara tube at her. She dodged, her instincts honed by years of living with a houseful of Little League pitchers, and headed for the bathroom. I heard the water running in the shower, and the phone rang as Cesca began her customary cleansing concert.

"Tiger Woods, y'all . . . It's all good, y'all . . ."

I snatched up the cordless phone in the kitchen, pressed it to my right ear, and plugged the left ear against Cesca's a capella hip-hop.

"Hello?"

"Gwen?" asked an all-too-familiar male voice. "It's Alex Coughlin."

I pounded on the bathroom door. "Shut up, Cesca!"

She shut up.

He cleared his throat. "Is this a bad time?"

I headed back to my bedroom. "Not really. I'm just getting ready to go out."

He laughed a little stiffly. "Hot date?"

"Um . . ." I admired the blond bombshell reflected in the mirror and the closet devoid of exorbitantly priced wedding dresses. "Yeah, kind of."

"Oh. Then I won't keep you. Bye."

"Wait." I turned my back on the blond bombshell. "Why'd you call?"

"I just wanted to check on your car. Make sure you got the brakes fixed."

"Oh, yeah. My brakes. Well . . ."

He groaned. "I knew it. Gwen, you cannot put this off. Good brake pads are critical to—"

"I know, I know. Life and death. I'll do it tomorrow. Have no fear."

There ensued a long pause, during which I thought I could discern Leo shouting in the background.

"So . . ." I took a deep, cleansing breath. "Anything else, then?"

"No."

"Oh."

He finally broke the silence. "Who's the lucky guy?"

"No one you know. It's not a big deal. I mean, I hardly even . . . it's totally casual."

Someone picked up an extension on Alex's side of the connection.

"*I want another cookie!*" Leo screamed, directly into my ear.

Alex sighed. "Leo. I told you to start getting ready for bed."

"You're not my mom! I wanna cookie! And I'm not going to bed. You can't make me!"

"Whoa." I held the receiver away from my ear.

"*I want my mooom!*" Leo slammed the receiver down, giving the dramatic gesture everything he had.

"Ouch," I said. "Has he been like this all day?"

Alex sounded like he'd spent the last twelve hours digging a ditch under the blazing sun. "Put it this way: remember when we first met, and I said I wanted to have five kids?"

"Yeah."

"I no longer want five kids."

I laughed. I couldn't help myself.

"I have to go," he said.

"No, hang on. It's been like this ever since Harmony left?"

"The kindergarten production of *Apocalypse Now?* Yes."

"I'm never, ever goin' to bed as long as I live," Leo howled in the background. *"Buy me a bunny!"*

"Aw, the special bond between father and son."

"Don't start with that," he warned. "I didn't know what to expect from fatherhood, I admit that. I thought I'd go fishing with my kids. Build birdhouses. Make dioramas and papier-mâché models of the planets."

"What? You guys haven't built any birdhouses yet?" I asked innocently. "How's the apple pie situation?"

"Let me tell you something: those stupid parenting books aren't worth the paper they're printed on. Where's the chapter on psychotic temper tantrums?" He did not seem to be seeing the humorous side of all this. "My God. How can one tiny person have so much lung power? How does he have room for any other internal organs? He's one big rampaging lung. Are they all like this?"

"Children? Yeah, pretty much."

"Well, they should put *that* in the books."

Leo howled away in the background. "I want Mommy! When's Mommy coming home?"

I glanced at my alarm clock. Ten minutes until Officer Paul

knocked on my door. And I still had to paint my toenails. Time to get off the phone and get back to *my* life. Caterwauling five-year-olds and ex-lovers not included. Alex was a dad now; let him figure out how to parent. This wasn't even remotely my problem.

And yet.

"Do you need any help?" I heard myself asking.

"No. I have everything under control."

Leo started wailing like an ambulance racing down Wilshire Boulevard.

"It doesn't *sound* like everything's under control." I decided to multitask, grabbing a bottle of polish and hunkering down on the bed with the phone wedged between my shoulder and my ear. "Have you tried giving him a time-out?"

"What's a time-out?"

"Oh my God. I thought you said you were reading up on this."

"I *am*. Listen, I'll figure it out. If I can handle the bottom dropping out of the Asian market, I can handle this."

"If you say so. But just bear in mind—"

"I told you—I don't need help."

"Will you knock it off? You know the Asian market, I know preschoolers." I shifted my weight, the Revlon bottle tipped onto the mattress, and pink frost oozed everywhere. I swore under my breath, then resumed my crash course in child development. "The most important thing is to . . ."

I broke off, wincing, as I heard a door slam with terrific force on the other end of the line.

"Alex?"

"Yeah, hang on."

A rattling sound, a series of hollow poundings, then Alex said, "He's locked himself in the bathroom. I better go."

I heard Leo's muffled voice yell, "I'm never, ever coming out," and then what sounded like the bathtub faucet running.

"Leo? Leo, open this door!"

"Nuh-uh! You're not the boss of me."

"Are you *sure* you'll be okay over there?" I asked.

"Of course," he snapped. "Just as long as—"

The bathroom faucet stopped and Leo called, "I'm running away again. I'm gonna fly off the roof. Like Fider-Man!"

"Don't you dare open that window." Alex sounded surprisingly calm for someone facing a locked door and a small child hell-bent on air travel. "Come out of there immediately. Do you hear me?"

No response from Leo. I know, because I held my breath and waited.

Alex muttered something I didn't catch.

"What? Did you get the door open?" I demanded.

"No. But I think I hear the window opening in there."

"Up, up, and awaaay!" Leo crowed.

I tossed the phone on the bed and ran for the door.

17

A few illegally run red lights later, I arrived at Harmony's house. Light blazed through all the open windows, and the marble koi in the driveway fountain sported the wilted paper crown that Leo had worn last week. A vague hint of jasmine wafted through the air. If it weren't for the eerie silence, I would've thought there was a party going on.

I rang the doorbell. After two full choruses of "Frère Jacques," a very fed-up Alex appeared, greeting me with, "I told you, I don't need any help. I have everything under control."

"Obviously." I peered over his shoulder to the foyer, which looked like a war-torn Toys "R" Us. Robots and dump trucks and what appeared to be Uno cards were confettied across the floor and up the stairs. I could hear water sloshing, along with the steady rhythm of someone repeatedly opening a door, then slamming it shut with all possible force.

Alex closed his eyes and rubbed his forehead. "That kid. Is driving. Me crazy."

"What happened? Did you get him out of the bathroom?"

He started up the stairs and beckoned for me to follow. "In a manner of speaking."

"What's that supposed to mean? He didn't . . . I mean, you stopped him before he jumped, right?"

He turned around, smiling grimly. "The flight risk has been neutralized. I'll show you."

The intervaled door-slamming ceased when we hit the landing. I trailed behind Alex down the hall to the bathroom door. Or, at least, to what had once been the bathroom door. The doorframe now sported several ugly gashes, empty hinges, and no door. The interior was a disaster area of wet towels, child-size clothes, slippery tile, and a bathtub overflowing with bubbles. The stench of jasmine was overpowering.

I gave him a thumbs-up. "Hey, good for you. How'd you get the hinges off? Did you find a screwdriver?"

"Harmony has no screwdriver. No screwdriver, no fire extinguisher, no list of emergency contacts. As far as I can tell, she doesn't even have a flashlight."

"A situation that you plan to rectify in the near future," I predicted.

He clenched his jaw. "Along with a lecture series on the importance of home safety."

"Boy, am I ever sorry I'm going to miss that." I paused. "So what's with the door slamming?"

He examined the fresh gouges in the wood. "That would be the work of my son. My firstborn and, if there is a God, my *only* son."

I examined the disemboweled doorframe. "So what finally happened?"

"As you can see, the perp stripped naked and dumped all of Harmony's perfume into the tub, along with an entire bottle of shampoo. He then neglected to turn off the faucet and fled onto the roof."

"The roof? Still naked?"

He nodded. "Probably for the best. Bare feet gave him extra traction on the shingles."

"And meanwhile, you were . . ."

"Trying to figure out how to pick a lock that rusted over in nineteen eighty-five and using my car key to take the hinges apart." He reached into his pocket and showed me the gnarled, paint-stained remains of his Audi key. "I would have climbed onto the roof through the French doors in Harmony's balcony, but of course, those were painted shut."

"But you did get him down."

"Eventually. I had to climb out there next to him. We had an illuminating little chat about the differences between Spider-Man and real life."

"And he saw your point and came inside?"

"Nah. I bribed him."

I laughed. "What'd you have to give him?"

"I promised him waffles before he went to bed. Apparently,

he loves them, and Harmony refuses to contaminate her house with Eggos." He shrugged. "But then I couldn't deliver, and that's why he's slamming the door."

Right on cue, a door slam echoed down the hall.

"Knock it off!" Alex yelled.

"I hate you!" Leo yelled back.

Norman Rockwell, here we come.

"So now what?" I asked.

"I did promise him, so I guess I better whip up some waffles." He exhaled loudly. "There must be a recipe in one of the cookbooks downstairs. I understand some sort of hot iron is involved, but after that, I'm out."

We both winced as a door slam rattled the windows.

"Tell you what," I said. "Give me directions to the nearest grocery store, and I'll pick up some waffles for the kid."

His gaze sharpened. "You said you had a date."

I flushed. "Yeah. That ended up not happening."

"Why?"

The truth of the matter was that I had fled the apartment while Cesca was still in the shower, leaving her a Post-it explaining that a young life was on the line and asking her to make my excuses to Officer Paul. Cowardly? Yes. Incredibly stupid? Yes again. I'd stood up a perfectly chiseled hunk of manhood in favor of a little boy who couldn't even print his own name. And I'd have to spend tomorrow morning listening to Cesca (along with Mike, most likely) rant and rave about whatever happened to common courtesy.

But I would die before I explained all this to Alex. I didn't want him to get the wrong idea. Or any idea at all. Anyway, I'd done it for Leo's sake. Not his.

So I restricted my remarks to, "Mind your own business."

"What happened?" he pressed.

"You want waffles or not?"

He held out his hand. "I want waffles. Give me your keys. I'll make a Ralph's run."

"What's wrong with your car?"

He showed me the mangled Audi key again. "I don't think I'll be getting much use out of my car tonight."

"Daddy? Who are you talking to?"

Alex glanced down the hall. "Gwen's here. I'm showing her what you did to the bathroom."

Two huge eyes peeked around the corner, then Leo barreled down the hall and surgically attached himself to my legs.

"Hi, Miss Gwen! Hi!"

I looked down at him. "How's it going?"

He widened his eyes and smiled angelically. The only thing missing was a little golden halo. "Good."

I raised my eyebrows. "You're being a good boy for your daddy?"

"Uh-huh." He nodded emphatically.

"Really."

"Oh, yes. I'm *very* good."

Alex snorted.

"So you're not tormenting Daddy just a little bit?"

"Nooo." He motioned for me to lean over, and when I did, he whispered, "Daddy doesn't know time-outs."

"That's all going to change," I promised him. "No more playing Daddy for a sucker."

"Hey!" Alex objected.

I gave him a look. "The kid destroys the bathroom, climbs out on the roof, flouts all discipline and bedtime attempts, and you promise him waffles. What would you call that?"

He shrugged. "A performance incentive."

"Just get to the store, chairman. And while you're gone, this kid is going to clean up the mess he made."

Leo's grin vanished. "Clean up?"

"That's right. There's water all over the floor, and it smells like a French—"

"It smells like Mommy," Leo supplied, cutting me off just in time.

"Well, you're going to clean it all up. And then, when you're done, we'll make waffles."

The grin reappeared. "Waffles!"

"That's right. So get crackin', buddy." I pointed him in the direction of the bathroom. "Grab a towel and start mopping. I'll help you."

"This really isn't necessary," Alex said as Leo started down the hall.

"Oh, yes, I forgot; you're the man who doesn't need any help." I turned toward him. "Listen. You have a choice. You can either take Leo to the store, where I guarantee he'll have another meltdown in the candy aisle because he's overtired, or you can go grab some Eggos while he cleans up his own mess and learns to take responsibility for his mistakes. Which sounds like the better option to you?"

He folded his arms. "You want blueberries in those waffles?"

I smiled sweetly. "Blueberries sound delightful. And don't worry about my brakes."

His gaze went steely. "You *are* getting new brake pads. I'm making you an appointment with my mechanic for Monday morning, and you better show up."

I knew when it was time to back down. "If you insist."

"I do." He looked supremely frustrated. "I may not have mastered time-outs yet, but brake pads I can deal with."

"Miss Gwen, I dropped the toilet paper in the bathtub," Leo hollered down the hall.

"Coming." I started for the bathroom, calling back to Alex, "It's been a little slice of heaven."

And the sick thing was, I kind of meant it.

The Eggos went over big. I tried to explain that placing the frozen disks in the toaster was, in fact, easy, but both Leo and Alex persisted in treating the finished product as some sort of culinary miracle. Even the fake maple syrup elicited oohs and ahhs.

There they were, two males in a state of carb-loaded bliss, Leo with syrup smeared all over his chin, and Alex studying the directions on the package as if they were hot new stock tips.

"I think it's somebody's bedtime," I announced.

"It's your bedtime in Fiji by now," Alex told Leo.

Leo licked a dot of syrup off his wrist. "What's Fiji?"

"It's an island near Australia. Which is in a different time zone." He stood up and offered his hand to Leo. "Which means you should have gone to sleep a long time ago."

"But I did a good job cleaning up the bathroom and the hall," Leo said proudly.

"Yes, you did. But you're still overdue for bed."

Leo clomped off toward the stairs with his dad. "But who lives in Fiji? Is it cold there?"

"Actually, it's very warm," I heard Alex reply as they left the room. "You'd like it—you wouldn't have to wear much."

They seemed to have the bedtime routine down pat, so I left them to what Harmony would have called "the bondy thing" and tried to use hot water and all-natural, eco-friendly cleanser to wipe up the syrup spills on the counter.

I checked my watch. Still plenty of time to head back to Westwood and meet up with Cesca at the sports bar. Or just curl up with the TV remote and a big bowl of ice cream. If I listened closely, I could actually hear HBO and Ben & Jerry's Phish Food calling my name from across the hills.

But I dawdled. I sat down on a dainty white stool in Harmony's dainty white kitchen, and admitted to myself that I didn't want to leave. A big part of me wanted to hang in limbo here, suspended in the gap between what could be and what had to be.

There was a certain safety in this situation Alex and I had created—we were free to let our imaginations run wild, because we could never take action. Desire without risk. Attraction without disappointment. An intoxicating alternative to our real lives.

I piled the last of the pink-rimmed china into the sink. My fear of being alone had railroaded me into someone else's light, white house. None of this was mine: not these dishes, not the father and child upstairs, not the sense of love and security I felt tonight.

This was wrong. Regardless of the current state of Alex and Harmony's sleeping arrangements or compatibility, they had decided to be a couple. Who the hell did I think I was, making waffles in her kitchen?

I had to stop *telling* myself to leave; I had to *actually* leave. So I did. I slipped out into my car, careful not to slam the door, and sped away.

I left without saying good-bye, and I knew it was the right thing to do, both for Alex and for me.

I was nobody's fallback. I deserved to come first. I deserved to be in a relationship where nobody ever had any doubts, or baggage, or overly fertile ex-fiancées. This was L.A.—I should be looking for a relationship that was soft-focus and well plotted, just like a movie. Right?

Right?

When I returned to the apartment, I found a mess the likes of which had not been seen since El Niño hit the California coastline. Cesca's clothes, my shoes, and rainbow-colored Sweetarts were strewn all over the kitchen and living room.

I had read enough true-crime books containing the sentence "The killer entered through the window of a first-floor apartment" to fear the worst. But when I reached for the phone to call 911, I saw the yellow Post-it note stuck to the refrigerator.

A Post-it in response to my Post-it? Touché.

Gwen—

Had a great time tonight. Taking a quick detour to Vegas, baby, Vegas! Be back Sunday. I'll play a few hands of blackjack for you.

C.

P.S.—took your wedding dress with me!!!

She had drawn a little smiley face next to the p.s. This in and of itself was as shocking as the contents of the note. Cesca DiSanto did not do smiley faces. She had very strong opinions on this matter; even e-mail "faces" composed of colons, parentheses, and dashes were verboten.

I checked the fridge's interior for alcohol of any kind before I reread the note. We had a splash of chardonnay left, so I uncorked it and swigged right from the bottle. Mike Jessup would be proud.

I slammed the empty wine bottle back on the countertop.

Cesca. Mike Jessup. Vegas. My wedding dress. Put those things together, and you had yourself a nightmare straight out of Edgar Allan Poe.

What to do? Who to call?

Cesca, obviously, on her cell. But she wasn't answering her

phone. Oh God. I was going to have to hire one of those professional "deprogrammers" who rescued cult members.

The cordless phone rang. I snatched it up.

"Hello?"

"Hey, G-dog! What up?"

I frowned. "Mike?"

"You know it. Is C. around?"

"Isn't . . . isn't she with you?"

"No. Why would I be calling you if she was over here with me?"

"That's what I was wondering."

"'Cause, like, if she was *here,* then I'd know that she wasn't *there.* 'Cause I'd be able to see her. Get that?"

"I get it," I snapped, "but I'm confused because she left a note for me saying she was headed to Vegas. With my wedding dress. I assumed she went with you."

His voice leaped up about two octaves. "What? She's in Vegas? And she took a wedding dress?"

"That's what I said."

"G-dog! How could you let her do that?"

I threw open the cabinet doors in search of more wine. "I'm not her warden. Besides, I wasn't here."

"I'm disappointed in you," he informed me.

"Then I'm hanging up."

"No! I'm sorry!" He always backed down. One of the things Cesca liked most about him. "Let's put our heads together and figure this out."

I grimaced but held my tongue.

"If C. went to Vegas . . . with a wedding dress . . . then . . ."

"Yesss?" I prompted, waiting for the epiphany to dawn.

"Oh my God! She's gonna get hitched!"

I rolled my eyes. "Ya think?"

"Yeah! That's it! She's getting married." There was the muffled sound of head scratching. "But who's she marrying?"

"Well . . ." I tried to break this news as gently as possible. "She might be marrying my date for the night. Paul something; I forgot his last name. He's a police officer. She hadn't met him before tonight, but I guess they hit it off."

He took a moment to mull this over. Then:

"Chicks are *whack,* man."

I thought about how I had spent my evening. "No argument here."

Mike was silent for so long that I thought we might have lost the connection. But then he piped up again. "That's it. I'm going to Vegas. And you're coming with me."

18

I agreed to go to Vegas because my concern for Cesca exceeded my irritation with Mike.

Just barely.

We took my car, bad brakes and all. I couldn't deal with the thought of five straight hours in Mike's rusty VW death trap. It was bad enough that I had to tolerate five straight hours of his conversation.

"So," he said as I merged onto the 15 Freeway. "Tell me about this Paul dude. Could I take him?"

"Probably not. He's a police officer."

"Is he good-lookin'?"

I debated sharing my *Baywatch* theory with him, then decided against it. Mike had never been my favorite person, but

I knew what it felt like to be dumped with spine-jarring suddenness. "Um . . ."

"No way can he be as good-lookin' as me." He checked out the redhead going ninety in the Corvette next to us and rummaged through the grimy duffel bag he'd brought.

My stomach growled. I checked the dashboard clock and realized that my lunch and dinner had consisted of a solitary Eggo. "Got any food in there?"

"Naw. Just the essentials."

I knew what that meant. "This is a no-smoking car."

He reclined his seat back and flopped around like a toddler. "Aw, *man*."

We hadn't even been on the road a full hour. I was starving, he was jonesing . . . *damn* that Cesca.

His hand snaked over to the stereo.

"What do you think you're doing?" I swatted his wrist away.

"We need some tunes. I got Warrant right here."

I sped up to pass a fleet of trucks. "No."

"Poison?"

"No."

"Europe?"

"Double no. Triple no."

We finally settled on Guns n' Roses' *Appetite for Destruction*. When Axl and the boys reached the final chorus of "Paradise City," I turned down the bass and told Mike to try Cesca's cell phone again.

"I'm sure that we're just jumping to conclusions. Silly, unwarranted conclusions," I said, doing my best P.R. spin.

"She's probably off on a girls' weekend with, you know, some of the wild psychologists we work with."

He turned the stereo off. "With a wedding dress?"

Why? *Why* had I told him about that?

"Maybe she's going to sell it to a casino chapel," I supplied. "Or, I know! Maybe one of her friends is eloping!" Hey, this was good stuff. Even *I* was starting to believe this.

He contemplated this for a minute. "But if she took off with her friends, wouldn't she have invited you?"

"Well . . ." I coughed. "How the hell are you planning to find her out there, anyway?"

"Oh, I know where she is." He said this so matter-of-factly that I wondered if he had tagged her with a homing device, like a panda in a nature preserve.

"You frighten me."

"She's at the Monte Carlo." He nodded smugly. "Every time we go to Vegas, she's all up in that place. She's got a fetus for that place."

I cleared my throat. "Perhaps you mean a 'fetish'?"

"A fetish. Whatever. That's where she'll be. And then, after I whup this police officer dude, her and *me* are getting married."

I checked the rearview mirror. The freeway behind me was dark and empty. No headlights. I could do a 180-degree U-turn over the median and head back right now.

My cell phone rang. Dear God, let it be Cesca.

"Can you get that?" I asked Mike. "I'm going eighty-five."

"Sure." He picked my phone up. "'Lo?"

He listened intently for a few seconds, then said, "Well, she's here, but we're on our way to Vegas right now and she's driving . . . Uh-huh . . . Uh-huh . . . the Monte Carlo, okay? Sure . . . right, see you there."

I pounced as soon as he hung up. "That was Cesca? Is she okay?"

He turned the stereo back on. "Nah. It was some chick named Harmony. She wanted to talk to you, but when I told her we're going to Vegas, she said she'll meet us there."

I slowed down to seventy. "She's meeting us *where?* Vegas?"

"Yeah. Says she needs to talk to you. And I gotta tell you, she sounds freaky deaky." He leaned over, filling my personal space with his ashtray breath, and gave me an elaborate wink. "What'd you do to her?"

The red taillights in front of me went blurry as panic set in. "Nothing! I did nothing! Why? What did she say?"

"Not much. But she sure seemed pissed. I guess she'll meet us at the Monte Carlo tomorrow morning. She's flying in from Mexico or some shit. Listen, can we stop for a burger now?"

I'd slammed back not one, not two, but six Diet Cokes by the time we vroomed into Sin City. The dashboard clock read 3:45 A.M. We'd made horrible time because *someone* had to stop for a snack, a cigarette, or a restroom break every thirty minutes (well, okay, the restroom breaks were mine . . . stupid Diet Cokes). The floor mats were littered with CD cases and fast-food wrappers. The lyrics of "Livin' on a Prayer" were permanently tattooed on my brain.

I floored it down the Strip, made an illegal left turn into the entrance of the Monte Carlo, yanked the parking brake, and handed my keys to the valet.

The sudden stop jolted Mike out of his peaceful nap. "It's probably cheaper to self-park, ya know."

"Get out or you sleep in the garage." I slammed the door and headed to the trunk for the overnight bag I'd packed.

"Jeez." He blinked his bloodshot eyes at me. "Crank-ee. And you know, your brakes don't sound so great. Might want to get them checked out."

I hoisted my bag over my shoulder and shuffled into the lobby. Even in the middle of the night, the hotel was blindingly bright and bustling with activity. Metallic *cha-chings* emanated from the casino down the hall. Scantily clad cocktail waitresses finishing shifts clicked by in their high heels.

I slapped my credit card down on the reception desk and asked for a room. The cheaper, the better.

"How many beds?" inquired the chipper brunette behind the counter.

"Two." Mike Jessup tossed his duffel bag down on my foot.

I glared at him, then turned back to the reservations clerk. "One bed will be fine, thank you."

Mike put both hands up. "Whoa. I think you're aces, G-dog, but I don't think the big C. would like it if—"

"Forget it. We're not sharing a room," I hissed. "Get your own."

"But I can't afford a room," he whimpered.

The last of my I'm-okay-you're-okay veneer evaporated.

"Listen to me. I just spent all night driving you out here in *my* car, paying for gas with *my* debit card, looking for *my* roommate, and now I am going to get some sleep in *my* bed, in *my* room. *Figure something out.*" I pounded the counter for emphasis.

The reservations clerk took a step back.

His eyes widened. "But—"

"Sir, I'd do as she says," the brunette advised.

I smiled. "Thank you. Listen, is there a Francesca DiSanto registered here?"

She frowned at the computer screen and punched a few buttons. "I don't see her name. Does she have any other traveling companions?"

"Yeah, but I forgot his last name." I sighed. "I'll just take my room key. Thanks, anyway."

Mike threw a tantrum that would do any preschooler proud. "Aw, *man!* Come on, I won't snore or anything! Come on, G!"

"I'm going to take a quick look around the casino for Ces, and then I'm going to bed. I better not see your face again until tomorrow morning. Meet you right here at ten," I told him, gathering up my bag and purse. *"Adios, muchacho."*

My deep, dark slumber (featuring nightmares of being chased by Jon Bon Jovi and Bret Michaels) ended abruptly at 8:38 A.M., according to the luminous alarm clock on the nightstand. I rocketed into a sitting position, scared and disoriented, and as my racing pulse slowed, I realized three things:

1. I was in a Vegas hotel room.
2. Someone was pounding on the door.
3. I was going to have to maim Mike Jessup.

I groped for the lamp switch, pulled on the pair of jeans and the tank top I'd worn last night, and prepared to confront the traveling companion from hell.

I flung open the door and recoiled from the harsh fluorescent light in the hallway. "This had better be good, or I swear to God—"

"Gwen! Hi! Did I wake you?"

Both hands flew to my mouth as I backed away from the willowy curves silhouetted in the doorway. "Oh. No?"

"Great." Harmony swished around me into the hotel room and started flicking all the lights on. " 'Cause I really need to talk to you. I ordered room service—they'll be right up with breakfast. That'll give you a minute to . . . brush your hair."

I didn't even bother asking what was wrong with my hair. I just snatched my comb off the dresser and started raking away at my scalp. "So. Harmony."

She curled up on the edge of my rumpled bed, tossed her hair back, and tucked one leg underneath her. "Yes?"

I concentrated on pulling on my socks and not making eye contact. "I thought you were filming down in Mexico."

She nodded. "I am. I have to be back there tomorrow night. But I have today off, and I need to talk to you."

Words to strike terror in any ex-girlfriend's heart.

She leaned forward, stacking her red-manicured hands under

her chin. "I'll get right to the point. I talked to Alex last night. I heard you were over at my place making frozen waffles."

"Yes, well . . ."

She whipped a nail file out of her purse. "Waffles are poison."

I could see the tabloid headlines now: "Bottle-Blonde Slashed in Monte Carlo: Cops Seek 'Nail File Killer.'"

I threw myself on her mercy. "Harmony, I apologize. I shouldn't have interfered with your parenting style. I'm sorry. I know you want to keep Leo healthy."

"Well." She smiled but kept that nail file pointed in my direction. "I was raised on milkshakes and candy bars and it never did me any harm. Besides, I know how Alex eats. He and Leo have probably had nothing but pizza and takeout for the past week."

She fixed me with that strong, glittering gaze again. "It's just very sad, nutritionally. And Western health care is so far behind."

"So far behind what?"

"Synchrona, of course." She regarded me with great pity. "I just thought I should let you know about waffles. Poison! Also bread, red meat, cheese, processed sugar, citrus fruit, cow's milk . . ."

I stared at her. "How have you not died of rickets?"

"Oh, I'm very centered. Anyway, that's not what I flew out here to talk about." She paused. "I want to talk about Alex. You and Alex."

I opened my eyes as wide as they would go, hoping this made me appear innocent and guileless. "What about us?"

She brandished the nail file again. "Like you need to ask!" Her laugh, though girlish and light, seemed forced. "I know what's going on between you two." The smile vanished. "And I have some questions."

As would any woman aspiring to become the fiancée of a man who spent his evenings talking car maintenance, child care, and Eggos with his recently dumped lover.

I kept a wary eye on the silver glint of the nail file. "Harmony, I assure you—"

The knock at the door made both of us jump.

"Room service," announced a muffled voice from the hall.

"Excellent!" Harmony leapt to her stiletto-clad feet and minced over to let the uniformed delivery guy in. He unveiled a linen-draped tray bearing fresh o.j., fruit, yogurt, granola, and some unidentifiable beige glop.

I tipped him on his way out, then frowned down at the ecru mess on the china plate. "What on earth is that?"

"A soy and eggplant omelet. No actual eggs, of course."

Great. Now she had armed herself with a knife and fork. She took a seat at the circular table in the corner and motioned for me to join her.

I spooned up a bite of yogurt, squared my shoulders, and decided to deal with this head-on, the way I should have from the beginning.

"All right," I said. "Let's talk about me and Alex."

"Let's." She finally put down the sharp metal objects and placed her hand over mine. "Alex loves you."

I dropped the bowl of yogurt. Live, active cultures splattered my shirt, my jeans, the carpet.

She started to laugh. "*Chérie!* Don't look so horrified."

"But I'm—no, he doesn't," I sputtered.

"Sure, he does. Well, he did, anyway. And I can see why."

"You can?"

"Sure." She shrugged. "You're the opposite of all the other women he's dated before. Even me."

I tried to look surprised. "You don't say."

"Honest! He used to be into the rescuer role or whatever. He had a thing for drama queens who would screw up his life. Can you believe it?"

"I can't believe that. That's unbelievable."

"But you're different. You're stable, you have a real job, and you look, you know, like a real person."

Through herculean effort, I managed not to react to this. "Harmony. What can I help you with?"

"Well . . ." She beckoned me closer. I leaned over the table and tried to stay upwind of the omelet.

Even her throat-clearing was dainty and delicate. "Alex and Leo adore each other. Obviously."

"Obviously," I agreed, although the only thing obvious to me was that no one had told her about the waterlogged state of her upstairs bathroom.

"And, I mean, of course Alex adores me too." She beamed and jingled her diamond-studded bangle bracelets.

"Uh. Huh." Two direct hits to the stomach.

Alex adored *her?* But she just said . . .

"He's so romantic," she gushed. "Just yesterday, he sent me flowers on the set. All the way from L.A.! Imagine that!"

"I'd really rather not."

"And you know our history. We picked up right where we left off in the romance department."

I wrapped my hand tightly around my butter knife. In the space of ten seconds, I had gone from fearing for my own life to contemplating murder.

"That sounds . . ." I swallowed back the bile flooding my throat. "That sounds . . . words fail me."

She pursed her Angelina Jolie lips. "Right where we left off. That's the problem. We didn't leave off in a very good place. I guess we were in love or whatever, but mostly we just fought. He kept saying I was *irresponsible*."

"Get out of town."

"I know! And he couldn't stand it when I flirted with anyone in front of him. Not even his friends! He drove me crazy with all his talk about maturity and responsibility! Hmph!" She shook her head and chugged her entire glass of ice water. "Anyway, cut to present day. Now that we have Leo, the man is still like a broken record. Maturity, morality, blah blah blah. I do my best to get along with him, but honestly! It's like herding kittens!"

I was still fixated on the bombshell she'd dropped a few sentences back. "But what about those flowers he sent you?"

She started fiddling with her spoon. For the first time since she'd barged in, she looked a little unsure of herself. "Oh. Well, the card only had Leo's name on it. But Alex must have ordered them, 'cause I'm pretty sure Leo hasn't figured out how to use my credit cards yet."

"But you said Alex was romancing you."

She sighed. "I might have exaggerated a *wee* bit."

I pushed back from the table, then leveled my gaze at her. The power dynamic in this relationship had flip-flopped in the space of thirty seconds. "Harmony. Why are you screwing with me?"

"All right, okay! I'm screwing with you! I confess!" She tossed her spoon to the carpet. "But it's only because Alex loves you more than me! I need your help!"

I coached my expression into my patented Therapist Poker Face. "What do you need my help for?"

She was sobbing prettily, one tiny fist pressed to her lips. "I need you to tell me how to make Alex love *me!*"

"Excuse me?"

"He doesn't love me the way I am now! He thinks I'm flighty and frivolous!"

"Now, let's not project," I lectured. "How do you know that he thinks that?"

"Because he told me I'm flighty and frivolous! He doesn't even like me. And I can't stand him, either! He is, like, the grand prize, lifetime winner of the Wet Blanket Award."

"Uh-huh. Well, given that you can't stand him, why do you want him to fall in love with you?"

"For Leo, of course. I'm gonna do whatever it takes to be a kick-ass parent, and if Alex is willing to put up with my shit, then I guess I'm willing to put up with his."

"Very magnanimous of you."

"I know. But I can't spend the next thirteen years living like this while we wait for the kid to head off to college." She dabbed her eyes with the bedsheet, musing, "Although, his preschool teacher said he's practically a genius, so maybe he can skip a grade, and then it'd only be twelve years . . ." She shook her head. "Whatever, every conversation at our house is like a frickin' Aesop fable. I can't possibly put up with it unless I'm getting some."

"Some what?" I asked, praying that her answer would be "aromatherapy" or "stock dividends" or "prescription tranquilizers."

"Sex." She tilted her head and grinned at me. "I'll sacrifice a lot for my little Pookie, but I think a celibate marriage is asking too much, don't you?"

I just looked at her.

"Especially with Alex C. He's killer in bed." She nibbled her bottom lip. "Or, at least, he was five years ago. You would know, Gwen! How's he now? Still mind-blowing?"

"I am not having this conversation," I said to myself as much as to her. "I am not even here right now."

"You two are perfect for each other. So *discreet!*" She giggled. Good to see that this discussion was only scarring one of us for life. "Well, anyway, if I'm marrying him, he's gotta worship me like the goddess I am. So I need you to teach me how to be a good fiancée. Starting now."

I shook my head. "Listen. Seriously. I can't help you. First of all, you can't make anyone love you, and second of all, this is so sick and wrong on so many levels."

"Oh, come on!" She wrung her hands. "Just give me a few pointers on how to be more like you."

"You want to be like me? Okay, here goes: find unsuitable man. Fall head over heels. Realize too late that your judgment is worse than Mary Jo Buttafuoco's. Repeat."

"No, you know what I mean! Come on, Gwen." She leaned forward. "Don't you want Alex to have a happy family?"

I crossed my arms over my chest. "Yes."

"Well, so do I. So teach me how to be the kind of woman he wants for his wife. I'll do whatever you say. Even if it goes against Synchrona."

I arched an eyebrow. "Wow."

"Yeah. I'm desperate."

Technically, I had no professional conflict of interest here. I could chat with her casually, refer her to books and other resources. This wasn't the same as being her therapist. But if I helped Harmony to become a woman of purpose and substance, I was effectively putting the final nail in the coffin for whatever Alex and I had together. Plus, what I said before about it being so sick and wrong on so many levels.

Then, the coup de grace. "Don't you want *Leo* to have a happy family?"

"Harmony," I said, "for someone who's not Catholic, you certainly have mastered the art of the guilt trip."

"Ohmigod, how did you know?" She laughed. "I went to

parochial school back in Wyoming! Lott County Sacred Heart, class of . . . well, obviously, I can't give you specific dates. My publicist would freak. But yeah, I grew up Catholic. Nuns, Latin mass, the whole enchilada."

"And now you've gone over to Synchrona?"

"Yep."

I nodded. "That explains a lot."

"That's exactly what my agent says."

Catholic guilt meets New Age rationalization? I was hopelessly outgunned in this little psychological skirmish, graduate degree or no graduate degree. Resistance was futile. "Oh, all right. I'll give you a reading list. But I'm not sharing anything personal. And after today, you're on your own, got it?"

She rummaged through her purse and whipped out a little notebook with a leather cover embossed with the Prada logo. "Deal! Let the spiritual growth begin! Where do you want to start?"

Harmony's cell phone rang two hours later, by which point we were deep into our fourth mimosa. And the discussion about fidelity had devolved from the level of Mars and Venus to Brenda and Dylan.

"I know you don't want to hear it, but flirting with other men is second- or third-degree cheating." I slurped the pulpy dregs from the bottom of my champagne flute. "Plus, it just pisses people off."

She scribbled this down. "I can't even flirt? Well, there goes my career."

"Welcome to monogamy, babe." I opened my mouth to continue, only to be cut off by a high-pitched, electronic version of "Isn't She Lovely?"

"Hang on." Harmony frowned down at the phone's digital display, then headed for the hallway. "Gotta take this. It's my Pookie."

"Well, don't tell him I'm here," I said. With Harmony gone, I had a moment to collect my wits, at which point I realized two things: one, I was getting pretty chummy—not to mention buzzed—with the enemy, and two, it was almost eleven and I hadn't heard from Mike.

Right on cue, the hotel room phone rang. Before I could even get the receiver all the way to my ear, I heard Mike hyperventilating.

"G-dog! G-dog!"

"What?" I demanded. "Did you find her?"

He stopped gabbling long enough to draw breath. "Find who?"

"*Cesca.*"

"No, but oh my God, G-Dog, guess who's playing the Hard Rock Casino tonight?"

I waited.

"Daddy Long Legs!"

I frowned. "Who?"

"Daddy Long Legs! The best metal band that ever walked the earth. And"—he gasped for air—"guess what else?"

I smote my forehead. "You're the worst boyfriend ever?"

"They're looking for roadies! They're hiring for their comeback tour!"

"We're supposed to be looking for Cesca. Remember her? The woman you pledged your undying love to?"

"I'm gonna apply to be a roadie for Daddy Long Legs." His voice was hushed with awe. "They *have* to hire me. It's . . . it's my dream come true. A miracle."

I glanced at the door. Harmony showed no sign of returning. "Listen up, Mike. We came all the way out here to find Cesca, and you're not leaving—especially not with a band sponsored by Aqua Net—until we find her. Got it?"

Big, annoyed sigh. "I guess. But I don't see how we're ever gonna track her down. It's like finding a needle in a—oh, wait, there she is!"

"What?" I barked. "Where?"

"She just came into the lobby. With your wedding dress and some tall black guy I've never seen before."

Harmony started knocking at the door. "Gwen? I'm ready to come back in."

I focused all my energy on the phone.

"Do not let her get away," I commanded Mike. "I'll be right there."

19

"Good Goddess." Harmony gasped as I raced into the hall, slamming the door behind me. "Where's the fire?"

"Down in the lobby. Come on." I dragged her toward the elevators. En route, I gave her the rundown on who Cesca was, why we were looking for her, and how to behave around Mike Jessup.

"Just pretend he's not there," I advised, all the while jabbing at the illuminated button marked L. "And if he won't stop ogling your chest, try pointing across the lobby and gasping, 'Isn't that Vince Neil?'"

"Don't worry. I learned how to handle those guys back in my beauty pageant days." She flashed me a dazzling Miss America smile. "And F.Y.I., hitting that button over and over won't get us down there any quicker."

I paced the perimeter of the tiny mirrored elevator while it stopped at every single floor to pick up passengers.

"Don't mind her," Harmony cooed to the bespectacled old couple with cameras around their necks and plastic cups of nickels in their hands. "She's a *psychologist*."

"Say." The man squinted at Harmony. "Aren't you that actress from *Chicago?* The Welsh one?"

"No, no," corrected the thin, pale teenage girl who stepped in at floor 19. "She's Harmony St. James, from *Twilight's Tempest.*"

There was much rejoicing among the populace of Elevator Number Five. Harmony glad-handed everyone, the anemic teenager posed for a photo with her soap opera idol, and the elderly couple marveled over their good fortune.

"Imagine! We just get on the elevator and run smack dab into the rich and famous," the old woman crowed.

"This is what makes America great," her husband agreed.

Harmony shook her golden curls back and laughed. "Did you hear that, Gwen? I make America great!"

"Totally," echoed the awestruck teen. "Your show was the only thing that kept me going through sophomore year. My teachers kept hassling me to go see a counselor or a psychologist or something, but none of them ever helped me as much as *Twilight's Tempest.*"

"Psychologists," grumbled the old man. "Pack of liars and charlatans. 'Mental health.' Hogwash."

"Can't compete with a good dose of hard work and common sense," his wife agreed.

"It's not even a real science." The teenager rolled her eyes.

I scowled at them and drummed my fingers on the brass handrail.

"What's *her* glitch?" the teenager muttered.

"She's a psychologist," the old woman stage-whispered back.

They all regarded me with real pity.

When the doors finally opened at the ground floor, I couldn't sprint out of there fast enough. But Harmony stayed right on my tail. I could hear her stilettos clicking on the marble floor.

I swiveled my head from side to side, gazing past the groups of tourists and hungover bachelor partyers, searching for any sign of Cesca or Mike. "Where is she?"

"Look!" Harmony grabbed my arm, practically drawing blood with her manicure. "It's Carter Nicholson!"

I followed her gaze to an impossibly tall man surrounded by a phalanx of flashbulbs and fans. "From the Lakers?"

"Yeah." She squinted across the lobby. "Who's that woman he's kissing?"

The sea of photographers shifted, and I caught a glimpse of Carter's companion.

Cesca DiSanto.

Wearing the designer creation formerly known as my wedding gown, looking impossibly petite next to the six-foot-six point guard, and smiling for the cameras. On her left hand, she sported a diamond ring so colossal, I was surprised she didn't need a sling.

In a trice, Harmony had her Chanel gloss out of her purse and onto her lips. "Let's go!" But she froze in midstrut, regarding me with guilty eyes. "Oh. I'm not supposed to flirt with married men anymore, right?"

"Right," I said when I recovered the power of speech. "Especially that one, because I think . . . I think he's married to Cesca."

"That's your roommate?" She squealed. Heads turned our way. The male heads stayed turned. "Oh, she's adorable! She's like a little fairy princess!"

"More like a ninja. Surprise attacks with no warning." I gaped at Cesca and the stately hunk beside her.

"You know, I met Carter at a record release party last month. Let's go say hi!"

One thing I had to say for Harmony St. James, she could really shove her way through a crowd. She jabbed her bony little elbows through the media throng with the ruthless efficiency of a New Yorker cramming into a subway at rush hour. No doubt she'd had years of practice cutting a swath to the bar at premieres and award ceremonies.

I peered over a photographer's shoulder, trying to catch sight of Cesca. I couldn't see her, but I could hear her telling the reporter, ". . . And it was just love at first sight. He looked at me, and he said, 'I seem to have lost my phone number; can I have yours?' . . ."

I stopped jockeying for position long enough to gag.

". . . And then he bought me a glass of wine, and then . . . we just knew. So here we are."

"Oh, that is so sweet," Harmony gushed, right in my ear.

I rolled my eyes. "He must have slipped something into that wine, because this is not the Cesca DiSanto I know and love. This is a twisted parody of a DeBeers ad."

"That's quite an engagement ring," the reporter said. "Mind if I ask how many carats?"

"Mind if I ask if that's your real hair?" Cesca shot back.

I smiled. "Now *that's* the Cesca DiSanto I know and love."

When the reported backed off, I shoved past him and came face-to-face with my soon-to-be-ex-roommate. "You know, Ces, if you wanted to move into a nicer apartment, there are subtler ways to tell me that than marrying a Laker."

"Gwen!" She pounced on me. I started getting a contact high from all her perfume and euphoria. "What are you doing here?"

"Tracking you down like a dog in the street." I leaned in and whispered, "With your *boyfriend,* I might add."

"Who?" She looked genuinely puzzled for a moment. "*Mike?* Oh, that was never serious. Come on."

"'Never serious'? What the hell?"

Her big brown eyes went distant and dreamy as she turned to her new husband. "I was just waiting for my true love to come along. My prince."

At this, His Royal Highness smiled indulgently and kissed the top of her blond-streaked head.

I stared at them. "What have you done with the real Cesca?"

"I ditched her at the state line." She laughed. "Meet my husband, Carter Nicholson."

"Pleased to meet you." Carter's hand was about four times the size of mine, but I tried to shake it anyway. "I've heard so much about you."

"You have?" My gaze bounced from him to Cesca. "How long have you two known each other?"

Carter consulted his diamond-studded Rolex. "About ten hours."

"I know this seems a bit . . . rash," Cesca said.

I nodded. "Just a bit."

"But it is so right, Gwen. I can feel it. Can't you see it?"

And I had to admit, she did look different. Her cheeks glowed, her eyes sparkled brighter than the diamond on her finger. She looked like I had felt when I still thought I was going to marry Dennis—lit up from the inside. Eager for the rest of her life to unfold.

"Yeah." I hugged her back. "I do see it."

"Plus, how gorgeous am I?" She struck a pose for the photographers, who snapped away. "I make this dress look *good*."

"It's an aisle, Ces, not a catwalk."

Carter laughed at this. I was warming up to him already.

"How did this *happen*?" I asked. "I thought you were going to wait at the apartment and make my excuses to Paul."

"I did!" She threaded her arms through Carter's and leaned into his black wool lapel. "Look, let's get out of this rat hole and go get a drink. We'll explain everything."

I raised an eyebrow. "'Rat hole'?"

She did her best Zsa Zsa Gabor imitation. "Dahling, we're moving to a penthouse suite at The Palms tonight. Less riffraff, you know. We're just going to grab my bags and pay the bill here."

I pouted. "But I'll have to go back to Westwood all by myself. Who will eat breakfast with me in our little firetrap by fraternity row?"

She tugged at Carter's hand. "I know! Gwen can come live with us in Brentwood, right? And live in the guest house and have breakfast with me every day while you're on the road!"

Carter laughed but did not, I noticed, agree.

I tried to emulate their enthusiasm. "Let's go raid the minibar at The Palms."

She shivered with delight. "I love minibars!"

"Then you're gonna love being married to me," Carter assured her.

I gasped as five razor-sharp nails sank into my forearm. "Ow-wow-wow."

"Oh sorry, *chérie*, did that hurt?" Harmony sidestepped around me and turned her ice blue eyes and freakishly thick eyelashes on Carter. "Hi, Carter. You might remember me from the RCA party at Fenix? I'm—"

He cleared his throat and took a wild guess. "Uh . . . Catherine?"

She batted her eyelashes again. "Not quite. I'm—"

"Harmony St. James! Fancy meeting you here, ya little minx!" A white-blond metalhead with black leather pants and a southern accent tackled Harmony. He had BIOHAZARD tattooed on his forearm and too many years of hard living etched into the deep lines of his face.

I backed off, repelled by both his unpredictable lunging and his pungent body odor.

Harmony peeked out from the half nelson he'd pinned her in. "Roy?"

"Rock and roll, baby!" His laugh sounded like a rusty muffler dragging against asphalt.

"I can't believe you're still alive!" She threw her arms around him. This elicited a frenzy of flashbulbs from the photographers.

She turned to me. "Do you know who this is?"

I considered asking about the possibility of a Keith Richards and Daisy Duke love child, but decided that this might be taken the wrong way. "No."

"It's Roy Rob!" Mike, practically foaming at the mouth, materialized at my right elbow.

I blinked. "The Scottish hero of lore?"

"No, dude. *Roy Rob.* Lead singer of the Daddy Long Legs. My personal idol." Mike's eyes glazed over. "I love you, man."

"Somebody slap him," Cesca commanded.

Roy sized up Mike with the practiced coolness of a man accustomed to Fatal Attraction fans. "You're crazier'n a treed raccoon, buddy. Far out." He dug around the back pockets of his leather pants and produced a laminated square of paper. "We're playing the Hard Rock tonight. Here's a backstage pass."

A match made in Hair Band Heaven.

Mike accepted the pass with an air of quiet awe. "I'll be there, my man. I'm in a band too."

Cesca snorted. "No, you're not."

"I am so! It's called Three-Hour Tour. Just like that line from *Gilligan's Island.*" Mike squinched up his face and screeched falsetto. "A three-hour tour . . . A three-hour tour."

"You played once, at your brother-in-law's barbecue, and the neighbors called the cops." She hiked up her gown and leaned into Carter. "Take me away from all this."

The two of them exchanged a scorching, honeymoon look.

So there I stood, surrounded by: newlyweds who'd been acquainted for less time than it took to prepare a Thanksgiving dinner, a half-pickled headbanger, a jilted groupie with a major jones for pilfered Diet Coke, the *paparazzi,* and my ex-boyfriend's ex-girlfriend, whom I was coaching to be his future wife.

Life just doesn't get any freakier, right?

And then the ex-boyfriend and his son walked into the lobby.

20

"What are *they* doing here?" I yelped.

Harmony followed my gaze to Alex and Leo. "Oh! Well, Leo really missed me. When I talked to him on the phone yesterday, I told him I was going to be in Vegas, and he wanted to come out and see some spider exhibit at the Shooting Star, so . . ."

"So why are they standing in the lobby of my hotel?"

She shrugged. "They just called me from the airport. I told them to come on over. But don't worry—I didn't tell them you were here."

"I think they figured that out all by themselves."

Leo was pointing at me and hopping around excitedly. Alex seemed less enthusiastic. His was the expression of a man about to face a prolonged technical interview by Senate subcommittee members.

Our plan to avoid all contact was officially a failure—first Eggo night, now this. And every time we were thrown together, extricating myself got more excruciating. Maybe Alex could set aside the feelings we'd had for each other and make his peace with the baby mama drama. Harmony definitely could (reading piles of soap opera scripts probably helped to keep things in perspective). But I could not. And I was through with pretending otherwise.

Leo's sneakers squeaked across the marble as he raced over to us. "Hey! Everybody's here!"

"Hi, Pookie!" Harmony swooped down for a jasmine-scented hug, but he wriggled away to share his news with me.

"We're in Las Vegas." He tugged on my hand with sticky fingers to make sure I appreciated the magnitude of this. "And know what's in Las Vegas?"

"Fear and loathing?" I ventured. I tried not to stare at Alex. I could feel his gaze on me.

Leo ignored this and carried on with breathless delight. "The desert! We're in the desert! There can be radioactive spiders out here!"

"You don't say."

"Yeah! Just like the ones that bit Fider-Man! And me and Daddy are gonna look for 'em, and maybe we'll find one and . . ."

Harmony patted his head. "Isn't that sweet? They've bonded."

"Yeah, it warms my heart." I turned to Mike. "I'm heading back to L.A. Right now. You coming?"

"No way." Judging by the vacant look in his eyes, Mike Jessup had, for all intents and purposes, already left the building. "Roy Rob said he might hire me as his personal assistant. I'll have a real job and travel the world. Working for Daddy Long Legs. Can you believe it?"

"Righteous." Roy contorted his right hand into what I was pretty sure was a satanic salute.

"All right, then. I'll see you both on VH1: Behind the Music." I pivoted and dashed for the elevator.

"Hey!" Cesca shrieked. I heard the rustle of a tulle crinoline as she ran after me.

She caught me by the elbow. "What are you doing, Gwen? I thought we were going to celebrate?"

I jerked my head toward the latest addition to the party. "I can't stay here with them."

She nodded slowly. "Oh I guess this must be . . ."

"Exactly. I'll see you at home. Enjoy your honeymoon." I resumed my charge toward the elevator banks.

"Can't you just stay a few hours? Don't you even want to hear about the wedding? Don't you want to help me figure out how the hell I'm going to tell my parents about this?"

"I do, but I have to leave. We'll talk when you get home."

"But . . . I won't live there anymore." She said this slowly, as if the truth of the statement were just dawning on her. "I'll be moving out."

I swallowed. "I know."

"Oh, Gwen." Her eyes filled up with tears. "You'll be there all alone."

I glanced down and shrugged. "Nah. I'll have all the frat boys I can handle to keep me company at three A.M."

She wrapped her fingers around mine. "This is really sad."

My smile was bright and breezy. "Just give me a call when you're on your way back and we'll decide how to break the news to your family. My advice? Think public places with lots of witnesses."

I risked a glance back at the fray in the lobby. Alex had disentangled himself from Harmony's embrace and was heading toward the elevator. "Ces, I've got to go. I can't deal with him right now."

She nodded, swiping at her eyes with her hand. "Go. Don't worry, I'll distract him 'til you're on the elevator."

But I should have known that Alex could not be deterred when he had his mind set on something. He reached my side before the elevator doors slid open and demanded, in a voice roiling with frustration and fatigue, "Where are you going?"

"Back to my room." I kept my eyes on the floor and my voice level. "Have fun with the radioactive spiders."

I felt his fingertips brush my shoulder.

"I didn't know you were here," he said. "Harmony never said anything about it."

I cleared my throat. "I know."

"But I have to ask. *What* are you and she doing in Vegas together?"

"She'll explain." I finally swung my gaze up to meet his.

"Listen. Not to be a complete sap, but good luck with Leo. And everything. Good luck with everything."

He waited a long, loaded moment before he nodded. "Because I'm not going to see you again."

I kept my mouth shut as the wood-paneled doors slid open. Then I stepped into the elevator, offering a wave and the snappiest farewell I could muster. "It was fun while it lasted, right?"

My attempt at a grin would have chilled Hannibal Lecter to the bone.

I hit the CLOSE DOORS button. My smile evaporated when I met Alex's eyes. He started to say something.

The doors closed.

I leaned back against the smoky mirrors. The UP arrow illuminated with a cheery ding. And then I had twenty floors' worth of silence to contemplate the solitude that waited for me back in Los Angeles.

In truth, the whole "solitude" thing didn't really kick in until two weeks later. It's true that the five-hour drive back to Westwood was no great shakes—I had to pull over every forty-five minutes to have an emotional meltdown with a side of French fries—and I spent the remainder of the weekend curled up with the remote control, my *Pulp Fiction* DVD (oddly soothing for frayed nerves), and an entire case of Diet Coke.

But come Monday, Cesca showed up with Carter for the great move-out. She brought along her entire family. Both parents, four brothers, and enough homemade goodies to feed the Lakers for an entire season.

According to Ces, after the initial shock wore off and they had vented their spleen in a two-hour screamathon about how their only daughter had cheated them out of the chance to throw a "proper wedding" and was consequently disowned, the DiSantos had calmed down and welcomed their new son-in-law with open arms. Her brothers were ecstatic to have a real live pro athlete in the family.

"Gwendolyn! You're wasting away!" Mrs. DiSanto announced the minute she walked through the door. "Have some manicotti. Where are the plates?"

I shook my head and lied through my teeth. "Oh thank you, Mrs. DiSanto, but I just had lunch. Really."

She glowered at Cesca. "Doesn't she eat?"

My roommate brushed this off with the nonchalance of a woman who has known since age three that she will never be able to eat enough to placate her mother. "I do what I can, but you know Gwen. She's hooked up to the Diet Coke IV. I don't even know if she can chew solid foods."

Carter smiled at me and tried to run interference. "I would love some manicotti, Mrs. DiSanto."

Mrs. DiSanto beamed. "Such a nice boy."

Cesca rolled her eyes at her new husband. "Brownnoser."

Carter laughed at this, but Mrs. DiSanto looked horrified. "I did not raise you to speak to your husband that way."

"Forget it, Ma. She was born sassy and she's going to die

sassy." Tony and David DiSanto hauled a chest of drawers out of Cesca's bedroom.

Another brother emerged from behind a pile of boxes. "Yeah, good luck, Carter. You're gonna need it."

Mrs. DiSanto tuned out her children's bickering, the better to interrogate the new son-in-law. "Carter, I'm very sorry to keep asking, but *how* did you two meet, again?"

Carter sighed. He had already been through this with Cesca's brothers, Cesca's father, Cesca's grandparents, and a sportswriter for the *Los Angeles Times.* But he finished his bite of pasta and started, "Well, one of my buddies from high school—"

"Paul Brenneman," Cesca supplied.

"Yeah. Paul came over here to see Gwen."

"But Gwen wasn't here. I was." Cesca beamed. "And when I told him that Gwen had left for the night, he looked so sad that I asked him if he wanted to go to Maloney's with me to watch the end of the Lakers game."

Mrs. DiSanto held up a hand. "What is Maloney's?"

"It's a sports bar," Cesca admitted.

Her mother covered her face with her hands. "My only daughter. My little girl, going to a sports bar with strange men." She turned and appealed to Carter. "*You* get her under control."

Cesca shushed her. "Anyway, Paul said we could do better than Maloney's, since he knew some guys from the team, so we went over to the Staples Center, and it was love at first sight."

Carter caught up his new bride in a hug. "Love at first sight."

Mrs. DiSanto narrowed her eyes. "But what happened to Paul?"

Carter seemed startled. "Oh yeah. He's still trying to hook up with Gwen, I guess." He crossed his arms and gave me a look. "You really should call him after standing him up like that."

"Yeah, that's just plain rude," Cesca chimed in.

"Oh, shut it," I told her. "If it weren't for me standing him up, you'd still be living on frat row here."

She giggled and threw her arms around her husband. "That's true."

Mrs. DiSanto regarded me with soft eyes. "What are you going to do now?"

"Don't worry, Ma." Cesca dug her stash of Oreos out of the cabinet. "I'll keep chipping in on the rent until our lease runs out. She's not gonna have to go live in the streets."

"But she'll be all alone." Mrs. DiSanto placed a hand on my forearm. "With nobody."

Just what a girl wants to hear after she's been left by not one but two men for ex-girlfriends, and her roommate moves into a mansion with a professional basketball player.

I gritted my teeth. "For the last time. I don't mind being alone. In fact, I *love* being alone. Just think, I'll never have to ruin another slice of pizza with pineapple and Canadian bacon."

"Philistine. You don't know what you're missing," Cesca insisted for the ten-thousandth time since our freshman year of college.

Carter raised an eyebrow at his new bride. "You put that on your pizza?"

"You'll learn to love it."

Mrs. DiSanto wasn't ready to let me off the hook just yet. "But won't you be lonely?"

"Of course not."

And this was not a total lie. Cesca and I had shared our living quarters for lo these many years, but I could see some definite advantages to going it alone. No more waiting for the shower. No more arguments over how we could watch *I Love the Eighties* and the Raiders game at the same time. I could spend an entire weekend in a single pair of hideous flannel pajamas. Hell, I could wear the red track pants every single day for the rest of my life, and no one would get on my case.

Cesca watched me mull this over. "You're going to wear those horrible pants every day now, aren't you?"

I smiled. "Maybe."

"I'm sending a SWAT team from the fashion police," she warned. Then she locked eyes with her new husband and forgot all about Adidas atrocities. "Oh, sweetheart, we've got to get ready for dinner, right?"

Carter consulted the wristwatch that could have paid for all my graduate schooling. "Yeah. We better get going."

She beamed as her brothers straggled through the door. "We're having dinner tonight. With *Phil Jackson*."

Tony looked like someone had just twisted a dagger between his ribs. "I can't believe you get to have dinner with *Phil* and you didn't even think to invite us."

"*I* should've married a Laker," David grumbled.

And as quickly as they had trooped into the apartment, they all trooped out. Cesca and her husband and her parents and her brothers locked the door behind them, leaving only a half-eaten pan of manicotti. My roommate—make that my *ex*-roommate—had gotten a life and left me behind in the corner I'd painted myself into.

Well, no use being melodramatic about it. Or starving myself to death. For the first time in three days, I felt a faint stirring of hunger, so I grabbed a plate, tossed some manicotti in the microwave, and headed into my bedroom to usher in the Golden Age of the Red Pants.

21

Two weeks later, I ended up calling Officer Paul Brenneman because my adviser, Dr. Cortez, basically made me.

I spent those two weeks working through the all-too-familiar stages of breakup recovery; from undereating to overeating, from pathetic self-pity to murderous rage, from living in track pants to straining my credit limit at the Beverly Center boutiques, from listening to the Smiths to blasting Gloria Gaynor.

I showed up at the clinic, did the best work of which I was capable, and avoided anyplace where there was the remotest chance I'd run into Dennis, Alex, or anyone who'd want an update on either my dissertation or my roommate. I saved nearly twenty bucks per week in coffee expenditures alone.

I didn't hear from Alex and he didn't hear from me. Cesca, however, heard plenty. At odd hours of the night, when I couldn't sleep and there was nothing good on TV, I'd call and interrupt her wedded bliss with Dark Tales from the Newly Single.

She handled this with her customary generosity of spirit and badness of attitude.

"You're lucky we had to delay the honeymoon 'til after the play-offs, 'cause I'm screening my calls when we get to St. Croix," she'd say. "Now why don't you just come and stay over here tonight? Carter's on the road, and I'm all alone in this giant house and we have like four guest rooms and a casita."

"Eh. You live far away now."

"Oh, come on. There's no traffic this time of night even if you take Sunset. I have a big box of Belgian truffles with your name on it."

"Forget it. I'd have to get up at the crack of dawn to make it to the clinic on time tomorrow. I'd rather complain over the phone."

"You just don't want to hear my lecture about those track pants again. You're wearing them right now, aren't you?"

"Maybe."

She always, always took my calls, feigned interest in my grievances, and then contributed little nuggets of wisdom like, "This sounds like what I went through the third time Mike and I broke up. It's the gambling hall theorem all over again."

"The gambling hall theorem?"

"Yeah, you know. You have to leave the gambling hall before

you get in too deep. If you're on a losing streak, then digging in at the craps table isn't going to help you—it's just gonna get you deeper into debt. You took a chance on Alex, and you lost, but you didn't lose big—only two hundred dollars or so. Now, with Mike, I kept going back to the table trying to change my luck. I was in the hole thousands of dollars. The casino enforcers were breaking my kneecaps out in the alley."

"Uh-huh." I yawned. Nothing like a good, long Mike story to lull me back to sleep.

"In fact, I'm still losing money on that man," she fumed, starting in on a few greivances of her own. "Do you realize that he just spilled his guts to the *National* fucking *Enquirer* so they could do a story on my *wedding?*"

"He did?"

"Check out the tabloids next time you hit the grocery store."

"Ugh. How Rick Salomon of him."

"And it was lies! All lies! The man said that Carter was a thug and that I was *prone to violent outbursts.* He said I threw plates with no provocation. Can you believe that?"

I glanced at the dustpan I had used to sweep up the shards of ceramic. "Has he no shame?"

"That boy's lucky he's touring with the latest inductee to the Anemic Rocker Hall of Fame, is all I have to say. When I find him . . ." She broke off, and I heard rustling plastic on her end of the line.

"Twizzlers?" I guessed.

"Bingo. Consider them an appetizer for the truffles—are you *sure* you don't want to come over?"

I closed my eyes for a moment, wishing that she hadn't progressed to the next stage in her life. Wishing that we were having this conversation here in the apartment with a veritable concession stand of sugary goodness piled up between us. Wishing that Carter had never swept her off her feet and into a fairy-tale ending in a gated community by the glittering waves of the Pacific.

That's right. I, Gwen Traynor, was secretly hoping my best and oldest friend's marriage would fall apart for the sole reason that I was lonely and scared of my own shortcomings.

Not exactly my finest hour.

"I'm not driving all the way over there right now, but let's have lunch tomorrow. How's married life, anyway?" I asked nonchalantly. "Are you having any trouble adjusting? I mean, I know it's a huge change . . ."

She laughed. "Honey. I married a Laker with a degree in biochemistry from USC and leopardlike prowess in bed. This whole marriage thing *kicks ass*." She chomped into another Twizzler. "My adviser even said I could have the rest of the summer off and reschedule my qualifying exams for the fall."

"Oh." The leopard part was news to me. "Well, that's great."

"And that reminds me. What's going on with Paul? Did you ever call him?"

"No."

She gasped. "Rude! Well, I hope you have a good excuse."

"No, not really."

"So you're stubbornly sitting home alone? Even though you have a cute policeman on tap?"

"That's right."

"Gwen! You can't hole up like a hermit forever." I could practically hear her eyes rolling. "I'm giving you two more weeks of grieving time for Alex, and then I'm personally taking charge of your social life."

"I'm not grieving, and I've got to go," I said as my call-waiting beeped. "But I'll say this one last time: My dating days are through until I get out of the City of Exes."

But I spoke too soon. The caller on the other line turned out to be Dr. Cortez, who informed me that the clinic board was throwing a benefit ball, at which my attendance was mandatory.

"Um . . ." I couldn't help glancing at the clock. Almost 11 P.M. "Can we talk about this tomorrow?"

But social decorum had never been his strong suit.

"Heather Vaughn was supposed to go, but now there's a conflict in her schedule," he snapped, as if Heather had deliberately schemed to foil him. "And we need a presence from the lab to explain the importance of our work to the donors. So whatever you're doing next Friday, cancel it."

"As it happens, my Friday nights are completely free," I bragged. "Except, of course, for all the extra hours I put in on my research."

"Well, then, your dissertation should be finished by now, shouldn't it?" he shot back.

Oooh. Well played.

"So I'll see you next Friday," he commanded. "Bring a date and a delightful attitude."

"A date?"

"That's right. It's a social event." He sounded very put out by this fact. "Bring a date. Meet and mingle. I want you to chat up the board members."

My breath caught. "The board members?"

"Yes. One of them spoke very highly of you."

Would that be the one who'd had sex with me, by any chance?

I tried to bail with all my might. "You know, actually, now that we're talking about it, I think I might be out of town next Friday. I'll have to check and get back to you—"

"Ms. Traynor," Dr. Cortez said in his snottiest headmaster voice, "I will see you next Friday at the benefit."

I could tell from his tone that any further argument would result in mind-boggling theoretical questions and unprecedented verbal laceration at my next oral exam.

"Okay, then!" I chirped. "I'll dig out my dancing shoes. Bye!"

I hung up, pitched the cordless phone clear into the hall, and spent a few minutes fuming over the indentured servitude that is graduate school. Then I got to my feet, called Cesca back, and asked for Paul's number.

"Your roots need retouching," Cesca announced as she zipped me into my little black dress two hours before the benefit.

I frowned at her. "If I wanted scathing criticism, I'd call Dr. Cortez."

"I'm just saying. It takes a little extra maintenance to be a blonde." She fastened the hook at the top of the zipper and instructed me to twirl. When I did so, she frowned.

"What now?" I demanded.

"You should have borrowed my Zac Posen."

"Stop name-dropping your wardrobe."

She grinned. "Who? Me?"

"I get it, I get it. You shop on Rodeo Drive now." I stepped into my shoes and strode over to the mirror. "I think I look pretty damn good. And you know where I got this dress? T.J. Maxx. Forty bucks, on clearance."

She nodded, impressed. "Who's the designer?"

"Label whore."

"I just think that if you borrowed the Zac Posen, you'd be sending a message to Harmony and Alex."

"Yeah. And that message would be, 'This hem is way too short for me and I'm too insecure to dress according to my station in life.'" I stuck my tongue out, and rummaged through my cosmetics drawer for lipstick. "Let Harmony prance around in Zac Posen or Roberto Cavalli or whomever. I'm a scientist, and I'm dressing like a scientist. Dark roots and all."

"You're a hard woman, Gwen Traynor." She shooed me back toward the bed, brandishing a mascara wand. "I can see why Alex zeroed in on you with his big Nick at Nite fantasy."

I closed my eyes as she moved in to beautify my lashes. "Oh really?"

"Yeah. You're never going to be a real L.A. woman. You're just too midwestern."

"If you're implying that I'm frumpy . . ."

She finished applying mascara and attacked me with

blusher. "All I'm implying is that you're never going to be one of those women who thinks a three-carat engagement ring is a good idea."

This was true. When Dennis had first broached the subject of marriage, I had said that I wanted to wear my grandmother's ring, with its tasteful sprinkling of antique diamonds. But Dennis had insisted upon what he called "going big"—the iceberg from Tiffany & Co. Something we could show off to his friends and his parents.

"Big diamonds are pointless." I could hear an echo of my mother in my voice. "At the end of the day, it's a piece of *rock*. A piece of rock that's going to catch on all your sweaters."

"See? I rest my case." She paused to admire the blingtastic jewel adorning her own ring finger. "But to each her own. My sweaters will just have to take their chances."

I changed the subject. "What time is it, anyway?"

"Six-thirty. What time are you supposed to be there?"

"I'm meeting Paul in the hotel lobby at eight."

"He's not picking you up here?"

"Remember what happened the last time he tried to pick me up here?"

"Yes I do." Cesca's eyes filled with dreamy delight. "I found my ideal man, season tickets to the Lakers, and a lifetime supply of Zac Posen all at once."

"So . . . uh . . . do you like seviche?"

I shifted my weight from foot to foot and kept my eyes on the velvet-draped entrance to the ballroom. No sign of Harmony and Alex yet. "I'm not really sure what that is," I admitted.

"Oh." Paul scuffed the burgundy carpet with his shoe. "It's like, fish with lime and grape seed oil and stuff. It's great when you make it with halibut."

"Oh." I nodded. And once again, the conversation ran drier than the Mojave. I sneaked a surreptitious glance at Paul's watch. Nine o'clock. We were looking at three more hours, minimum, of awkward pauses and door glancing.

Don't get me wrong—he seemed a nice enough guy. And he looked good in a tux. The raffish charm of Mark McGrath meets the cool debonair of Armani. This was not lost on the other female guests—lonely hearts postdocs kept coming up to me, making eye contact with Paul and purring, "Hi there. Didn't I see you at the neuroscience symposium last week?"

If only he had the small-talk skills to back it all up.

If only I could devote my undivided attention to plumbing the depths of his knowledge about limes and marine life.

But he didn't, and I couldn't, so my date with Officer Paul collapsed like a house of cards. The initial physical attraction wore off five minutes after we stopped discussing the miraculous courtship of Carter and Cesca, whereupon we realized that we had nothing to talk about. And I do mean *nothing*.

I smiled at him. He smiled at me.

I glanced at the door again, and when I turned back, I caught him checking his watch.

Luckily, Dr. Cortez swooped down upon us, preempting any further attempts at conversation.

"Gwendolyn. You're here. Good." He regarded Paul with the

sneering hauteur a sommelier might reserve for a bottle of Boone's Farm. "Hello."

"Hey." My hunky date extended his hunky right hand. "Paul Brenneman."

"*Doctor* Richard Cortez." The sommelier deigned to touch the hunky date. "I apologize for whisking Gwendolyn away like this, but duty calls."

"Good Goddess! Paul!" Harmony St. James shoved Dr. Cortez aside like a linebacker in lamé and barreled right into Paul's arms. "Chérie! How are you?"

"Harmony?" Crimson seeped into Paul's cheeks. "What are you doing here?"

"Oh, I'm very into charity," she assured him, waving her Louis Vuitton wallet. "It's all about the kids, you know. By the way, Leo says hi." She grabbed my shoulders and air kissed both sides of my face. "Gwen! You look fabulous!"

"Wait." My gaze bounced from my current date to the woman who'd ruined my last foray into the romantic arena. "You two know each other?"

"Hey." Paul pointed one index finger at me, the other at Harmony. "*You* two know each other?"

"Of course!" She readjusted the neckline of her dress, which had dipped dangerously low, and winked at me. "Paul and I hung out together a few months ago. Just, you know, casually. Before Alex C. came back into the picture."

Paul's face fell upon hearing this description of their relationship.

So my new rebound man was still hung up on the woman

that my *last* rebound man had dumped me for. In about ten—make it twenty—years, I would be able to tell this story and laugh, but right now was more like primal scream time.

She threw an arm around him and nodded at me. "And then Gwen and I met when I took Leo to—"

"No need to go into details," I said firmly. "Let's just say I know Leo."

She gave me a conspiratorial look. "Yes. She knows Leo."

Paul gave up on trying to understand the social intricacies of the situation and fixated on his ex. "You look beautiful."

"Beautiful" was not the word. The woman could give Elizabeth Hurley an inferiority complex. Her gown was a masterpiece of gold sequins and strategic flashes of flesh.

"How did you two meet?" I asked, deciding that if the answer to this question turned out to be "He pulled me over on a major thoroughfare and asked for my number," I was going to rampage right here and now.

"You don't know? Paul used to be my costar on *One Life to Live*! That was years ago, but he had the biggest crush on me for, like, two seasons!" She swatted him with her beaded evening bag. "You didn't tell her you're a celebrity?"

"*You're* the celebrity," he said, yanking at his shirt collar. "I never even liked acting that much. I don't miss it at all. Besides. The guys at the station would never let me live it down if they knew."

"How is that going, anyway?" She breathed, batting her eyes.

But I missed Paul's response because Alex had appeared on the horizon. He caught my eye and started toward me. Snippets of our brief but intense relationship flashed through my mind.

Then I shook my head and snapped out of the soft-focus fantasy.

Because the bottom line was, whatever I'd thought we'd shared was just that: a fantasy. Something I wanted to believe so desperately that I'd ignored all the red flags. After you cut through all the excuses and extenuating circumstances, he'd turned out to be the same as Dennis—a man who could never love me the way I needed to be loved.

"Gwen," he said softly.

I set my jaw and stared at the chandelier dripping with crystal. "Fancy meeting you here."

Clinking glasses and frenetic chatter welled up around us, filling the long silence. And after about thirty seconds, I realized that Harmony and Paul were both staring at us.

I cleared my throat. "Paul Brenneman, this is Alex Coughlin. Alex, this is Paul. He's my . . . he's . . . I was just leaving."

Alex nodded. "Paul. I see you've met Harmony."

"His *fiancée*," she added, flashing a left-hand diamond ring of glacial proportions.

"You two are getting married?" Paul's expression was that of a little boy who has watched somebody run over his puppy, back up, and run over it again. "Congratulations."

Still staring at the chandelier, I excused myself from the conversation and took a few tentative steps toward the bar.

So they were getting married. *Big surprise.* They were living together, they had a child, Harmony had been talking weddings since day one. What had I expected?

Time for a very, very strong drink. I bellied up to the bar. "Vodka on the rocks, please. Make it a double. A triple."

The burgundy-jacketed bartender raised his eyebrows. "Why don't you start with a single and work your way up?"

I nodded. "Yeah. Okay. Whatever."

He paused. "You all right?"

"Yeah. Okay. Whatever."

"Gwen." Alex materialized by my right elbow.

I closed my eyes and gripped the cool brass rail bordering the bar area. "Go away."

"I want to talk to you."

"Well, I *don't* want to talk to you." I opened one eye. "Actually, I do have one question: you're really, officially engaged to her?"

He waited until I opened both eyes to answer. "Yes."

Fortunately, the bartender handed me my vodka just then.

"Do you love her? Scratch that—do you even *like* her?"

He held my gaze in silence.

"Are you guys, you know, in the same bedroom now?"

More silence.

I drained my glass, tossed it back on the counter, and signaled to the bartender. "*Now* can I have a double?"

The bartender, who had apparently overhead the tail end of our conversation, nodded. "Coming right up."

Alex rested a hand on my shoulder. "I know you're upset. But we need to talk. I heard you gave Harmony some kind of relationship syllabus?"

"And how did you hear that?"

He sighed. "She told me."

I pulled away from his grasp. "Where the hell is that double?"

"Here ya go." The bartender took aim and slid the glass across the bar toward me, Old Western-style.

But Alex intercepted the drink before I could grab it. He tossed it back like a dehydrated James Bond.

"Hey!" I protested.

"God, I needed that." He raised an eyebrow at my outraged expression. "And you already had one."

I crossed my arms over my forty-dollar dress. "Mr. Coughlin. Perhaps you are not familiar with the Official Breakup Code of Greater Los Angeles, but it clearly states that the dumper must forfeit to the dumpee all joint property, anecdotes which depict the dumper in an unflattering light, and available alcoholic beverages."

"But I never dumped you."

I stared at him. "Are you new here? Leaving the woman you're sleeping with to reunite with and marry your ex-girlfriend is the very definition of dumping." I nodded crisply at the bartender. "Let's try that double again."

"What should I have done, Gwen? Left my four-year-old son to grow up in the New Age equivalent of *Moulin Rouge* just because I thought you were hot?"

The bartender had fled to the far end of the bar, which was fortunate, since any drink I'd had would have ended up in Alex's face.

He kept talking in a low, even tone. "That didn't come out

the way I intended. All I'm saying is, we had a few weeks. And they were—well, you know how they were, but how can I put that ahead of my son? Regardless of what I want, Leo has to come first. He *has* to." In his eyes I saw the angry determination of a boy who had been abandoned by his own father.

"It's not that cut and dried, and you know it," I shot back. "Haven't you ever heard of joint custody?"

"Joint custody? Where the child spends ninety percent of his time with his mother and the odd weekend and holiday pretending to bond with his father while he wishes he were back home playing with his friends? That is not a family. That is a legal stopgap."

"Whatever you say. But keep me out of it from now on."

"Listen. I never thought I could give Leo that—a family. Because of Harmony. You've seen the way we are together. We broke up for a good reason. Many good reasons, in fact. But ever since she talked to you in Vegas, things have been different. She's changing. She's been reading books on parenting and marriage. She's been talking about consistency." He grinned. "The words 'delayed gratification' actually came out of her mouth."

My smile was brittle.

"And she says it's all because of you." I couldn't identify the emotions sparking in his eyes. "I wanted to thank you. If it weren't for you, this engagement never would have happened."

"You're *so* welcome." I spun on my heel and stalked back across the ballroom toward my date, who was exclaiming over Harmony's wallet-size pictures of Leo.

". . . And here we are at the zoo in Santa Barbara," Harmony gushed. "Isn't he cute?"

"He looks just like you." Paul seemed oblivious to the rage radiating from my every pore. He turned to me. "Can you believe what a great mom Harmony is?"

I just glowered at them.

He shook his head. "Incredible. Well, tell him I said 'hey.' I miss the little guy."

"I'll tell him." Harmony crooked her index finger to motion us deeper into her jasmine-scented aura. "And, don't tell anyone, but he's going to have a brother or a sister pretty soon."

I backed out of the aura.

"You're planning to have more kids after you get married?" Paul asked.

She winked. "Not exactly."

His eyes bugged out. "You mean you're . . ."

"Yep! I'm pregnant!" She hugged us both at once. "Isn't that insane?"

22

Clearly, the only appropriate response to this announcement was to flee for the exit and call it a night. Little did I know that I was about to double down on the insanity.

"Gwen?" A familiar voice filled my ear as a hand brushed against my lower back. "You're blond?"

Just what I needed to make my night complete. The *other* fucking ex.

I whipped around to glare at Dennis. "What the hell are you doing here?"

He looked rumpled and tired, like he'd just finished a thirty-six-hour call and thrown on a tux. Which he probably had.

He couldn't seem to look away from my newly blond bob. "Your hair. It's . . . You look so . . ."

I arched my back away from his touch. "I'm in no mood for this. What do you think you're doing here?"

"I know some of the psychiatric residents, and they invited me . . ." He broke off, shaking his head. "That's a lie. The truth is, I was looking for you. I know this is your turf and I'm being a little ballsy right now . . ."

I considered darting past him and making a break for the valet booth, but I could see Dr. Cortez hovering nearby, so I tried to pretend I was deeply mired in a pleasant, fund-raising sort of chat.

"I know you hate me." He hung his head. "And I deserve it. What happened between us was . . . it was bad."

"No. 'Bad' is a flooded basement or a severe allergic reaction. What happened between us was more along the lines of the 'Totally Unforgiveable.'" I smiled big for Dr. Cortez and lowered my voice to a razor-sharp hiss. "So if this is about Cesca shaking you down for five thousand dollars—"

"It isn't." He grimaced as if his appendix had just burst. "Cesca said you were engaged to a lawyer named Chet."

"You actually believed that?" I burst out laughing. "*Hel-lo,* she was obviously lying."

This puzzled him. "Why would she do that?"

"Because she's been my best friend for almost a decade and she can't stand you. Chet. Good Lord. I can't believe you bought that." I crossed my arms and started tapping one foot. "I'm on my way out, so if there's nothing else I can help you with . . ."

"Lisa broke up with me."

This news did not elicit the surge of triumph I would have expected. All I felt was a slow, sinking disbelief—all that grief and fury, all those tears and broken catering contracts . . . for nothing?

He cleared his throat. "Aren't you going to say 'I told you so'?"

I sighed. "Apparently not." When I scanned the crowd, I saw Dr. Cortez circling to the right, still eyeing us suspiciously. And Alex was fighting the tide of the crowd, making his way toward me. "I can't deal with this right now. I'm out of here."

"Don't go." Suddenly, Dennis seized my shoulder and went in for a kiss on the lips, which I managed to deflect with my cheek. "I miss you, Gwen."

I froze. *"What?"*

"Lisa was a mistake. I don't know what I was thinking. I got scared, and I . . ." He shrugged helplessly. "Give me another chance. Let me explain."

"There's nothing to explain. I was there, I know what happened. So does everyone on our guest list," I reminded him.

"I know. I was an asshole." He kissed my forehead, which I let him get away with because I was too stunned to protest. "But I need to talk to you. Just talk. Please. I can't sleep, thinking about how I treated you."

I looked at his worn, pinched face and knew he was telling the truth. The heat of the ballroom and the buzzing in my ears overwhelmed me for a moment. "Okay, fine. We'll talk." I glanced nervously back at Alex, who had stopped his approach when I let Dennis kiss me. "But not tonight."

"Meet me at the Spanish Kitchen tomorrow at seven," he instructed. "You won't be sorry."

But as I caught Alex's eye across the ballroom, I already was.

"You're telling me that Dennis just *happened* to show up at the benefit ball?" Cesca pushed up the sleeves of her huge Lakers sweatshirt. "That's quite a coincidence."

"No coincidence. He talked to his friends who work with the clinic. Planned the whole thing." I helped myself to another Oreo. Brunch at the Nicholsons' had been rather hastily thrown together at 9 A.M. this morning when I called her to discuss the many new twists in my life.

"So he admits he's stalking you." Carter, who was currently in training and thus banned from cookies, bit into an apple and slouched against the kitchen cabinets. "Don't forget to work that into the police report."

I rolled my eyes. "He's not stalking me. He doesn't have time. The man's a third-year resident."

A hush fell over the kitchen as Cesca and her husband considered this. Carter's sprawling stucco mansion contained many professionally decorated dining nooks and parlors, along with a den equipped with the best entertainment system money could buy, but old habits die hard—Cesca and I preferred to talk in various states of disarray in the kitchen.

"What did he have to say for himself, anyway?" Cesca demanded, then turned to Carter. "This guy is *such* a jackass."

"He dumped you the night before your wedding, right?" Carter asked.

I nodded.

"Want me to administer a good, old-fashioned ass kicking?"

"Not with your sore wrist, sweetie," Cesca admonished. "But I'm sure that any of my brothers would be happy to take care of it."

"Nobody's kicking anybody's ass. He wasn't being obnoxious, really. He just seemed sad. He said he's been feeling bad about the whole thing."

"Aw." She pulled a face. "Somebody call the whaaambulance."

"You didn't see him, Ces. He looked awful. And I guess Lisa broke up with him—"

My attempts to continue that sentence were drowned out by Cesca's cackling. "That is so perfect. Roadkill from the karma bus. I love it." She cocked her head. "So why aren't *you* laughing?"

"I was, at first," I said. "But now I'm just confused. He's begging me to get together tonight to talk about stuff."

"No way you're doing that," Carter said.

"*No. way.*" Cesca narrowed her eyes. "You're *not.*"

I sighed.

"Uh-oh." Carter took a sip of coffee.

Cesca gasped in outrage. "Gwendolyn Traynor, what the hell? Do you remember nothing from the last year? How can you even consider—"

"Ease up," I said quietly. "I once loved this man enough to marry him."

"Yeah, and look what he did to you. If you think that he's going to change his ways just because—"

"I'm not expecting him to change his ways," I insisted. "I'm a psychologist too, remember? I know the score. But he left me high and dry, with no warning, and I deserve some answers. If it had been you, Ces, wouldn't you want to do an exit interview?"

"I might," she conceded. "But one thing's for sure. If I was looking for closure with the guy who dumped me in front of all my friends and family, I'd be packing a little heat."

"I'll keep that in mind," Carter decided.

"I think the Spanish Kitchen frowns upon gunplay," I said.

"I know the manager there," Carter volunteered. "Want me to request an extra-sharp knife for you?"

"Or just a rusty spoon?" Cesca smiled sweetly.

"I've got it under control," I assured them. "Anyway, that's not my real news."

"I don't think I even want to hear the real news." She shuddered.

"I ran into Alex and Harmony at the ball. They're engaged. Officially."

"Time-out." Carter refilled his coffee mug and glanced out the window at the sparkling blue ocean. "Weren't they engaged before? When they were first dating?"

"Not according to Harmony." Cesca's voice dripped with venom.

"Who, as it turns out, also used to go out with Officer Paul," I added.

"Get out!" Cesca whirled to face down her husband. "Paul used to date Harmony? Did you know about this?"

"No. How would I know who the man dates?"

"Because you're *friends.*" Cesca, who could list the middle name, car model, and sexual eccentricities of every boyfriend I'd ever had, raised her eyes heavenward.

I forged ahead to the point. "Well. Apparently, she and Paul will never get a chance to reconcile, since she's wearing an emerald-cut Rock of Gibraltar on her left hand. She and Alex are really going to get married."

Cesca shook her head. "This is outrageous."

"And she's pregnant."

Everyone took a moment to digest this bit of information.

"That *would* explain a lot," Carter said.

Cesca shook her fists. "That bastard! How dare he hand you that family values bullshit while he was whoring around with his fiancée!"

The housekeeper peeked in the doorway, took one look at Cesca's face, and kept on walking.

"The audacity! Pretending that moving in with her was some huge sacrifice when all the time he was getting his lying, cheating, double-dealing rocks off!"

"That's pretty cold," Carter agreed.

"I guess I'm naive but . . ." I turned up my palms. "I still can't believe Alex would do that."

"*I* believe it," Cesca said.

"So do I," Carter agreed. "That Harmony is pretty fine." Then he remembered whom he was talking to. "I mean, not as fine as my beautiful wife, of course, or you, Gwen, but—"

"Oh, save it," she told him. "Gwen, if the man is going to marry her, I'm pretty sure he's going to have sex with her."

"But they weren't even getting along until two weeks ago at the earliest," I said.

"Trust me, a man doesn't have to get *along* with a woman to want to get *with* her." Carter laughed.

Cesca shot her new spouse a withering glare. "Carter, do you *want* to sleep alone tonight?"

"No, I'm just . . . agreeing with you."

"Well, do yourself a favor and stop agreeing." She turned back to me. "He does have a point, though. It only takes one slipup. One quick attempt at reconciliation. And Alex probably justified it with some platitude about self-sacrifice and community service: 'I've got to bag this hot chick for the sake of the greater good.'"

I had to admit, this line of reasoning did sound like typical guy logic. "So you're saying that I'm the only one surprised by this little tidbit."

"In a word, yes. I know it's hard to hear." She sat down next to me on the floor. "I don't want to be the bitch here. But don't waste too many tears on this guy. Just be glad you escaped. You were right: he's no better than Dennis."

"Men are pigs," Carter added. "Take it from me."

I sighed and leaned my head on Cesca's shoulder. "How could I be so stupid?"

"You're not stupid. You were 'in love.'"

"You say to-may-to, I say to-mah-to."

23

All right, I admit it—I got my roots retouched before I headed off to the big showdown with Dennis.

Vain and pointless? Yes and yes. But I had my reasons. Tonight was not going to be a repeat of the showdown at The Bomb Shelter. There would be no cell phone throwing. I would stay cool, calm, and collected. I would make him rue the day he let a catch like me slip away. I'd demand some answers. At knifepoint, if necessary.

Then I'd implement Phase II: slip away into the night, burn rubber to Cesca's house, and consume half a pineapple-and-Canadian-bacon pizza.

I surrendered my car to the Spanish Kitchen valet twenty

minutes after the agreed-upon meeting time. Fashionably late, without being (very) passive-aggressive.

But when I strutted into the warm, muted candlelight reflecting off the varnished bar, I didn't see Dennis.

So he had stood me up again. *Again.*

The bartender, an erstwhile model-actress in a frilled red blouse and a topknot, smiled at me. "What can I get you?"

At this point, I had a choice: I could walk out, smothered by my own sense of shame, or I could sit down and behave like a sophisticated single girl about town who was confident enough to stake out the bar all by herself.

I sat down. "I'll start with just a cranberry juice."

"Thank God you're still here." Dennis pulled out the stool beside me. "I was stuck in traffic on San Vincente, and I was afraid you'd leave."

I gave him a look. "My cell phone didn't ring."

He had the decency to flush. "I know, I should have called. But the Yankees game went into overtime, and the guys wouldn't let me leave . . ."

I yanked my wallet out of my bag and threw a twenty down on the bar. "You know what? I don't have to listen to this anymore. Why should I sit here with you and pay twelve bucks per drink when I can go bang my head against a brick wall for free?"

He grabbed my hand. "Don't go."

I rolled my eyes but sat back down. "You've got five minutes. This better be good."

He opened his mouth. Closed it. Opened it again. "God, you look beautiful."

I pointed to the door. "Brick wall's right out there."

"I mean it, Gwen." He folded my hand between both of his. "You were always pretty, but smart-pretty. Now you're gorgeous." He paused, soaking me in. "You're the total package."

I sneered at him. "Why? Because I'm *blond?*"

"No. Because you're sexy and sweet and funny. I don't know how to say it. I guess no one else ever made me feel the way you did. You were it. The One."

I could feel my heart thawing out, so I compensated with the iciest sarcasm I could muster. "I see. That explains why you humiliated me in front of my family and friends and took off with Lisa. When *did* you decide to get back together with her, anyway?"

He stared at the shelves of tequila bottles behind the bar. "I ran into her at the Standard. During my bachelor party. The month before the wedding."

A *month* before . . . ?

"You ass." I slammed my open palm down on the bar.

"I know." He caught my gaze and held it. "I was an idiot. I got scared. I was confused, I was cracking under the pressure of med school and the wedding, and I threw away the only thing that mattered."

And the horrible thing was, he was totally sincere. I could see it in his eyes.

I snatched my hand away from his. "Listen. If you were so unhappy . . . if you were so confused . . . Dennis, I was going to be your *wife*. Why didn't you talk to me about it?"

He shook his head and uttered the phrase responsible for countless relationship casualties. "I couldn't talk about it."

"But you could tell Lisa about it?"

"No. Lisa was a mistake. When I was with her, I felt different. But it wasn't real. It was never like you and me." He reached over and gulped some of my cranberry juice. I noticed tiny beads of sweat forming across his forehead.

"Lisa broke up with me because I couldn't stop talking about you."

I was not going to pretend that this admission wasn't a little gratifying.

"Gwen." He downed the remainder of my drink and went for broke. "I love you. I love you more than I've ever loved anybody, and I need a second chance. I know I don't deserve your trust, but I'll earn it back."

The joyful, frenetic beat of salsa music blaring through the restaurant's speakers was so inappropriate against the strained, stale pause that followed that I almost laughed.

"Dennis . . ." I sighed. "No."

"I'll never give you reason to doubt me again," he pledged. "And I still love you as much as I did when I asked you to marry me."

Tears burned my eyes, but I didn't blink as I shook my head.

The look on his face when I shook my head flayed my heart raw. "Please. I'll do whatever you want. Counseling. You name it. We can fix this."

"But I don't want to," I said softly. "I've moved on."

He crumpled up the damp napkin next to my drink. "You're seeing someone else."

"Actually, I'm not. I'm alone. All by myself."

"You're lying to spare my feelings." His eyes were bleak. "I can tell there's someone else. You're smiling."

"I wouldn't lie." I shook my head. "A girl can smile when she's by herself. Because it's better to be alone than attached to the wrong man."

And with that, I hopped off my stool, put my feet on the ground, and closed the door on that chapter of my life.

Two weeks later, as I sat in my clinic office, poring over client notes and nursing a giant cup of coffee, I heard a woman's scream down the hall, a series of muffled thumps, and then a light rap at my door.

Oh no. Dr. Cortez had finally snapped and murdered Heather, and now he'd come for me.

Another tap at the door. "Miss Gwen?"

I opened the door to find Leo beaming up at me from under the brim of his Spider-Man cap. His outstretched hands were cupped together, and his little pink tongue darted in and out of his mouth in an attempt to wiggle what appeared to be a loose tooth.

"Leo." I peered down the empty hallway. "What a surprise! How did you—"

"Miss Heather saw a fider in her office. I caught it to show her, and she screamed." He looked inordinately proud of himself.

"I heard her," I said. "Where is she now? And how did you find my office?"

"I remember from before. And besides." He pointed to the

wall placard bearing my name and title. "I know letters. *G* is for *Gwen*. And *goose*."

"That it is," I agreed. "But don't you think Heather is wondering where you are?"

He shrugged and strolled into my office, stopping to marvel at the state of my desk. "Wow. It's messy in here."

"I think you may have mentioned that before."

"Wanna see my spider?" He parted his hands and deposited an enormous brown-and-white-striped arachnid on my desk. "Lookit. It's a zebra spider. They eat moths."

"Oh my God." I backed up against the window. "Why don't we put him back outside where he can be with his other spider pals?"

"Zebra spiders don't like other spiders. If they see one"—he twisted his face into a fang-baring grimace—"they attack!"

Staring at the spider trying to scale the side of my Styrofoam coffee cup, I could understand why Heather had screamed. The thing looked like it should be hiding out in the Amazon jungle somewhere, exploding out of the underbrush and eating unsuspecting missionaries.

I snatched up the empty UCLA coffee mug perched on my bookshelf, turned it upside down, and clapped it over the eight-legged monstrosity. As soon as I hustled Leo out of the room, it was curtains for this freakish beast.

Leo, perhaps sensing my murderous intent, stalled for time as I ushered him toward the door. "Miss Gwen . . . um . . . I have to tell you something . . ."

"Yes?" My voice was tinged with the tiniest hint of impatience. I kept one eye on the inverted mug, half expecting the spider to push it off the desk and lunge at me.

"Um . . ." His eyes darted from side to side as he tried to come up with a conversational hook. "Do you wanna come to my birthday party?"

"Your birthday party? Kiddo, your birthday was last month."

"Yeah, but Mommy got back from Mexico and said we could have a big party. So Daddy's taking me and Gilbert and Patrick to Disneyland."

I couldn't help but smirk, picturing Alex spending hour after hour standing in line under the afternoon sun with three five-year-olds, all overstimulated and begging for churros. "Well, tell your dad I said good luck with that."

"And he said I could invite one more person." Leo doffed his hat and scratched the back of his little neck. "So I'm asking you."

"Oh, sweetie. I think your dad meant one of your friends from school. I'm sure he didn't mean me."

"He said whoever I want. It's *my* birthday. So I can ask you."

I shook my head. "Sounds like fun, but I can't. Now let's get you back to Heather. We can talk about this later."

Desperate to delay the inevitable, he went for broke. "And, um, you know what else? Someday soon, I'm gonna be a big brother. I'm gonna have a baby sister."

I stopped shooing him toward the hallway. "A baby sister?"

"Yuh-huh." He nodded vigorously. "Mommy wants to name her Paisley."

I coughed. Twice. "Really. And what does Daddy have to say about that?"

"Daddy who?"

I stared at him. "You know. Your daddy. The guy who lives with you? In your house? With your mommy?"

"I have two daddies now. My real daddy and Daddy Paul."

I sank down into my office chair. "You have . . ."

"And when Paisley gets here, Daddy Paul's gonna be her daddy."

"I see," I said, not seeing at all. "So if Paul is going to be . . . Paisley's daddy, then who will be your daddy?"

He gave me a condescending look. "My daddy is always gonna be my daddy."

"Right. Okay. Just checking."

He smiled, and I saw a glimmer of the happy, confident child emerging from the anxious, moody little boy I'd first met. "My daddy loves me sooo much. And my mommy loves me too. No matter what."

"That's right. But let me ask you this—"

"Gwen!" Heather appeared at my door, buttoned up and exasperated as always. "What are you doing with my client?"

Leo gave her a syrupy sweet smile. She quelled him with her ornery schoolmarm look and ordered him back to her office, shutting the door behind them.

I hadn't managed to work out all the logistical details yet, but one thing was certain: if Officer Paul had been introduced to Leo as "Daddy Paul," then some big changes had gone down over in the hills. Which left Leo and Alex and Harmony . . . where?

My usual impulse under these circumstances would be to speed-dial Cesca or even Alex himself. But not today. Today I decided to handle the turbulence in my life on my own.

I tipped my head back and let the warm summer sunlight filter through the window and onto my face, trying to ignore the mutant bug clamoring against the confines of a coffee mug. Then I shrugged and got back to work. And I didn't call anyone at all.

24

When I got back to the apartment that evening, I discovered that I had left my house keys at my office. Retrieving them would necessitate trekking back through the bowels of the underground garage, fighting rush-hour traffic, and returning to the clinic, where I would probably run into Heather and/or Dr. Cortez, both of whom would be eager to load me up with a few extra journal articles to read or grant proposals to review.

Off to have a word with the building superintendent, then.

I was giving the doorknob one last, futile twist when Alex walked around the corner in his suit and tie. He stopped for a moment when he saw me, then resumed his pace.

He wasn't smiling. In fact, he looked like a stockbroker

preparing to tell his client that the market had bottomed out and their portfolio was no longer worth the paper it was printed on.

"Oh good," he said. "You're here."

"I'm here. But I'm locked out. Hey, maybe you can do that trick with your car key again?"

He dropped his calfskin briefcase on the carpet. "Stand aside." He jiggled the lock, then stepped back to scrutinize the construction of the door. "What's with you and Leo and the locked doors?"

"What can I say? We like a challenge."

He frowned, which emphasized the tension etched across his face. "I probably *could* get this open for you, but it might ruin the paint job."

"Then forget it. I'm not about to forfeit my security deposit. I'll just go ask the super for the spare key. So. Anyway . . ." My voice trailed off in a question mark.

"You're wondering what I'm doing here."

"Well." I leaned back against the wall. "Yeah."

He waited until I glanced back at him. "I have to tell you something. To your face, not over the phone. I don't want you to hear it from anybody else."

I nodded. His voice told me everything I needed to know. "Harmony's pregnant."

He didn't seem surprised so much as exhausted and defeated. "Yes. How did you know?"

"She told me at the benefit ball. And then I ran into Leo at the clinic."

He rolled his eyes. "That kid is worse than Page Six with gossip." He returned the full force of his focus to me. "But yes. Harmony is pregnant."

I puzzled over the defensive edge in his voice, and then realized that he was waiting for me to unleash hell. So I simply asked, "Who's the father?"

He looked stunned.

I waited.

Finally he asked, in tones of deep suspicion, "Don't you think *I'm* the father?"

I shrugged. "I don't know. That's why I'm asking."

"But how . . . ?"

"When you told me you weren't sleeping with Harmony, I believed you. Well," I amended, "I believed you for a while; then I just thought you were a lying scumbag. But I sat down this afternoon and thought it through. Being a researcher, I thought it was only fair to look at the actual data. And realistically, even if you guys *have* been having sex, it still wouldn't be enough time for her to be sure she's pregnant. Never mind find out the baby's gender."

"But . . ." He opened his briefcase and dumped out a stack of legal documents covered in microscopic print.

"I know. Nancy Drew would be proud, huh?"

"But I was prepared to take the DNA tests and file all sorts of official . . ."

I furrowed my brow. "Why?"

"Because I didn't want you to think I would, you know, misrepresent myself."

I laughed. "You mean, you didn't want me to think you were a cheating pathological liar even though we broke up?"

His expression was embarrassed but determined. "That about sums it up."

"Well, I do appreciate all the effort you were prepared to put into this." I leaned against the wall. "But it's really not necessary."

"So you believe me? You're actually going to take my word on something this preposterous?"

"I just can't seem to stop giving people the benefit of the doubt. It's a curse, really. Besides. You are hopelessly honest."

"I can be inscrutable," he insisted.

"*Hopelessly* honest. Sorry to disappoint you." I raised my eyebrows at him. "Still engaged?"

"Harmony is. To Paul."

"What?" My eyebrows arched still higher. "Damn. That was fast."

"Apparently, he's been pining for her since they first met. They were dating right before she and I got together. And after all that work she's done on improving her relationship skills . . . she wants to put them into practice with him."

"Ah, the irony."

"Ever since you sat down with her in Vegas, she's gotten much more grounded. More . . ."

"Sane?" I suggested.

"I wouldn't go that far. But she's a much better parent. She says she wants to 'do things right' with the new baby. A real mother and father and all that. My own idealism has come back to bite me in the ass."

"Wow. And here I thought you were the designated father."

"I'll always be Leo's father. I even offered to talk to my co-op board so that she can buy a condo in my building."

"Hold up. She's willing to give up that cute little house in the hills for a *condo?*"

"A condo in a prime location by the beach," he pointed out. "She practically started drooling when I suggested it. I want Leo to grow up with both parents and stability, but architectural proximity seems to be the best we can do. Family's all about compromise, you know?"

I cupped a hand to my ear as if deaf. "I beg your pardon?"

"Compromise," he repeated. "Flexibility."

"And what happened to all your big talk about moving to Colorado with the Stepford wife and the never-ending supply of baked goods?"

He grinned. "There's nowhere to surf out there, anyway."

And then he kissed me. Our bodies came back together with an ease that surprised me. The spark and the heat I remembered; the sense of comfort was new.

But I pulled away. "Hey. Don't think we can pick up right where we left off just because your ex ran off with *her* ex. I have my pride, you know."

He sighed in mock frustration. "We can't pick up where we left off? What a shame."

"A tragedy." I nodded. "But I'm not your type, anyway."

"No, you're not. And that's too bad. Because, in the immortal words of *The Partridge Family,* I think I love you."

I froze. "You do?"

"I do."

I heaved a theatrical sigh of my own. "Well, you're not my type either. But it's possible I love you too. Even though you quote *The Partridge Family* at inappropriate moments."

More kissing, with a little extra groping thrown in for good measure.

"Damn it," he growled. "Why the hell did you lock us out of your bedroom?"

"I think it's a sign. Look at the evidence: locked doors, crazy exes, unexpected children popping up left, right, and center . . . . Fate is against us."

"It does look that way."

I smiled. "Maybe it's just not meant to be."

"Maybe." He seemed unconcerned.

"Well, what are we going to do now?"

He took my hand in his. "There's only one thing *to* do."

"Consult our horoscopes and wait 'til our rising signs are in alignment?"

"Guess again."

25

"God. Who knew that getting married was such a hassle?" Alex opened the Audi's passenger-side door and I ducked inside, shaking raindrops from my newly brunette hair.

"I tried to tell you," I reminded him, tucking the skirt of my blue silk dress under my legs as I sat down. "Didn't I tell you?"

"She told you, Daddy," Leo piped up as Alex buckled him into the car seat.

"See? I have witnesses. And this was only the rehearsal dinner. Wait until Saturday."

We had opted to do the rehearsal dinner on Wednesday instead of Friday in the hopes of cutting down on last-minute wedding chaos. This plan had failed spectacularly.

"Turn the heat on," Leo begged as Alex slammed the driver's-side door and jammed the key in the ignition. "I'm *freezing!*"

"What?" I gave him a look of horror. "You think this is cold? It's sixty degrees! You just wait until we go to my parents' house in Chicago for Christmas next year."

My soon-to-be-stepson looked delighted. "Will it be snowy? Can I go sledding with Daddy?"

"Of course." I turned to Alex and smiled. "Daddy loves winter. Wait 'til he shows you his killer snowboarding moves."

"Oh man." Alex shook his head. "I thought we could just go to Hawaii for Christmas. I could teach you to surf, Leo. How about that?"

"No! I wanna go sledding." Leo started kicking the back of Alex's seat.

"Hey, you wanted a family, you got it." I laughed. "That's what real families do during the holidays—schlep around airports and complain. Besides, my mom is dying to do all the Christmas traditions with Leo."

"Your mom, my mom . . ." He pulled off his tie and tossed it back at Leo, who giggled. "We should have eloped."

"If you cast your mind back, you may recall that I did warn you, but *somebody* was all 'it's important to have a traditional ceremony.'"

"Well, that was before I found out that planning a traditional ceremony is like trying to mobilize the Russian Army. And now we have to go to Chicago in December?"

"My mom loves you. It'll be just like Currier & Ives. If you play your cards right, maybe you'll even get pie."

He stopped fiddling with the dashboard heater and gave me a long, hot look. "Pie is not what I want."

"Oh really?" I feigned girlish innocence.

"Leo, you're sleeping at Mommy's tonight."

"Okay," Leo chirped. "But I don't want to be the reindeer anymore."

"It's 'ringbearer,'" Alex corrected.

Leo stuck out his chin. "I don't want to be it. Can't make me."

"We know," I assured him. "We read you loud and clear."

After weeks of breathless chatter about his tuxedo and his duties as ringbearer, Leo freaked out when our wedding planner showed him the church aisle he'd have to walk down. The prospect of fifty ("*only* fifty," as we'd tried to spin it) staring guests had been the dealbreaker, and he now insisted that he would spend the ceremony in his Spider-Man shirt, tucked away from prying eyes with Harmony in the front pew. Further attempts to include him in the service had been met with extreme resistance and disdain.

"Oh my Goddess, it is pouring down there!" Harmony threw open the back door and clambered in next to Leo.

"May we help you?" Alex asked politely as wet wind gusted through the car.

"Yes! We'd like a ride home, please!"

"Thanks, man, you're the best." Paul climbed in on the other side of Leo. "Hey, little buddy, you must be getting excited about the wedding."

Leo narrowed his eyes. "I'm not being the reindeer."

"Good job setting boundaries, Pookie." Harmony stroked her hugely pregnant belly.

Alex sighed, put the car in gear, and started to pull away from the curb.

"*Wait!*" Harmony shrieked.

All of us startled except for Paul, who simply put a hand on Harmony's arm and asked, in the calm tones of a man who deals with murder and mayhem on a daily basis, "What's the problem, babe?"

"I left my purse in the restaurant."

"Be right back." He unbuckled his seat belt, but before he could open the door, I heard tapping at my window.

Cesca, safe and dry thanks to the ministrations of her personal umbrella holder, a.k.a. Carter Nicholson, motioned for me to roll down the window.

"You forgot this." She tossed Harmony's sparkly, rainbow-striped purse into my lap.

I handed it back to Harmony. "Thanks, Ces. And thanks for helping me get organized tonight."

"Girl, I am a born enforcer." Behind her, Carter nodded in agreement. "Between me and the wedding planner, there's nothing to worry about. Although, frankly, you could have given us all a little more notice."

"Oh, but a whirlwind wedding is so romantic," Harmony gushed.

"It wasn't really whirlwind," I protested. "I mean, getting engaged after four months of dating isn't so unheard of."

"Yeah, but then you gave us two months to plan the wedding." Cesca shook her head. "Two months! That *is* unheard of!"

I gave my future husband a look. "Well, well, well. Look who's lecturing us on the perils of spur-of-the-moment weddings."

"That's right; I planned my wedding in twelve hours . . . because my parents weren't involved!" She pointed a finger at Alex. "No offense, but your mom is a piece of work." Then she turned to me. "And *your* mom . . ."

"We know, we know." Alex threw his hands up. "Believe me, I'm reconsidering elopement right now."

"Go for it," Cesca advised me.

"Amen to that," Carter said.

"Oh, don't be so negative," Harmony admonished. "Your moms are absolute dolls. You just need to learn serenity."

"Well, your fabulous matron of honor needs to go home and watch Sports Center," Cesca announced. "Any last requests?"

I looked at the water stains on my silk skirt, the torrential storm outside, and the motley assortment of family members in the car. "Five minutes of peace and quiet?"

She shrugged. "Okay. Done. Hey Leo, want to go for a ride in a Porsche?"

"Yeah!" Leo scrabbled to escape the confines of his seat belt. "Yeah, yeah, yeah!"

"Can I ride in the Porsche too?" Paul begged.

"No. You and Harmony are going in my car. Carter, you take Leo's car seat, and I'll meet you at their condo. Everybody move, move, *move!*"

And they moved. Within forty-five seconds, the Audi's

backseat was vacant. I'd never seen a six-foot-six basketball star react so fast.

"Wow." Alex whistled long and low. "She really could mobilize the Russian Army."

"Believe it," Cesca assured him. "I'll get them all back to Santa Monica safe and sound. See you on Saturday, you crazy kids." She blew us a kiss and vroomed off with a caravan of people so closely and convolutedly related to us, we couldn't begin to describe them with words like *ex* and *step*. They were all just family now. For better or for worse.

"God bless Cesca," I said in the sudden calm.

"It's just you, me, and your dress, which I must tell you is see-through when wet." He turned the ignition off, placed his hand on my bare knee, and inched the hem of the dress up my thigh.

"Alex! We are in a parking lot!" I gasped in what I hoped was a convincing tone of outraged modesty.

"Yes. A dark, secluded parking lot with no kids or exes or psychotic bridal moms."

"I thought we were 'taking a break' until the wedding night?"

"That's three days away. I'll never make it that long." He paused, then gave me a wicked grin. "Screw this. Let's go to Vegas."

I started to laugh. "Are you kidding? Right now?"

"Right now. Just you and me. We'll go get hitched and hole up in a suite at the Bellagio."

I was starting to like this idea. "Can we raid the minibar?"

"Like a plague of locusts." His grin got bigger. "We can say our vows to Elvis."

"Then we can hit the craps table and make back everything we spent on the minibar." I paused. "But what about our moms? They'll be heartbroken if we cancel the wedding."

Ever the long-term planner, he already had an answer for this. "We won't cancel it. We'll be back by tomorrow afternoon, and no one will ever be the wiser. All I want are a few hours alone with you. We get married for us tonight. We get married for the family on Saturday."

I thought this over, then nodded. "I'm in a Vegas kind of mood. Let's go."

"You're sure?"

"I'm sure. Floor it."

And that was the beginning of our own perfectly imperfect, postmodern, Elvis-presided version of happily ever after.

Up Close & Personal with the Author

ADMIT IT: YOU STILL LISTEN TO OLD GUNS N' ROSES AND BON JOVI ALBUMS ON THE SLY, DON'T YOU?

I admit nothing! I have the right to an attorney! Okay, I will confess that to this day, I treasure my old Wham! albums, along with George Michael's "Faith." That thing has aged like a fine wine. And, when the occasion calls for it, I have been known to do a very dramatic—and very loud—rendition of Don Henley's "Boy of Summer" (don't tell anyone, okay?).

UNTIL THE MIDDLE OF THE BOOK, GWEN KEEPS HER UNUSED WEDDING DRESS IN HER CLOSET AND RECOILS AT THE SIGHT OF IT EVERY MORNING. WHY WOULD SHE HANG ON TO SOMETHING THAT BRINGS BACK BAD MEMORIES?

I have a theory that women's closets are a giant collage of the important moments in their personal histories. For instance, I recently went through my wardrobe in an effort to make room for stylish new arrivals, and I was surprised to find how emotionally attached I was to certain items, like the dress I was wearing when my husband proposed and the dress I was wearing when I won the Golden Heart award. These are fancy dresses that I'm never going to wear again (I compulsively acquire cocktail dresses the way other women compulsively acquire shoes), but I just couldn't bring myself to put them in the bag marked for Goodwill. I think that Gwen had that same kind of emotional attachment to her wedding gown, except, in her case, the gown represented what *could* have happened—an imaginary alternative to a very difficult time in her life. Plus, let's face it: who's really going to toss a three-thousand-dollar silk gown?

BOTH *EXES AND OHS* AND YOUR PREVIOUS NOVEL, *MY FAVORITE MISTAKE,* FEATURE PRECOCIOUS LITTLE BOYS. WHAT'S YOUR DEAL? ARE THESE CHARACTERS BASED ON REAL KIDS YOU KNOW ?

None of the characters in my books are based on real people. Sometimes I will write about intriguing habits or idiosyncrasies I notice in friends or family members (like Cesca's sports fanaticism), but my characters are all a mishmash of things I've seen on TV and read about in magazines and overheard in department store dressing rooms (prime eavesdropping territory!). As to where the child characters come from . . . I don't have children of my own, but I spent a lot of time working in preschools while I was in grad school. The kids constantly surprised me with the sophistication of their questions and the accuracy of their emotional perceptions. I had a great time getting to know them, and I think all writers should spend a lot of time with children. They give you such a funny, fresh view of the world and remind you to constantly ask "What if . . . ?" questions.

DID YOUR PROFESSIONAL TRAINING AS A PSYCHOLO-GIST MAKE IT EASY TO WRITE A CHARACTER WHO'S A THERAPIST?

If only! When people hear "psychologist," the first image that comes to mind is a bearded man sitting in a room plastered with fancy diplomas and droning, "Tell me about your mother . . ." But the truth is, I'm trained as a cognitive researcher, so I spent a lot of time in the lab and none in a therapist's office. Gwen, on the other hand, is a practicing clinician, so I had to track down people in that field and pester them with questions about protocol and professional ethics. (And I'm sure I got some of it wrong.) Otherwise, the character was fun to write—I think that psychologists, like writers, are drawn to their career because they're interested in relationships and emotional domino effects.

AT THE END OF THE BOOK, WE FEEL LIKE GWEN AND ALEX ARE SET FOR A HAPPY MARRIAGE. BUT WHAT ABOUT CESCA AND HER NEW HUSBAND? AND HARMONY AND PAUL? DO YOU THINK EITHER OF THESE COUPLES IS GOING TO MAKE IT TO THEIR FIFTIETH ANNIVERSARY?

Cesca and Carter are going to go the distance. I know this for a fact because, hey, I'm the author and they have to do what I say! It's true that they had a very abbreviated courtship, and love at first sight doesn't work out in every case, but they're compatible on so many levels and, as we know, Cesca is not one to give up without a fight. Paul and Harmony, on the other hand, have a more twisty-turny road ahead of them. At the end of the day, their temperaments complement each other—he's calm and contemplative; she's spontaneous and energetic—and they both have good intentions and forgiving hearts. I think that their first year or two will involve a lot of adjustment and revision of unrealistic expectations, but in the end, he loves her exactly the way she is, which no one else ever has. That goes a long way toward creating a harmonious relationship. Plus, despite her colorful past, Harmony is really making an effort to change for Leo's sake. She's willing to admit her faults and strive to correct them, and that means that, at her core, she's very strong and will probably "grow up" into a very good mom. But I doubt she'll ever admit that's she's old enough to be celebrating a fifty-year-old relationship!

Good books are like shoes...
You can never have too many.

American Girls About Town
Lauren Weisberger, Jennifer Weiner, Adriana Trigiani, and more!
Get ready to paint the town red, white, and blue!

Luscious Lemon
Heather Swain
In life, there's always a twist!

Why Not?
Shari Low
She should have looked before she leapt.

Don't Even Think About It
Lauren Henderson
Three's company... Four's a crowd.

Hit Reply
Rocki St. Claire
What's more exciting than an I.M. from the guy who got away...

Too Good to Be True
Sheila O'Flanagan
Sometimes all love needs is a wing and a prayer.

In One Year and Out the Other
Cara Lockwood, Pamela Redmond Satran, and more!
Out with the old, in with the new, and on with the party!

Do You Come Here Often?
Alexandra Potter
Welcome back to Singleville: Population 1

The Velvet Rope
Brenda L. Thomas
Life is a party. But be careful who you invite...

Great storytelling just got a new address.

downtOwn press

PUBLISHED BY POCKET BOOKS

11656

Be the Next Downtown Girl
Contest Rules

1) ENTRY REQUIREMENTS:

Register to enter the contest on www.simonsaysthespot.com. Enter by submitting your story as specified below.

2) CONTEST ELIGIBILITY:

This contest is open to nonprofessional writers who are legal residents of the United States and Canada (excluding Quebec) over the age of 18 as of December 7, 2004. Entrant must not have published any more than two short stories on a professional basis or in paid professional venues. Employees (or relatives of employees living in the same household) of Simon & Schuster, VIACOM, or any of their affiliates are not eligible. This contest is void in Puerto Rico, Quebec, and wherever prohibited or restricted by law.

3) FORMAT:

Entries must not be more than 7,500 words long and must not have been previously published. Entries must be typed or printed by word processor, double spaced, on one side of noncrasable paper. Do not justify right-side margins. Along with a cover letter, the author's name, address, email address, and phone number must appear on the first page of the entry. The author's name, the story title, and the page number should appear on every page. Electronic submissions will be accepted and must be sent to downtowngirl@simonandschuster.com. All electronic submissions must be sent as an attachment in a Microsoft Word document. All entries must be original and the sole work of the Entrant and the sole property of the Entrant.

All submissions must be in English. Entries are void if they are in whole or in part illegible, incomplete, or damaged or if they do not conform to any of the requirements specified herein. Sponsor reserves the right, in its absolute and sole discretion, to reject any entries for any reason, including but not limited to based on sexual content, vulgarity, and/or promotion of violence.

4) ADDRESS:

Entries submitted by mail must be postmarked by July 31, 2005 and sent to:

Be The Next Downtown Girl
Author Search

Downtown Press Editorial Department
Pocket Books
1230 Sixth Avenue, 13th floor
New York, NY 10020

Or Emailed By July 31, 2005
at 11:59 PM EST as a
Microsoft Word document to:

downtowngirl@simonandschuster.com

Each entry may be submitted only once. Please retain a copy of your submission. You may submit more than one story, but each submission must be mailed or emailed, as applicable, separately. Entries must be received by July 31, 2005. Not responsible for lost, late, stolen, illegible, mutilated, postage due, garbled, or misdirected mail/entries.

5) PRIZES:

One Grand Prize winner will receive:

Simon & Schuster's Downtown Press Publishing Contract for Publication of Winning Entry in a future Downtown Press Anthology, Five Hundred U.S. Dollars ($500.00), and

Downtown Press Library
(20 books valued at $260.00)

Grand Prize winner must sign the Publishing contract which contains additional terms and conditions in order to be published in the anthology.

Ten Second Prize winners will receive:

A Downtown Press Collection
(10 books valued at $130.00)

No contestant can win more than one prize.

6) STORY THEME

We are not restricting stories to any specific topic, however they should embody what all of our Downtown Press authors encompass—they should be smart, savvy, sexy stories that any Downtown Girl can relate to. We all know what uptown girls are like, but girls of the new millennium prefer the Downtown Scene. That's where it happens. The music, the shopping, the sex, the dating, the heartbreak, the family squabbles, the marriage, and the divorce. You name it. Downtown Girls have done it. Twice. We encourage you to register for the contest at www.simonsaysthespot.com in order to receive our monthly emails and updates from our authors and read about our titles on www.downtownpress.com to give you a better idea of what types of books we publish.

7) JUDGING:

Submissions will be judged on the equally weighted criteria of (a) basis of writing ability and (b) the originality of the story (which can be set in any time frame or location). Judging will take place on or about October 1, 2005. The judges will include a freelance editor, the editor of the future Anthology, and 5 employees of Sponsor. The decisions of the judges shall be final.

8) NOTIFICATION:

The winners will be notified by mail or phone on or about October 1, 2005. The Grand Prize Winner must sign the publishing contract in order to be awarded the prize. All federal, local, and state taxes are the responsibility of the winner. A list of the winners will be available after October 20, 2005 on:

http://www.downtownpress.com

http://www.simonsaysthespot.com

The winners' list can also be obtained

by sending a stamped self-addressed envelope to:

Be The Next Downtown Girl
Author Search
Downtown Press Editorial Department
Pocket Books
1230 Sixth Avenue, 13th floor
New York, NY 10020

9) PUBLICITY:

Each Winner grants to Sponsor the right to use his or her name, likeness, and entry for any advertising, promotion, and publicity purposes without further compensation to or permission from such winner, except where prohibited by law.

10) INTERNET:

If for any reason this Contest is not capable of running as planned due to an infection by a computer virus, bugs, tampering, unauthorized intervention, fraud, technical failures, or any other causes beyond the control of the Sponsor which corrupt or affect the administration, security, fairness, integrity, or proper conduct of this Contest, the Sponsor reserves the right in its sole discretion, to disqualify any individual who tampers with the entry process, and to cancel, terminate, modify, or suspend the Contest. The Sponsor assumes no responsibility for any error, omission, interruption, deletion, defect, delay in operation or transmission, communications line failure, theft or destruction or unauthorized access to, or alteration of, entries. The Sponsor is not responsible for any problems or technical malfunctions of any telephone network or telephone lines, computer on-line systems, servers, or providers, computer equipment, software, failure of any email or entry to be received by the Sponsor due to technical problems, human error or traffic congestion on the Internet or at any website, or any combination thereof, including any injury or damage to participant's or any other person's computer relating to or resulting from participating in this Contest or downloading any materials in this Contest. CAUTION: ANY ATTEMPT TO DELIBERATELY DAMAGE ANY WEBSITE OR UNDERMINE THE LEGITIMATE OPERATION OF THE CONTEST IS A VIOLATION OF CRIMINAL AND CIVIL LAWS AND SHOULD SUCH AN ATTEMPT BE MADE, THE SPONSOR RESERVES THE RIGHT TO SEEK DAMAGES OR OTHER REMEDIES FROM ANY SUCH PERSON(S) RESPONSIBLE FOR THE ATTEMPT TO THE FULLEST EXTENT PERMITTED BY LAW. In the event of a dispute as to the identity or eligibility of a winner based on an email address, the winning entry will be declared made by the "Authorized Account Holder" of the email address submitted at time of entry. "Authorized Account Holder" is defined as the natural person 18 years of age or older who is assigned to an email address by an Internet access provider, online service provider, or other organization (e.g., business, education institution, etc.) that is responsible for assigning email addresses for

the domain associated with the submitted email address. Use of automated devices are not valid for entry.

11) LEGAL Information:

All submissions become sole property of Sponsor and will not be acknowledged or returned. By submitting an entry, all entrants grant Sponsor the absolute and unconditional right and authority to copy, edit, publish, promote, broadcast, or otherwise use, in whole or in part, their entries, in perpetuity, in any manner without further permission, notice or compensation. Entries that contain copyrighted material must include a release from the copyright holder. Prizes are nontransferable. No substitutions or cash redemptions, except by Sponsor in the event of prize unavailability. Sponsor reserves the right at its sole discretion to not publish the winning entry for any reason whatsoever.

In the event that there is an insufficient number of entries received that meet the minimum standards determined by the judges, all prizes will not be awarded. Void in Quebec, Puerto Rico, and wherever prohibited or restricted by law. Winners will be required to complete and return an affidavit of eligibility and a liability/publicity release, within 15 days of winning notification, or an alternate winner will be selected. In the event any winner is considered a minor in his/her state of residence, such winner's parent/legal guardian will be required to sign and return all necessary paperwork.

By entering, entrants release the judges and Sponsor, and its parent company, subsidiaries, affiliates, divisions, advertising, production, and promotion agencies from any and all liability for any loss, harm, damages, costs, or expenses, including without limitation property damages, personal injury, and/or death arising out of participation in this contest, the acceptance, possession, use or misuse of any prize, claims based on publicity rights, defamation or invasion of privacy, merchandise delivery, or the violation of any intellectual property rights, including but not limited to copyright infringement and/or trademark infringement.

Sponsor:
Pocket Books,
an imprint of Simon & Schuster, Inc.
1230 Avenue of the Americas,
New York, NY 10020